I0846590

Cracked Glass

BOOK 1 OF THE CRACKED GLASS TRILOGY

Cracked Glass

The Sin of Silence

Kimberly Cummings

The Cozy Scratchpad

Copyright Page

To God and my family

Therefore to him that knoweth to do good, and doeth it
not, to him it is sin.

James 4:17 KJV

Table of Contents

Chapter 1: The State Calls
Luna Turner

The gavel cracked like a gunshot.

"All rise," the bailiff's voice carried over the wooden benches. Reporters shuffled their notebooks, cameras clicked from the gallery, and the scent of polished oak mixed with too many bodies crammed into the Red Leaf City Courthouse.

Judge Nancy Lampson entered, her black robe rippling as though it carried the weight of the entire trial. She adjusted her glasses, surveying the packed courtroom with the same authority she had carried for twenty-five years. Outside, protestors roared loud enough to bleed through the windows, some chanting "Justice for the Children," others holding signs in support of Francine Grove, the politician's wife, who had become a reluctant symbol of betrayal and innocence in the city.

"Be seated," Judge Lampson ordered. The benches creaked as bodies sank, but the tension never softened.

At the prosecution's table sat Jackson Hill, his navy tie too tight against a determined jaw. Beside him, his second chair, Lucas O'Hell, shuffled a neat stack of notes, ready to pounce on any inconsistency. Across from them lounged the defense: Jasper McMichaels, sharp-eyed, and his second chair, Clair Winston, and paralegal, Wyatt Reddings. Next to them, Benjamin Grove sat stone-faced, the former golden politician turned accused criminal, cuffed at the wrists and ankles, his jaw clenched as if the world owed him silence.

Hill rose. "Your Honor, the State calls Luna Turner."

A ripple went through the room. From the front pew, a woman in her mid-thirties stepped forward. Her navy blazer was pressed, her hair tightly pinned back, but the tremor in her hands betrayed her calm. She walked with a social worker's posture: shoulders squared by years of case files, home visits, and heartbreak.

"Ms. Turner," Judge Lampson said, "please raise your right hand."

Henry Printerson, the court reporter, watched with practiced neutrality as the oath was given. Luna swore to tell the truth; her voice was steady but quiet.

She sat down, exhaling slowly, her fingers brushing the edge of the witness stand.

Jackson Hill moved closer. "Ms. Turner, I'd like you to tell the court about the day your involvement in this case began."

"It was an ordinary day at Red Leaf City Social Services," Luna began. Her voice softened as though she was pulling the jury into her memory.

Her eyes unfocused, and suddenly, the courtroom dissolved into the rhythm of a local government office.

I had checked my calendar three times that morning. The phone lines were already buzzing before I could take my first sip of coffee. Five messages blinked on my voicemail light, each one waiting for my attention. I listened to them carefully, including an intake referral, a foster placement question, two schools inquiring about documentation, and one parent's request. I made notes, color-coded, because in this line of work, nothing could be dropped. Not when lives sat in the margins of paperwork.

Her testimony painted it like a diary entry.

"After lunch, I met with a foster parent who came in with concerns. She was worried about her foster son's nutrition. He said he had lost weight and wasn't eating properly. So, I filed a referral for health and wellness. That's what we do: we connect families with the services they need. No two families are alike, so every case deserves individual attention."

She paused, looking at the jury, her eyes shining. "I try to go the extra mile. Because if we don't, who will?"

Hill gave her space, letting the words linger.

"By the end of that day, after hours had already rolled past, my phone rang again. It was a foster mother named Lily Roberts. She reported that her foster child, Jonah Carter, had been missing for the last four days."

The jury stirred. Four days.

"I immediately became concerned. Our policy requires reporting any suspicious activity within twenty-four hours. But Lily hadn't seen him in nearly a week. Four days gone, and only now she was calling."

Luna's tone cracked, her flashback thick with memory.

"I asked her why she hadn't reported it earlier. She told me Jonah had gone missing before, and he would sometimes stay at a friend's house. That he usually came back by morning. She thought it was no big deal."

The silence in the courtroom was heavy, broken only by the scratching of pens. "I knew better," Luna whispered. "Every missing child is a big deal."

"Objection!" Jasper McMichaels snapped, rising to his feet. His voice sliced through Luna's memory like glass breaking.

Judge Lampson's head lifted. "On what grounds?"

"She's speculating about what constitutes a 'big deal.' That's not a fact; that's her personal opinion. The jury doesn't need her interpretation."

Hill braced. "Your Honor, the witness is explaining her decision-making process. That goes to credibility."

Lampson considered, then nodded. "Sustained in part. Ms. Turner, keep your answers factual." Luna's hands tightened in her lap. "Yes, Your Honor."

Hill gave her a reassuring nod. "Continue. What did you do next?"

"I stayed late," Luna said. Her voice steadied again. "Even though the office was closing, I filed the necessary paperwork to document Jonah as a missing child. I called law enforcement immediately. I wasn't going to wait until the next morning. A child's life was at risk."

Her mind replayed the late-night office with the hum of fluorescent lights and the clock ticking past seven. Fingers typing into the system: MISSING CHILD: JONAH CARTER, AGE 13.

"I told them everything Lily said. I was familiar with Jonah's case file, and it did not mention any prior disappearances. Nothing. Which meant Lily hadn't told anyone before. She had stayed quiet."

The last words weighed heavily. Hill leaned forward. "Ms. Turner, was Jonah Carter ever found?"

Luna swallowed. The courtroom seemed to lean in.

"Yes," she said, her voice breaking. "His body was discovered two weeks after the initial investigation was launched."

"And where was his body found?"

She drew in a shaky breath. "I was on-site when Detective Cane Walls first uncovered Jonah's body, buried on the property of Benjamin Grove."

Gasps rippled through the gallery. Grove's face remained stone, but his fingers clenched the defense table. Outside, the protestors must have heard Luna's words…. their chants swelled, pounding against the courthouse windows until the glass trembled.

Judge Lampson banged her gavel. "Order!"

The noise inside gradually subsided. Jackson Hill glanced at the jury, then back to the bench. "No further questions for this witness, Your Honor."

Judge Lampson struck the gavel once more. "Mr. McMichaels, you may proceed with cross-examination."

Jasper McMichaels rose slowly, smoothing his tie. His movements were deliberate, almost theatrical.

"Ms. Turner," he began, walking toward the witness stand, "you testified that Jonah Carter's body was found on my client's property. You didn't find it yourself, did you?"

Luna's hands tightened in her lap. "No, sir. I was present with the Red Leaf Police Department during the search."

"Present," Jasper echoed. "So, who actually located the body?"

"Detective Cane Walls," Luna said softly. "Along with Detective Otis Black."

Jasper nodded slowly, pacing in front of the jury box. "So, for the record, the detectives found the body. Not you."

"Yes, that's correct."

He paused, glancing briefly at the jury. "And when you arrived at the scene, Ms. Turner, did you witness my client, Mr. Grove, on the property?"

"Again, I was present onsite; I did not arrive after the fact," Luna said.

"Did you see him bury anything?"

"No."

"Handle anything? Shovel? Tools? Evidence of any kind?"

Luna hesitated, then shook her head. "No, sir."

"Then your entire statement, that Jonah Carter's body was found on my client's property, comes solely from what you were told by law enforcement?"

Hill rose quickly. "Objection. Mischaracterizes the testimony."

"Sustained," Judge Lampson said, her tone firm. "Mr. McMichaels, stick to facts."

Jasper inclined his head, voice softening with practiced control. "Understood, Your Honor." He turned back to Luna. "You said you were present during the discovery. So, you heard or saw the detectives confirm what they found?"

"Yes," Luna said. "I saw them uncover the body."

Jasper let the silence stretch, then stepped closer. "But you can't testify under oath that you know how that body got there, can you?"

Luna swallowed hard. "No, sir. I can't."

He smiled faintly, his expression controlled and confident. "No further questions, Your Honor." Jasper returned to the defense table, whispering something to Grove, whose jaw flexed but eyes stayed forward. The tension in the courtroom was thick enough to feel. Judge Lampson looked over her glasses. "Court will recess for lunch. We'll resume at 1:30 p.m. Jury is dismissed for lunch."

The gavel struck once.

Chapter 2: Discovery on Grove's Land

The courtroom settled as everyone returned from lunch. It seemed to breathe in unison when Jackson Hill rose again. "The State calls Detective Cane Walls.

Cane stepped from the aisle with the slow, deliberate walk of a man who had seen tragedies and refused to hurry past them. He wore a charcoal suit that didn't quite hide his broad-shouldered frame. His jaw looked set, as if from years of holding unpleasant truths in place. He took the oath from the bailiff, sat down, and placed a battered notebook on the rail, its leather cracked along the spine.

"Detective Walls," Hill began, "how long have you served with Red Leaf City Police?" "Twenty-five years," Cane said.

"And your assignment this past spring?"

"Missing Persons Task Force, seconded to Violent Crimes due to… volume." He didn't look at the jury when he said it. He didn't have to. The word volume did the work.

"Directing your attention to the evening of March 14," Hill said. "Did you receive a call from Red Leaf Social Services about a missing child named Jonah Carter?"

"I did not. Dispatch received the call and sent a unit to Red Leaf Social Services that evening to take the initial report," Cane said. "From Ms. Luna Turner. She reported the child had been unaccounted for four days. She'd already entered the case into the state database and requested immediate law enforcement response despite the hour. A unit was also dispatched to Lily Roberts' residence for an initial statement. That was the start of the investigation."

"Walk us through what you did next."

Cane's fingers tapped the notebook's edge once, a

drummer's count-in, and the courtroom thinned into memory.

It was cold for March, the kind that stung fingers and tempted shortcuts. He took none. That evening, a unit had been dispatched to Lily Roberts' home to take the initial statement. The next morning, he and his partner, Detective Otis Black, followed up and returned to the address. The house was a faded yellow two-story with a porch swing that squealed whenever the wind shoved it. Half the streetlights on the block were out. Lily answered with the chain still latched. She was small and bird-boned, her eyes darting at the notepad in Cane's hand like it might peck at her.

Cane offered a faint, reassuring nod. "Ms. Roberts, I'm Detective Cane Walls, and this is Detective Otis Black. We're following up on yesterday's report and have a few more questions about Jonah."

Her fingers fumbled with the latch before she opened the door a few inches wider. "Did you find him?"

"Not yet," Cane said softly. "We're doing everything we can." He paused, studying her trembling hands. "Can we come in for a moment?"

Once they stepped inside, the air hung heavily with the smell of coffee and something burnt. Papers and drawings cluttered the table.

Only then did Cane ease forward, his tone still careful. "I understand this has been difficult, but I need to ask… why did you wait four days to report Jonah missing?"

Lily's eyes darted toward the living room, where a video game controller still sat tangled in its cord. "I… he's run off before," she murmured, one hand twisting a worn washcloth that had seen better kitchens. "He goes to friends' houses sometimes. I thought he'd come back like he always does."

Her voice thinned, barely holding. "But this time… he didn't."

Cane exchanged a look with Otis. They took her statement

carefully, asking for the names of the friends Jonah might have stayed with.

While Otis paced the small living room, his eyes moved quietly over corners…. a pair of mud-caked sneakers by the back door, a bed made too neatly, a plate in the sink with a ring of dried ketchup.

Cane kept his tone measured. "Any reason he'd run?"

Lily shook her head. "No. Not this time."

"Anyone new around the house?"

She blinked, unsure of the scope of the question. "I… It's been just us."

Just us. And yet the house felt like a tide had dragged something away.

They left with a list of names and a sense of time bleeding.

By late morning, they arrived at Red Leaf Middle School. The front office smelled faintly of disinfectant and pencil shavings. The principal, Ms. Raynor, met them at the door, her expression tight.

"We've been worried sick," she said. "Lily called Monday, but there hasn't been any word since."

After a brief exchange, the detectives were escorted down the hall to Jonah's locker. A custodian unlocked it while they stood by. Inside: a spiral notebook with the cover torn off, a pencil stub wrapped with tape, and a crumpled flyer for the Red Leaf Community Resource Center…. Francine Grove's pride.

GED help. Résumé workshops. Youth mentorship.

The phone number and youth mentorship had been circled in blue ink.

"Francine's place," Otis said, meeting Cane's eyes. "Grove's wife," Cane muttered.

They called Luna Turner from the parking lot. She

answered on the second ring, her voice tightly controlled. They told her they had follow-up questions from yesterday's report and asked if she was available to speak with them.

"I'm here at the office," she said. "I cut my morning home visits. If you can come by, I've pulled Jonah's contact sheet, the school liaison notes, and two prior referrals that never closed."

They went straight over.

The fluorescent lights in social services made everything look the same color…beige walls, beige file folders, beige exhaustion. Luna wasn't beige. She pointed out patterns that hadn't looked like patterns until she spoke them aloud: unexplained absences clustered around specific dates; a youth-center volunteer ID that never quite checked out; a bus stop Jonah had started using a full mile farther from home.

"Who runs that stop?" Cane asked.

"Transit says it's a city route shared with the hospital but look." Luna tapped a page. "There's an alley camera a block over we can pull, and Jonah's file shows an intake at the Red Leaf Community Resource Center last month. That's Mrs. Grove's place."

Cane wrote it down. He noticed the way Luna's hand trembled after she finished tapping, the steadiness in her eyes anyway.

"Thank you," he said. "We'll pull it."

By early afternoon, they were back at the station. Chief Ezra Lightening signed off on a fast-track request for the alley-camera footage. At 4:47 p.m., the file came through…grainy, gray, unforgiving. A small boy with a backpack, head down, hands jammed in pockets, stood under a flickering streetlight. A dark sedan idled nearby, headlights off. The boy passed by; the sedan eased forward. In the next frame, the boy was gone.

Cane's stomach knotted. "Plate?"

Otis shook his head. "Too much glare."

"Badge it," Cane said. "Enhance every way you know how."

The tech grunted. "Working."

At 6:12 p.m., a side feed arrived from a traffic cam two blocks over, mostly a grocery sign and a sliver of road, but enough. A plate flashed, incomplete yet promising: BMG and a smear of numbers..

Otis leaned in. "BMG. What are the odds?"

"Benjamin M. Grove," Cane said flatly, because saying it out loud made denying it expensive.

In court, Cane didn't dramatize. He let the facts pile like bricks.

"We established probable cause to seek a search warrant for the Grove estate based on the camera evidence, Jonah Carter's file anomalies, and corroborating interviews," he said. "The request was submitted that same evening and signed by Judge Herron at 7:42 a.m. the following morning."

Jasper McMichaels rose from the defense table. "Objection to the characterization of 'probable cause,' Your Honor. The camera evidence was partial, and my client's initials matching a plate prefix is, at best, coincidence."

Hill didn't look at Jasper; he looked straight at Judge Lampson. "The warrant speaks for itself, Your Honor."

Lampson nodded. "The jury will receive the warrant. Overruled for now. Proceed."

"Detective," Hill said, "describe the execution of that warrant."

Cane glanced down at his notebook, then back up.

"Following the initial camera footage, we continued the investigation for nearly two weeks. We ran down the partial plate, canvassed nearby businesses, and reinterviewed witnesses connected to Jonah's school and the community center. Several tips came in, none conclusive, but each one pointed us back to the same area. By the end of that second week, we executed the warrant on the Grove property.”

Hill nodded. “And what time did you execute that warrant?”

“At 8:10 a.m.,” Cane said. “We did not alert the press. We kept a small footprint…. myself, Detective Black, two uniforms, Luna Turner, and a forensic tech team.”

“Why reserve?”

“In case we found… anything,” Cane replied. “We didn’t want to trample the very ground that might speak.”

“Tell us what happened when you arrived.”

The Grove estate sat behind a low stone wall and a higher hedge that pretended the city wasn’t real. The house was glass, steel, and money. Dew still clung to the manicured lawn; everything looked clean enough to deny the possibility of dirt.

They rang the doorbell. A house manager answered, cheeks flushed with sleep and offense. “Mr. Grove is away, and Mrs. Grove is out of town,” she said.

“Then you won’t mind if we look around,” Cane answered, handed her the warrant.

They split the grounds into grids. Otis took the north side, the orchard and the tool shed. Cane took the south side by the pool and the retaining wall. He noticed a patch of earth that hadn’t decided if it wanted to be wild or landscaped. The uniforms started recording, body cams blinking. The forensic techs waited by the van, half an eye on the sky.

The ground on the south side was wrong. It was a feeling before it was a fact…. the way the soil sank a little under Cane’s heel, the way the grass changed color from bright to bruised. He crouched and pressed his palm into the earth. The cold pushed back.

“Otis,” he called. “Here.”

Otis came at a jog, breath clouding. “What do you see?”

"Someone loved this spot," Cane said softly, the way men speak at graves. He pointed to the shoeprints: a pair, wide set, with one pivoting out as if the foot inside it had been impatient. "And someone came back to check."

They photographed before touching anything: wide shot, mid-range, close-up. A small flag went into the soil, E-01, and then another, E-02, for the neighboring patch that had been disturbed, too.

Cane took a spade from the tech he'd called forward. The first lift was slow and reverent. The soil slid like something swallowing.

"Bag it," Otis said, voice sandpaper. "Every layer."

They found plastic first, a corner of a contractor bag, black as denial. Then the smell, the one your body remembers before your mind allows the memory.

"Stop," Cane said, and the team froze. He backed away, swallowing bile, then called the medical examiner. The chain of custody began then: photographs, measurements, and sample collection. The work of honoring the dead is meticulous.

They peeled back the plastic only when the ME arrived. A small foot emerged, and all professional language temporarily failed. The tech, who had been all business, stilled her hands.

"Male," the ME said, voice hushed. "Preteen to Teen. We'll confirm at autopsy."

Otis turned aside and breathed into his sleeve. Cane didn't move for a long moment. The city's morning birds had the indecency to keep singing.

"Detective Walls," Hill's voice asked from the present, quiet but steady, "who was recovered from that grave?"

Cane's fingers tightened on the edge of the witness stand. "Jonah Carter," he said. "Confirmed by dental records later that day."

"Detective Walls," Hill's voice asked from the present…A hush rippled through the courtroom. Even Jasper didn't rise. The gallery seemed to hold its breath.

The morning light filtering through the trees, fog rolling low across the clearing. A forensic photographer clicks off a final shot. The boy's small frame, wrapped carefully now in a white sheet, is lifted into the coroner's van. The sound of the door closing echoes like punctuation.

"After discovering the body," Hill continued gently, "what did you do next?"

Cane's voice steadied, drawing from memory. "We expanded the grid. Preserved the scene. Notified the family liaison at Red Leaf Social Services and the District Attorney's office. Logged evidence, flagged the plate from the camera footage, and sent two uniforms to speak with the estate's morning staff. No one admitted to seeing anything."

Yellow tape catching in the wind; Black directing uniforms, his face drawn tight. Cane kneeling near the disturbed soil, the hum of tech machines filling the silence that followed grief.

"And after the scene was processed?" Hill asked.

Cane exhaled slowly. "I returned to the station. Detective Black stayed on-site. I filed the initial report and debriefed with the DA's office. The lab ran the partial plate against vehicle records, it matched one registered to Benjamin Grove's office fleet."

"Detective," Hill said, "did Mr. Grove return to his property that evening?"

Cane nodded once. "He did. Around seven forty-five. Patrol units were still on-site."

"Was he allowed entry?"

"No, sir," Cane replied. "He was advised the property was under active investigation and sealed until processing was complete. Forensic teams were still inside. He was instructed to remain nearby, and he chose to wait in his vehicle."

"Did he comply?"

"At first," Cane said quietly. "But his demeanor changed once Detective Black informed him the warrant named both his residence and his office property. He became defensive. Agitated."

"And what happened next?"

"Detective Black asked him to accompany him to the precinct for a formal interview. He agreed, voluntarily."

"Did you interview him that night?" Hill asked.

"Yes. At the precinct."

"And was he charged then?"

Cane's jaw tightened. "Not yet. We released him pending lab results. The warrant for his arrest came two days later."

"Where was he located?"

"At his office in City Hall."

Murmurs swept the gallery again. Hill paused just long enough for silence. "Detective," he said, "walk us through that arrest."

Cane's memory skipped again. City Hall smelled like old documents and new lies. They approached in plain clothes to keep the spectacle contained. It didn't stay contained.

Benjamin Grove saw them long before they reached him; power teaches a man to read a room before it reads him. He stood behind his desk, jacket buttoned, hair immaculate, eyes tired. For a moment, Cane thought he saw something like relief slip across the man's face, like a weight had finally agreed to be named.

"You could have called," Grove said wearily.

"We have a warrant and probable cause," Cane replied. "Benjamin M. Grove, you are under arrest for suspicion of homicide and related offenses. Turn around, please."

Grove did. His hands were steady. His assistant was not. She stammered something about lawyers; Otis told her to call whom she needed. Cane read Grove his rights. A rumor had already sprinted down the hall to the press corps' bullpen. By the time they walked Grove out, cameras were weeping light. Reporters shouted questions about children, corruption, and Francine. Grove kept his eyes on the middle distance as if there was a safer country there.

Outside, the first day of protests formed without rehearsal. Justice for Jonah signs appeared as if they'd been waiting in closets. On the opposite corner, a cluster held WE STAND WITH FRANNIE placards, faces anxious and protective. Police tape stretched along the steps. Chief Ezra Lightening himself stood at the top, jaw set, as if holding an entire city on a short leash.

Grove wasn't a man anymore in that moment; he was a story walking.

"Back to the scene, Detective," Hill said softly, steering away from the spectacle. "Let's talk chain of custody. What items did you recover from the grave?"

Cane referenced his notebook. "Plastic sheeting, length of nylon cord, remnants of duct tape, soil and insect samples, and the child's clothing…t-shirt, jeans, a sneaker. Each item was bagged, labeled, and logged: E-01 through E-12. Photographed before bagging. Hand-to-hand transfers all signed."

"Were there any prints or DNA recovered?"

"Partial DNA on the nylon and tape, mixed profiles. The lab will testify to the specifics." Jasper stood. "Objection to pre-trying the lab testimony."

"Sustained," Lampson said. "The jury will hear from the lab."

Hill nodded. "Understood. Detective, during your investigation, did any evidence emerge linking the burial to someone other than Mr. Grove?"

Cane considered the wording, then answered cleanly. "We investigated potential accomplices. The State has charged co-conspirators."

Hill stepped back from the lectern. "No further questions, Your Honor."

Judge Lampson gave a curt nod. "Mr. McMichaels, you may

proceed with cross."

Jasper rose with leisurely disdain, adjusting his cufflinks before speaking. "Co-conspirators who made deals to save their own skin," he said, strolling to the lectern as if it already belonged to him.

"Detective Walls," he purred, "twenty-five years…Missing Persons, Violent Crimes. You've seen a great deal."

"Yes."

"And you know the difference between evidence and a narrative, don't you?"

Cane didn't blink. "I do."

"Good. Because what I'm hearing is a story with many convenient cuts: a partial plate, an estate, and an assumption that ties them together neatly."

"No," Cane answered.

"You didn't witness him bury anything, handle a weapon, or speak with the victim?"

"No."

"Yet you concluded that the child's body, tragically…. on his property means Mr. Grove put it there."

Cane met his eyes. "I concluded that evidence placed there by human hands does not bury itself."

A murmur rippled through the gallery. Jasper smiled thinly. "Detective, you understand that circumstantial evidence can make a story sound complete even when it isn't?"

"I understand that facts speak whether anyone's listening or not," Cane replied.

Jasper tilted his head, feigning pity. "Or whether anyone's interpreting them correctly, Detective."

Judge Lampson's voice cut through the tension. "Mr.

McMichaels, move on."

Jasper paused just long enough to appear gracious. "No further questions at this time, Your Honor."

He returned to the defense table, expression unreadable. The courtroom exhaled, tension bleeding into the hum of side whispers and shifting chairs.

Judge Lampson glanced toward the jury. "Detective, you may step down."

The gavel struck once, echoing like a closing door.

Chapter 3: The Foster Mother

The murmurs hadn't settled since Detective Cane Walls stepped down. Reporters' pens prowled the margins; the gallery breathed in shallow, synchronized starts. Judge Nancy Lampson waited one beat longer than necessary, letting the room remember itself.

"Counsel?" she said.

Jackson Hill stood, smoothing a page that didn't need smoothing. "The State calls Lily Roberts."

A woman rose from the second row as if the bench itself were reluctant to release her. Lily Roberts was small and careful.... careful hair pulled into a loose bun, a careful skirt that hid a run in the stockings, and careful hands that kept finding each other at the waist, as though they could braid themselves into courage. She walked the aisle without looking at the defendant's table. She did not look at Francine either, though she must have felt the city's eyes move between them like a metronome.

Bailiff Caden Young administered the oath. Lily's voice floated, thin as a thread.

"Ms. Roberts," Hill said, gentler than he'd been with anyone else today, "thank you for being here. Please state your name and your relationship to Jonah Carter."

"My name is Lily Roberts," she said, lips barely parting. "I was Jonah's... I was his foster mother."

Her gaze dropped to the rail. The bailiff, a man whose job was to be unnoticeable, shifted his weight and looked down, too.

"Ms. Roberts," Hill continued, "I'm going to ask you some questions about your time caring for Jonah. If you need a moment, ask for one. If you don't understand a question, please let me know, and I'll rephrase it. All right?"

"All right," she whispered.

"Let's start with when Jonah came to live with you."

She nodded, eyes still on the wood grain as if it might remember for her. "Last November. He was removed from his biological mother on a long-term basis and placed through Social Services. It was… an emergency placement. They said he didn't have any relatives who could take him."

"And were you okay with the long-term placement?"

"I usually don't house children for longer than ninety days," Lily said. "The last four placements I had were short-term or emergency… less than a week. But I agreed to it."

"Did you feel you could handle the long-term placement, since this was your first one?" Hill asked.

"Yes, I was okay with it."

"So, Jonah was with you for about four months, would you say?"

"Yes."

Hill took a half step toward the jury, then backed away, letting them see her without making her feel seen through. "How would you describe Jonah when he arrived?"

"Quiet," she said. "Polite. He had a way of apologizing for being in a room. He folded his clothes and lined up his pencils. He asked where to put his shoes, like it was a test he didn't want to fail."

"Did he attend school during the time he lived with you?"

"Yes. He… he tried. Some days were good. Some days…" She swallowed. "He missed his mom."

"Food," Hill said softly. "Let's talk about that."

Her fingers clenched together once, a wring of invisible

water. "He wouldn't eat much. Some days, he'd pick at toast. He said food made his stomach feel 'too loud.' I didn't know what that meant. I tried soups. Eggs. He liked apples if I peeled them."

"Did you reach out to Social Services about this concern?"

"Yes. I went… I went in. After lunch one day, I left work. I went in." Her eyes flicked up, searching, and found Luna Turner in the front pew. Relief worked through her shoulders like a slow-acting drug. "I spoke with Ms. Turner. She gave me a referral for health and wellness. I was grateful."

Hill nodded. "You did the right thing to raise that concern. Now, I'd like to direct your attention to the second week of March. Do you recall the last day you saw Jonah alive?"

The word alive lifted, hovered over the room, and would not go down. Lily's bottom lip trembled. "March tenth. A Monday."

"What happened that day?"

"He came home from school, and I asked about his day. He said it was fine. He took off his backpack and put it on the chair. Sat down at the kitchen table and started his homework. I made him a peanut butter and jelly sandwich and poured him a glass of milk. He said he and his friends went to the playground after school for a bit, then came home. He asked if he could go to the park near the house before dinner, just for a minute. The park was only two blocks away, so I told him yes. I told him I needed him to stay close because I had laundry and was starting dinner. He nodded. He was so… agreeable." She winced at her own choice of words.

"Did he come back?"

A pause. "No."

"What did you do then?"

"I started to worry around the thirty-minute mark. At an hour, I called his phone. No answer. I walked the block. I asked at the corner store. I asked Mr. Patel if he'd seen Jonah that day. He said no. I told myself Jonah was at a friend's house, he'd done that before, stayed late, and then… then come home." Her voice dropped. "But he didn't come home that night."

"And you waited."

"I waited," she said, and there was a flake of defiance in the words, brittle but real. "I sat up on the couch. I called his name out the window at two in the morning like a fool. At four, I made coffee I didn't drink. I thought about calling then. But I didn't."

"Why not?"

"Because last time," she said in a rush, "he came back by morning. He'd gone to a boy's house, a classmate with a game system. His teacher said boys do that sometimes. She told me not to panic. She said it makes them run farther." The words came too fast, as if speed might make them more accurate. "The second night, I called the school. Left a message. I thought he'd show at first period. He didn't. The third day…" She pressed her mouth into a straight line. "The third day, I thought, if I call the police and he walks in while they're here, I'll look like I don't trust him. The fourth day, I knew I'd made a mistake."

Hill let the quiet sit with the jury. It sat in their laps like something that could not be put down. "What did you do on the fourth day?"

"I called Social Services. Ms. Turner answered. She… she didn't scold me. She told me to stay on the line while she filed the missing child report. She called the police, too. She told me the policy was twenty-four hours and asked me if anyone had told me that." Lily's throat worked. "I should have known. I should have known. It was in the packet. I read the packet. I thought I did."

"Ms. Roberts," Hill said, voice steady, "did you want harm to come to Jonah?" "No," she said, eyes fierce for the first time.

"No."

"Did you love him?"

"I was trying to," she said. "He made it easy."

Hill glanced at the bench. "Your Honor, the State would like to mark Exhibit 19 for identification, a series of text messages from Ms. Roberts' phone showing attempted calls to Jonah on March 10 and 11, and a voicemail to the school on the morning of March 11."

"Marked," Lampson said.

Hill didn't hand the messages to Lily; he didn't need to. "Ms. Roberts, when did you learn that Jonah had been found?"

"Ms. Turner called me. Her voice… I knew before she said it. She asked if I had someone with me. I said no. She asked me to sit down anyway. I sat on the floor. She told me they found… they found him." Lily's hands came apart at last and hovered uselessly in the air, like birds that had forgotten where to land. "She said they found him on… on Mr. Grove's property."

Hill let the name hang, then set it down. "Ms. Roberts, did you know Benjamin Grove personally?"

"No."

"Had Jonah ever mentioned him?" "No."

"Had anyone from the Red Leaf Community Resource Center, Mrs. Francine Grove's organization, been in contact with you about Jonah?"

"Yes," Lily said, surprising herself. "A pamphlet came home in his backpack. A volunteer called once about tutoring help for reading: I said we'd like that. I… I forgot to call back." Shame flushed her cheeks. "We had an appointment card taped to the fridge. It was for the next week. He never… we never got there."

Hill softened his tone another degree. "Ms. Roberts, I want

to ask you a hard question, and I'm asking it because the defense will." He didn't look at Jasper when he said it. "You waited four days to report Jonah missing. Do you understand that violates policy?"

"Yes."

"Do you understand that the delay made it harder to find him?" "Yes."

"Do you understand that the law may consider that negligence?"

A tremor passed down her arms, visible even at the back of the gallery. "Do you understand," she said, lifting her head at last, "that I am not the one who buried him?"

A charge ran through the benches. Jasper McMichaels was on his feet. "Objection…. nonresponsive, inflammatory."

"Sustained," Lampson said, but her voice carried an undercurrent of human acknowledgment. "The jury will disregard the witness's last statement. Mr. Hill, keep your questions within the lines."

"Yes, Your Honor," Hill said. He paused for a moment, allowing the temperature to drop back to a tolerable level. "Ms. Roberts, one final question. If you could speak to Jonah now, what would you say?"

Lily pressed her fingertips to her lips as if holding something precious behind them. When she lowered her hand, her voice was simple. "I would say I'm sorry I waited. I would say I should have called the police sooner."

"No further questions," Hill said and stepped away.

"Cross," Judge Lampson said.

Jasper approached as if he were touring a painting he intended to buy to burn. He offered Lily a smile that had no edges, because it lacked sincerity.

"Ms. Roberts," he purred, "you are familiar with the foster-parent handbook, correct?" "Yes."

"And you received training on reporting protocols." "Yes."

"So, when you waited, not one day, not two, but four…that was a choice."

"I was afraid," she said.

"Afraid of what? Of being embarrassed if he walked in while you were, what was it, 'panicking'?" He made the word into candy and poison. "Afraid of looking like you 'didn't trust him'?"

"I didn't want him to feel hunted," she said, and a few jurors flinched at hunted.

"Isn't it true," Jasper continued, "that Jonah had run off before and returned without incident?"

"Once," she murmured. "Someone brought him home."

"Someone? A friend? A neighbor? A mysterious Samaritan?" Jasper spread his hands. "You didn't verify where he had been?"

"I tried," she said. "He said a friend. He wouldn't tell me the name." "And you accepted that."

"He was… he was thirteen," she said, and the number sounded both big and devastatingly small.

Jasper paced a step, then another, turning for the jury. "You told this court you loved Jonah, that you were 'trying to.' Yet you did not follow policy. You did not call the police within twenty-four hours. You did not call Social Services until the fourth day. You did not follow up with the Red Leaf Community Resource Center, which offered him help. You did not verify prior disappearances.

You… didn't do a lot of things, Ms. Roberts."

A whisper of objection formed on Hill's lips, but he let it die; the jury needed to hear the ugliness said out loud.

"I made mistakes," Lily said, shoulders curving inward, making herself a smaller target for impact that would come anyway. "But I did not…"

"Bury him," Jasper finished for her. "Yes, yes, we've had the drama. But we're not here for drama, we're here for facts. Fact: You waited four days. Fact: You ignored policy. Fact: you told yourself stories to make the quiet feel safe." He let the last sentence linger, its cruelty tidy.

"Mr. McMichaels," Lampson said, a line appearing between her brows, "ask a question."

Jasper inclined his head, chastened by etiquette, not conscience. "A question, then. During those four days, Ms. Roberts, did you see any unfamiliar vehicles near your home?"

Lily blinked, thrown by the pivot. "I… a black car passed by more than once. I noticed because one of the headlights looked dull. The neighbor, Mr. Brown…. Dennis mentioned it, too. He said I should call if I saw it again."

"And did you?"

"No."

"Because?"

She looked at her hands. "Because I thought it was nothing." The words were ashes.

"No further questions," Jasper said, satisfied at last with the small ruin he had made. Hill rose for the redirect. "Briefly, Your Honor."

"Proceed."

"Ms. Roberts," Hill said, voice returned to human temperature, "when you went to Social Services about Jonah's eating, did you go to the same person who later took your missing-child call?"

"Yes. Ms. Turner."

"And did Ms. Turner file immediately?"

"Yes."

"Did she treat you with respect?" Lily's eyes found Luna's again. "Yes."

"Did she make you feel foolish?"

"No."

"Thank you," Hill said. "No further questions."

"Ms. Roberts, you may step down," Judge Lampson said.

Lily rose, then paused, hand on the rail. She turned toward the jury because there are things we say to strangers when we have failed the people we love. "He lined up his pencils," she said. "As if the world would be kinder if he were tidy for it."

"Ms. Roberts," Lampson warned softly.

"I'm done," Lily said, and left the stand like someone returning to a house that had learned how to echo.

The court recessed for fifteen minutes. The moment the gavel fell, the gallery detonated into whispers; the hall exploded into noise. Outside, the protest lines pulsed and collided…. JUSTICE FOR THE CHILDREN on cardboard, WE STAND WITH FRANNIE on foam board. A chant rose that had started as a plea and hardened into a verdict: "No more silence! No more silence!"

Jackson Hill stepped into the corridor with Lucas O'Hell at his shoulder. The air tasted like old coffee and new ink. A microphone shoved forward, then another.

"Mr. Hill, does the State intend to charge Lily Roberts?"

"No comment," Hill said, already moving, because sometimes a man keeps his humanity by rationing his words.

A young protestor with a knit cap and eyes too old shouted over the press. "Why didn't anyone help him? Why didn't anyone see?"

Hill didn't answer. He had answers; they weren't for cameras.

He felt, rather than saw, Jasper glide past in the opposite direction, phone already pressed to his ear, face made for TV. "We have a fragile foster system scapegoat," Jasper said to whoever paid to hear him. "And we have a city in love with an illusion." Lucas leaned in. "We're up next with Trenton Love," he murmured.

"If he's ready," Hill replied, his voice roughened by the weight of the case. "He was Jonah's best friend, the last person who saw him alive at school before he disappeared." He lowered his head slightly. "Lord, keep him steady."

At the end of the corridor, Francine Grove stood apart from the crowd, her fingers clasped so tight they'd gone white. Cameras shifted toward her like startled birds but stilled when she refused to speak. Her grief needed no microphone. She met Hill's eyes once, one silent exchange of strength, before a volunteer from her foundation guided her through a side exit away from the press.

Inside, the courtroom returned to its somber rhythm. Judge Lampson took the bench, the clerk called for order, and the jury filed in, their faces drawn and watchful. The silence carried the memory of a missing boy whose empty desk had become a symbol of the city's unrest.

"The State may call its next witness," Lampson said.

Hill rose. "The State calls Trenton Love."

A thin shadow appeared in the doorway, followed by a boy whose steps echoed too softly for his thirteen years. Trenton walked beside a counselor, shoulders hunched, sweater sleeves swallowing his hands. His shoes squeaked once as he reached the witness stand.

"Your Honor," Hill said, "for the comfort of the witness, the State requests permission to allow his support person to stand near the well."

"Granted," Lampson replied. "And the jury is instructed that the presence of a support person should not influence your assessment of credibility."

Trenton was sworn in. His quiet "yes" sounded like a door closing somewhere far away.

Hill approached, stopping just close enough to be a presence, not a pressure. "Trenton," he said gently, "you knew Jonah Carter?"

"Yes," Trenton whispered.

"You two went to school together?"

He nodded. "Since second grade."

Hill's tone softened further. "And you were friends?"

"Best friends," Trenton said, voice trembling. "We used to sit together at lunch. We walked home most days. Played basketball after school."

Hill gave a slow nod. "Trenton, I know this is hard. Take your time. Do you remember the last time you saw Jonah?"

Trenton swallowed hard. His fingers twisted the hem of his sleeve. "Yes, sir. It was after school… four days before he went missing."

"Where were you?"

"At the playground behind the gym. We were shooting hoops and talking about the science fair." He blinked rapidly. "Jonah said he had to get home before his foster mom started to worry. He only stayed for a little bit. He picked up his backpack and said, 'See you tomorrow.'" I stayed a little bit longer.

Hill waited. "Did he seem upset or scared when he left?"

Trenton shook his head. "No, just… normal. Laughing, actually. He said he'd text me about the project that night. But he never did."

The courtroom was still except for the hum of the air vents. Hill's voice broke the silence, careful and quiet. "And that was the last time you saw him alive?"

A tear slipped down the boy's cheek. "Yes, sir. That was the last time." Hill hesitated, then leaned slightly forward. "How many times had Jonah spent the night at your house?"

"Once," Trenton said softly.

"Do you think he ever told his foster mother, Lily Roberts, about that sleepover?"

Trenton's brow furrowed. "I don't know, sir. He never said anything about it."

Hill nodded, a quiet acceptance in his expression. "No further questions."

Jasper rose from the defense table, buttoning his jacket. He studied the boy for a long moment, then said, "No questions for this witness, Your Honor."

Judge Lampson inclined her head. "You may step down, Mr. Love."

Trenton slid off the witness chair, his sneakers whispering across the floor as the counselor guided him out. The courtroom remained hushed, the echo of his testimony lingering like a held breath.

Chapter 4: Broken Vows

The afternoon light slanted through the courthouse windows, catching the flecks of dust that hovered above the jury box. Judge Nancy Lampson lifted her gavel.

"Ladies and gentlemen of the jury," she said, her voice calm but edged with finality, "we will adjourn for today. The court will resume tomorrow at 9:00 a.m. You are dismissed until that time. Please remember the rules: do not discuss the case with anyone, refrain from consuming media coverage, and refrain from forming or expressing opinions until you have heard all the evidence. Bailiff, you may escort the jury."

The twelve jurors rose in unison and filed out through the side door. Their faces were lined with fatigue, shadowed by what they had just heard from young Trenton Love.

As the door closed behind them, the room exhaled.

Jackson Hill stacked his files, sliding them into his leather briefcase. Lucas O'Hell leaned closer. "Tomorrow will be heavier."

Across the aisle, Jasper McMichaels smirked as he gathered his papers. "Sympathy makes a weak case, Jackson. Let's see what happens when the tears dry."

Hill straightened, jaw tightening. "Truth makes a stronger one, Jasper. And truth doesn't dry."

Wyatt Reddings muttered something under his breath, too low for the gallery to catch. Lucas shot back with a sharp retort, and for a moment the air between the tables bristled. Judge Lampson rapped her gavel once more.

"Counsel, keep your tempers for the jury, not for each other. This court is adjourned."

Benjamin Grove, shackled at the wrists, rose with the defense. His face remained carved from stone, but his eyes flicked once toward the gallery, toward Francine. She didn't meet them.

Francine Grove stepped out into the roar of Red Leaf City. The courthouse steps were split down the middle: to the left, protestors chanted "Justice for the Children" with signs painted in black and red; to the right, a smaller cluster of loyalists held placards with her face and "We Stand with Frannie." Police barricades tried to keep the groups apart, but their voices collided in the spring air like rival choirs.

Francine pulled her blazer tighter and looked for a familiar face. A hand brushed her elbow, her foster mother, Julia Carpenter, steady and gray-haired, a woman whose voice still carried the warmth of lullabies.

"Let's get out of here," Julia said. "You look like you need a meal that isn't eaten under a spotlight."

They ducked into their cars, winding away from the courthouse chaos. Julia led the way to a café tucked between a florist and a bookstore, far enough from downtown to breathe. They parked and walked into the café together. Inside, the smell of fresh bread and onion soup wrapped around them like a shawl. They ordered quietly and took a booth in the corner. Francine stirred her iced tea with a straw she didn't plan to drink.

"Are you all right?" Julia asked, watching her daughter's face.

Francine gave a hollow laugh. "I don't know how to be all right, Mama. Every child they talk about up there makes me feel like I failed them. Like my name is tangled in Benjamin's crimes."

Julia reached across the table, covering her hand. "You didn't fail them. You built places for them when no one else would. You gave them a roof, a meal, a tutor, and a hand on their shoulder. Don't let his corruption steal your work."

Francine swallowed hard, nodding, though tears blurred her

vision. "I thought we were rebuilding, Mama. I thought he believed in me. In us. And now…"
She shook her head. "Now every brick feels poisoned."

The waitress set down two bowls of soup and sandwiches, but Francine's appetite was almost gone.

They were halfway through lunch when Frannie's phone rang, a shrill, old-fashioned jangle that made her heart stutter.

"Mama," she said cautiously. "It's the county jail. A… collect call." Julia stiffened. "You don't have to answer."

Francine's pulse thudded. She pressed her napkin into her lap, "I need to hear him, Mama. Just once."

At their booth, she swiped to the left and answered it. "This is Francine."

Benjamin's voice rushed through the line, low and urgent. "Frannie, it's me. I need to see you before visitation closes today. Please. Two hours. Don't let them turn you against me."

Her throat closed. "Benjamin…"

"I need you," he pressed. "Face to face. Just us. Please."

Francine gripped her cell phone, eyes squeezed shut. Julia's gaze burned across the table, pleading silently.

"All right," Francine whispered. "I'll come."

She hung the phone up; her face was lined with worry. "You don't owe him this," she said.

"I owe myself the truth," Francine replied softly. She touched her mother's cheek. "Thank you for lunch."

Julia rose, folding her daughter into a hug. "Promise me you won't let him break you twice." Francine kissed her mother's temple. "I promise."

They parted outside the café. Julia drove away, the taillights fading into the maze of Red Leaf City. Francine slid into her own car. Her hands trembled on the steering wheel as she started the engine.

The city stretched out before her, rows of crimson trees lining the avenues. They were beautiful, always beautiful, and yet to her they looked like bleeding reminders. The chants from the courthouse still echoed in her ears: "No more silence! Justice for Jonah!"

Francine's thoughts churned: her marriage vows spoken under vaulted ceilings, her mother's vow to keep her safe, her own vow to every child who walked through the Community Resource Center's doors.

Which vow still bound her now?

She drove on, past shuttered shops and children kicking a worn soccer ball down a cracked street, until the jail's gray walls rose ahead of her.

She pulled into the visitor lot and cut the engine. For a moment, she just sat there, watching the guard tower turn slow against the pale sky. Then she reached for her purse and stepped out.

The metal detector hummed as she passed through. Guards checked her ID, stamped her wrist, and led her down a corridor that smelled of bleach and despair.

She entered the visitation room, where glass partitions divided it, and telephones hung like relics. Benjamin Grove sat on the other side, in an orange jumpsuit, chains clinking as he shifted. His hair was mussed, his face pale, but his eyes… his eyes still hunted for control.

When he saw her, he leaned forward, pressing the receiver to his ear. Francine sat slowly, lifting the phone to her own.

"Frannie," he breathed, relief rushing out. "Thank God you came."

Her lips trembled. "Why, Benjamin? Why would you do this to me? To us?"

"I did it for us," he said quickly. "For power. For leverage.

We could fix the system if we were strong enough. You have to believe that.”

Her eyes hardened. “Fix the system? You corrupted it. You used me…used my passion, my story, to cover your filth. You knew why I started the center. Do you remember?”

Benjamin’s eyes flickered. “Of course.”

“I started it because I was one of them,” she said, voice breaking. “I was tossed from family to family until my fifth family gave me a home. They loved me. That center was my vow, that no child would feel the silence I felt. And you….” her voice cracked…. “you stole that from me.”

Benjamin pressed his palm to the glass. “I’m sorry. But it’s not too late. We can rebuild. If you stick with me…if you stay silent, we can recover.”

Her hand curled into a fist on her lap. “No, Benjamin. Silence is what killed Jonah.”

His face crumpled. “Frannie, please. Without you, I have nothing.”
Tears blurred her vision, but she set the phone down slowly and deliberately. Then she rose, refusing to lift her hand to the glass. Benjamin’s voice cracked through the receiver, muffled and desperate.
He struck the glass, shouting, “Stay silent, Frannie. Please… It’s the only way!” She turned and walked out, her footsteps echoing down the sterile hall.
Outside, the wind stirred the red leaves. They rustled like whispers, like a thousand children reminding her what silence costs.

Chapter 5: The Children's Place

The drive home should have been short, but Francine Grove could not bring herself to take the turn toward her neighborhood. The courthouse was still echoing in her chest, her husband's voice still clawing at her ear. Stay silent. Stay with me. We can rebuild.

Her hands tightened on the wheel until her knuckles bleached pale. Instead of home, she followed the road that curved past the rows of crimson maples and amber oaks. The trees of Red Leaf City never lost their color; they burned all year, reminders that beauty could hide rot if no one looked close enough.

She pulled into the gravel lot of the Red Leaf Community Resource Center.

The building stood proudly in its simplicity, two stories of brick and glass, its windows crowded with children's drawings, and flyers taped to the doors advertising GED classes and after-school programs. Inside, it always smelled of crayons and disinfectant, laughter tangled with the scrape of folding chairs.

Francine cut the engine but didn't move. She just sat, staring at the center she had built with nothing but a handful of donors and a vow. The nausea rose before she opened the door. She stumbled toward the nearest trash can, gripping the metal rim, and retched until her stomach emptied.

"Miss Frannie?"

She turned, wiping her mouth with the back of her hand. A boy no older than ten stood a few feet away, his face wide with concern. Behind him, three other children peeked from the doorway.

"I'm fine," she said, forcing a smile. Her voice was hoarse. "Something just upset my stomach." The boy pointed toward the hall inside. "Nurse Janet's got medicine for that."

The others laughed, and the sound was bright enough to make her chest ache. She straightened, brushing her hair back into place. "Tell Nurse Janet I'll keep her in business next time," she teased.

The children dissolved into giggles and scattered down the corridor.

Francine pushed open the door. The hum of the center wrapped around her.... voices reciting spelling lists, sneakers squeaking in the gym, the buzz of a copy machine. She inhaled deeply, steadying herself.

At the reception desk, Manny Alvarez, Program Director, looked up from a stack of grant applications. His face lit with warmth, though his eyes carried the fatigue of a man who had given too many evenings away to other people's children.

"Frannie," he said, rising. "Didn't expect to see you here today. I thought you'd be at court until late."

"I was," she admitted. Her voice trembled on the edge of exhaustion. "I just... needed to see this place. To remind myself why we do what we do."

Manny gestured toward the hall. "Want the tour? Or just the quick update?"

"Quick update," she said, though her feet were already carrying her toward the classrooms.

Manny followed, slipping into his well-practiced rhythm. "We've got twenty-three in GED prep now, fifteen high schoolers in after-school tutoring. Job placement programs are busier than ever.... We landed three interviews this week. The elementary and junior programs are full, and the kitchen served one hundred and forty-two meals yesterday."

Francine's lips parted. "One hundred and forty-two."

"Every one of them has a full belly by bedtime," Manny said with pride.

They passed the art room, where children hunched over sketchbooks. A girl held up a crayon drawing: a house with a door wide open, light pouring out. Above it, stick figures held hands.

Francine's throat tightened. "Beautiful," she whispered.

But with each laugh, each bright crayon, came the bile of betrayal. Her husband's shadow stretched long across these walls. He had taken her life's vow and twisted it for power, for profit. Her stomach rolled again, though there was nothing left to give.

They reached the small lounge, where teens tapped on laptops donated by a local bank. Francine leaned against the doorway, suddenly unsteady.

"When I started this program," she said softly, "there were only three children. Just three. I knew every shoe size, every birthday, every scar on their knuckles."

Manny waited.

"One of them is in prison now," she confessed, her voice splintering. "I tell myself I should have done more."

Manny shook his head gently. "We do our best, Frannie. We can't save the world."

Her eyes brimmed, but she refused to let them fall. "Then I'll save as much of it as I can." He rested his hand on her shoulder. "That's all any of us can do."

She looked out at the children again, their heads bent over textbooks, their laughter breaking against the walls. For the first time since the courthouse, she let herself breathe.

But as she walked back to her car, she pressed her palm against her stomach, whispering a vow no judge could silence, "I'm going to keep trying."

Chapter 6: The Phone Wouldn't Speak

The house was too quiet for sleep. Francine lay on her back and watched the red-leaf shadows shift across the ceiling, the city's strange autumn flickering through the blinds like a heartbeat she couldn't steady. The trial day had been a sandstorm; now the grains were settling in her chest, one anxious grain at a time.

The first call came at 11:12 p.m.

Her phone shivered on the nightstand. She rolled toward it, blinking at the screen. Unknown Caller. She swiped.

"Hello?"

Nothing. Not even breath. She listened to a hush that felt as though it had been placed there on purpose. "Hello?" she tried again, softer this time, as if gentleness might coax a human out of the line. The call disconnected.

She set the phone down and listened to her own home: the faint hum of the refrigerator, the water heater ticking once, her breath too loud in the too-quiet dark. She told herself it was the wrong number. It was easier than telling herself the truth.

The second call came at 11:28 p.m..

Another unknown caller, same silence. She didn't ask hello this time. She said, "Whoever you are, speak." The line, offended by her request, hung up on her again.

She stopped trying to sleep. She got out of bed and padded to the kitchen, poured water she didn't want, leaned against the counter, and watched her reflection tremble in the glass. Stay silent, Benjamin had pleaded across the jailhouse phone. Stay with me. The words clung like smoke. She had walked away.

Her legs still remembered walking.

At 11:43 p.m., the third call. She felt her pulse jump before the ring finished. She answered, saying nothing, and offered them the same mirror back.

Silence. Then…she wasn't sure, maybe the shape of breath. Perhaps the shape of someone smiling was a fluent language of fear.

The line went dead.

She stared at the black screen, then scrolled to Detective Otis Black. She hovered a second. It was late. She should leave a voicemail. She pressed Call anyway.

He picked up on the first ring. "Black."

She blinked. "Detective, it's Francine Grove. I…. I didn't expect you to answer."

"I keep my phone on." His voice was gravel and coffee and the hour. "What's happened?"

"They've called three times," she said. Her voice surprised her with how steady it sounded. "No voice. Just… quiet. I don't know why that's worse."

"It's worse because it lets your mind do the talking," he said. "Unknown number?"

"Yes."

"Any words at all?"

"No."

He was quiet for a beat that felt like him looking out a window at a dark street. "Mrs. Grove, listen to me," Detective Black said. "We know your husband is incarcerated, so that we can rule him out as the one making those calls. Stay calm, all right? We'll get to the bottom of it."

Francine nodded, her fingers tightening around the edge of her housecoat.

Her voice was small. "You think it's a prank?"

Black shook his head. "I think someone wants you scared. Let's make sure they don't get what they want."

"Keep your doors locked," Black said. "If the number calls again, don't answer. Let it go to voicemail and write down the time. We'll start a log and trace what we can."

"Thank you," she said, and meant it. Gratitude felt like the only door she could still close.

"Francine," he said, using her name carefully, not presuming it, "you did the hard thing today.... ignoring the press. That'll quiet them for a while."

She gave a faint laugh. "Quiet. How much louder can quiet be?"

"Loud enough to hear what matters," he said. "Get some rest if you can."

The call ended. She kept the phone against her ear for a moment, listening to the empty dial tone. Then she checked the doors, the windows, and every lock twice. When she finally lay down, the house was too still. Shadows crept across the ceiling until the dark began to unspool, and the room softened around her.

The night never really ended; it just changed jurisdictions. By morning, Black was sitting in the back row of a federal courtroom with a paper cup of bad coffee burning his palm...and an ache behind his eyes that meant he'd slept in the shape of a chair. The seal on the wall was different here, an eagle instead of the state shield, but the air carried the same lacquer of reverence and fatigue. Hudson Waters was brought in, shackled, the orange making him look almost theatrical. If Benjamin Grove had learned to wear power like a tuxedo, Waters wore it like a motorcycle jacket he'd been told to take off.

Otis wasn't here as a witness; he was here as a weathervane. He wanted to see which way Waters' wind would blow when Grove's name surfaced, because even men in shackles chased rumors like dogs chase cars.

Waters sat. He didn't look back. Men like Hudson had learned early that acknowledging the existence of back rows made them mortal. His attorney, a sleek man in a slate suit with eyes like shutters, leaned to whisper in his ear. Waters smiled without his mouth.

Proceedings clanked along. Words like continuance, discovery, and protective order stacked up until they made a wall between what everyone knew and what anyone could say. Otis scribbled in the margin of his notebook: Phone calls Fr. Grove Patrols. Then, Rumor: diversions at the Grove trial? He underlined diversions twice.

When the hearing adjourned, he rose with the pause of a man who would rather talk to a storm than to a defense attorney and made himself cross the aisle.

"Counselor," he said.

The slate suit turned. The man's smile arrived before his curiosity. "Detective Black," he said. He did not offer his hand, a small mercy.

"I'm not here to discuss the federal case," Otis said, because that was the only sentence that would open the next one. "I'm here about your client's reach."

"Ah," the attorney said, the way a man says mice when you've told him there are wolves.

"We're getting hang-up calls. Witnesses are nervous. If something happens…." Otis let the end of the sentence do its own work.

The smile didn't change shape. "If something happens, Detective, you'll investigate it."

"Is your client communicating orders from custody?"

"My client," the attorney said pleasantly, "is paying me to defend him, not to keep him in jail. He is entitled to speak with counsel. He is not entitled to make your job easy." He flicked his gaze toward the double doors. "If you have evidence of threats, bring it to the U.S. Attorney.

Otherwise… prove it."

And then he was gone, a gray slipstream of billable hours, leaving Otis with the cooling coffee cup and the sudden feeling that he had been talking to a building.

Outside, the wind worried the flag. Otis looked up at it and thought of a knot he'd been tugging since March that refused to loosen. If Waters is the shot caller, he wrote as he walked, then who's holding the phone? He didn't like the answer that came back: People who don't look like criminals when they sign the visitor log.

He headed for his car. He needed to be back across the county line before the afternoon session in Grove's trial. Rumor had it that the State intended to call Ruby Keys, Luna Turner's supervisor at Social Services. Rumor also had it that the defense would rather swallow thumbtacks.

The corridor outside the Red Leaf courtroom smelled like coffee and adrenaline. Otis arrived as the afternoon light angled toward gold. Through the glass, he saw the jury box empty, Judge Lampson's bench unoccupied, the clock hands doing their slow, patient walk to the hour. The gallery, though, was a hive: reporters adjusting lenses, protestors trying to look like concerned citizens in borrowed blazers, the odd city council member making sympathy faces.

He found Cane Walls leaning against the wall like a man who had promised himself he would not start smoking again. Cane lifted his chin in greeting.

"You see, Waters?" Cane asked.

"I saw his lawyer," Otis said. "The man's a raincoat."

"Any luck?"

"Depends on your definition. He told me to prove the weather." Otis's mouth tugged a humorless inch. "How are we here?"

Cane scrubbed his hand over his jaw. "We're not. Not yet.

Chapter 7: The State Calls Ruby Keys

The judge delayed the afternoon session by thirty minutes. Jasper claims he's got food poisoning from a bad oyster. Says he needs a recess to, what was the phrase, compose himself."

"Jasper eats oysters in Red Leaf?" Otis said. "That's an argument for the death penalty.

Cane snorted. "Clair is 'stuck in another proceeding,' allegedly. No second chair, just a plastic bag, an apology and Wyatt is only a paralegal. Meanwhile, the State's got Ruby Keys in the witness room with two Marshals and a paper bag to breathe into."

Otis felt the hair along his forearms lift. "They're stalling Ruby."

"Feels like it," Cane said. "And if I had to bet a month's pay, I'd say somebody whispered to somebody that today was the day."

Otis's gaze drifted to the frosted glass of the witness room door, where a shadow moved in restless loops…. Ruby Keys, Luna's supervisor. The woman who had smiled through staff meetings and told overworked caseworkers to "prioritize the priorities," as if children could be sorted like mail. Otis had never liked her, but not liking wasn't a crime. He had learned that the hard way.

Lucas O'Hell came up fast, shoes squeaking. "Judge is taking the bench," he said, breathless. "Jasper claims he can't proceed without co-counsel and also might faint. We're objecting to any continuance."

They moved in, the room drawing them like a magnet. Judge Lampson took her seat with the calm of a woman who had given up on being surprised by theatrics. Jackson Hill stood; Jasper rose more slowly, one hand pressed to his abdomen in a performance that would have earned a polite review if the audience hadn't been twelve people deciding whether a man would die in prison.

"Mr. McMichaels," Lampson said, "the court understands you're unwell."

"Your Honor," Jasper said, face arranged into pallor, "I apologize to the court and to the State. I am experiencing acute food poisoning and have been advised by my physician to seek immediate rest. My co-counsel is regrettably detained in another division. Given the gravity of today's witness…" he didn't say Ruby; he let the suggestion do the heavy lifting…. "we cannot proceed without infringing on my client's right to effective counsel. I respectfully request a continuance until tomorrow morning."

Hill was already shaking his head. "Your Honor, the State has a witness under subpoena who has traveled and who requires security accommodations. We are prepared to proceed. We object to the delay."

Jasper dabbed at his brow with a linen square. "I am not grandstanding, Your Honor. I simply cannot stand."

"You're standing now," Lampson observed.

A titter rippled through the gallery and died under her gaze.

Lampson looked from one table to the other as if weighing two knives. Then she sighed, which in Judge Lampson was the same as slamming a door. "This court is not a theater. Mr. McMichaels, if you are genuinely ill, you may sit. You may conduct a limited cross today and reserve the rest for the morning when your colleague is present. The defendant's rights will not be injured by an evening of soup and crackers. Mr. Hill, call your witness."

Jasper opened his mouth and closed it again. He sat. The linen made another lap across his forehead.

Otis felt the room tighten. Lucas slipped out to fetch Ruby from the witness room. Cane leaned forward, forearms on his knees, the posture of a man waiting for something either to break or to mend.

Jackson stood. "The State calls Ruby Keys."

The door opened. Ruby Keys walked in with a careful smile that didn't touch her eyes. She wore a navy suit that said, "Administration and I'm not afraid," along with sensible shoes that admitted she was. She took the oath with a tremor only the front row could see.

Otis watched her hands. They were steady enough. But when she sat, she didn't place them on the rail like most witnesses. She slipped them under the ledge, out of view. Hiding them.

Protecting them. He made a note he didn't need to read again: Hands tell on the mouth. "Ms. Keys," Hill began, "state your name and your position."

"Ruby Elaine Keys," she said crisply. "Supervisor, Red Leaf City Social Services, Family and Children's Division."

"For how long?"

"Seven years."

"Do you supervise Luna Turner?"

"Yes."

"Directing your attention to the period when Jonah Carter was reported missing, did Ms. Turner report concerns to you about irregularities she noticed, children disappearing and reappearing on paper without clear documentation, referrals unclosed, and outside parties requesting schedules for specific youth programs?"

Ruby's smile faltered for a fraction. "Ms. Turner is… thorough," she said. "She reports many concerns."

"And did you instruct her to pursue those concerns?"

A pause the length of a blink. "I instructed her to follow protocol." "Did you ever instruct her to stop digging?"

Jasper was halfway out of his chair before the last word finished. "Objection. Leading and assumes facts not in evidence."

"Overruled as to form," Lampson said. "Rephrase, Mr. Hill."

"Ms. Keys," Hill said, softer now, a scalpel instead of a hammer, "did you tell Ms. Turner to focus on other cases and leave Jonah Carter's file alone?"

Ruby's eyes did a quick, involuntary thing…. left, right, home. "I told her we were short-staffed and that resources had to be allocated efficiently."

"Efficiently," Hill repeated. "Did that efficiency include sharing program schedules with any person outside Social Services?"

"Objection," Jasper said sharply. "Compound and argumentative."

"Overruled," Judge Lampson said.

"No," Luna answered.

Hill let the no sit like a glass he intended to tap. "Did you ever receive money or gifts from any individual tied to the Grove campaign or to the Red Leaf Community Resource Center in your capacity as supervisor?"

"No," Ruby said again, quicker this time. "I donate to the Center like everyone else."

"Did you ever receive money from any associate of Hudson Waters?"

The name slid across the rail like a blade. Ruby's mouth thinned. "Absolutely not."

Otis watched her eyes again, not the blink, but the pause

after the blink. A half-beat longer than a lie needed. His pen found the margin: Stall on 'stop digging' Resource talk. Schedules?

A deputy slipped into the well and put a note on Lucas's table. Lucas read it, swallowed it, and handed it to Jackson. Jackson's jaw set.

"Ms. Keys," he said, voice still even, "we're going to talk about emails."

Jasper coughed into his linen as if his stomach had chosen that exact word to object. The gallery leaned forward as one body.

Otis felt his phone buzz in his pocket. He didn't look, but he knew what it would be: patrol confirming they were parked outside Francine's house, lights off, eyes on. He pictured the red leaves moving in the day like the hem of a robe.

Cane shifted beside him. "You think Ruby flips?" he murmured. "Ruby doesn't flip," Otis said. "Ruby calibrates."

"Then what happens?"

Otis watched Jackson lift the first exhibit. "We find out who's been holding the phone."

He could still hear the federal attorney's voice in the back of his skull: Prove it. The trouble with proof was never the what. It was always the who and the when: who handed whom a schedule, who asked for which child's name, when the call was placed, and when the call was answered.

In the front row, Luna Turner sat with her hands clenched in her lap, knuckles white under the strain of staying seated when everything in her wanted to stand and point. Two rows behind her, Francine had slipped in, pale but composed, the weight of a night with three silent calls tucked under her eyes. She did not look toward Benjamin. She looked at Ruby. She looked at the witness whose mouth might finally admit the shape of the machinery.

Somewhere, in another building with a different seal on the wall, Hudson Waters would be smiling without his mouth. Otis didn't need to see him to feel the tug of the thread. He sat forward, elbows on his knees, and let the courtroom gather the next breath.

On the wall, the clock's second hand climbed toward the mark where days either broke open or broke apart.

Chapter 8: Smoke

Ruby Keys clutched the rail like it might steady the part of her that words could not. Under the fluorescents, her navy suit looked a shade too dark…. the color people choose when they want to be believed. Jackson Hill held a thin stack of papers he hadn't shown yet. Jasper McMichaels sat on the edge of his seat for cross, one hand on his stomach, the other hovering over the lectern as if it were a prop he might lean on when the performance required it.

"Ms. Keys," Jackson said, voice patient, "you've told this court you followed protocol."

"Yes," Ruby said. "To the best of my ability."

"And protocol includes replying to emails?" He lifted his brows slightly.

"Yes."

Jackson glanced at the clock like a man timing a soufflé. "Did you ever email anyone outside Social Services about program schedules?"

"No," she said, too fast.

Jackson lifted the top page from his stack. "Your email, March ninth. Subject line: Schedules. Recipient: charliedeskers@....."

"Objection," Jasper snapped, the word too sharp for the room. "Foundation and hearsay. And we have not authenticated…."

"The court will see the exhibit," Judge Lampson said. "Overruled as to foundation.

The State may lay it by testimony. Mr. Hill?"

Jackson stepped closer, not menacing, but inevitable. "Ms. Keys, do you deny sending this email?" Ruby's eyes did that tiny left-right-left again, looking for an exit only she could see. "I… sent many emails."

"This one contained a list of program times and the names of children scheduled to be in the after-school room that week," Jackson said. "Do you deny sending it?"

"I don't recall."

"And the reply from 'C.D.'?" Jackson flipped the page.

"Quote: Got it. It will be easy to grab from the side alley."

A ripple moved through the gallery. Ruby flinched like the sound reached her before anyone else heard it. "I don't know who that is," Ruby said, but the words had splinters.

"Charlie Deskers is a charged co-conspirator," Jackson said evenly. "The jury will hear from him when his health permits." He paused, studying her.

Ruby stared down at her folded hands like they might teach her how to hold herself together. Jackson turned halfway toward his table, then looked back. His tone hardened just enough to slice through the silence.

"So, I'm going to ask you again," he said. "Did you ever accept cash or favors from anyone connected to Benjamin Grove's office or Hudson Waters?"

A long pause. Then….

"Yes."

The room erupted in gasps…. the scrape of shoes, the rustle of clothes, the dull click of camera shutters from the back row.

"Order," Judge Lampson commanded, gavel cracking once against the wood.

Jackson waited until the noise faded. His voice dropped,

steady and precise.

"Just so the record is clear, you lied earlier when I asked if you had ever taken money from Hudson Waters?"

Ruby's voice trembled. "Yes."

A murmur rippled through the jury box, low and disbelieving.

"Order," Judge Lampson said again, sharper this time.

Jackson didn't look away. "And you also lied when I asked whether, while serving as a supervisor, you accepted money from Benjamin Grove's office during an active investigation into a missing child?"

Ruby's eyes glistened. "Yes."

Jackson let the word settle. "No further questions." He returned to his seat, the hush of the courtroom following him like a verdict not yet spoken.

Judge Lampson called for the defense. Jasper didn't rise this time. He leaned slightly forward, elbows on the defense table, his tone smooth enough to sound reasonable.... almost kind.

"Ms. Keys," he began, "you've worked for Social Services... what, eight years?"

"Seven."

"Seven," he repeated, like a compliment. "And during those seven years, you've handled hundreds of case files?"

"Yes."

"Sometimes hundreds at once?"

"Yes."

"So, it's fair to say mistakes can happen.... misfiled notes, misplaced forms, misdirected emails?"

Ruby hesitated. "I... suppose."

He nodded slightly, as if agreeing with her. "You said you don't recall sending the email in question. That's honest. But you can't say for certain that you didn't, correct?"

She swallowed. "No, I can't."

"And you receive dozens of emails a day. Some from staff, some from outside agencies?"

"Yes."

"And if a name popped up you didn't recognize…. 'C.D.' for example, you might assume it was a volunteer, or another liaison?"

"Possibly."

"Possibly," Jasper echoed, leaning back. "Now, about this alleged payment, when you say you accepted money from Mr. Grove's office, are you referring to a check issued through the Red Leaf Community Fund?"

"Yes."

"That fund, Ms. Keys, provides community outreach grants to Social Services departments across the county, doesn't it?"

"Yes, but…."

"Just yes or no, please."

"Yes."

"So, what we have is a legitimate check, through a legitimate grant, not an envelope of cash in a dark alley."

Her eyes flickered down. "It wasn't like that."

"Exactly," Jasper said softly, almost sympathetic. "It wasn't like that. No further questions, Your Honor."

He sat back, folding his hands, and let the implication breathe, the idea that what had sounded like corruption might just be confusion written in bureaucratic ink.

Ruby's fingers trembled as she unlatched from the rail. At the judge's nod, she stepped down, head lowered and moved past the jury box toward the aisle. The murmur in the gallery followed her like static.

Judge Lampson's gavel struck once. "We'll take a ten-minute recess."

The courtroom buzzed with movement.... papers rustling, murmurs swelling as spectators stood. Wyatt Reddings stood and followed Jasper into the hallway, his phone face down between his legal pad and his thigh.

It vibrated once, then again.

He glanced at the screen.

A message from an unknown number:

Unknown: *Some people need to learn to keep quiet...*

For a heartbeat, he didn't breathe.

He slid the phone toward Jasper's elbow.

Jasper glanced down mid-sentence, then again, longer this time. The color drained from beneath his cheekbones. His jaw set.

"Who's it referring to?" Jasper asked quietly.

Wyatt's throat felt dry. "Ruby?" Jasper exhaled through his nose. "Could be. Could be someone trying to make it look that way." He lifted the phone, screen tilted so only Wyatt could see. "We need to alert Red Leaf PD. Now."

Wyatt nodded, already reaching for his phone. "I'll go to the bathroom and make the call."

"Make sure you tell them it came during court," Jasper said. "Chain of evidence matters."

"I'll keep playing sick," Jasper murmured, eyes still on the phone. "See if I can persuade Lampson to end early."

But before Wyatt could leave, Bailiff Young's voice cut through the tension. "Court will now resume."

They exchanged a quick look, the air tightening between them, and joined the others filing back inside.

"All rise."

Judge Lampson took the bench, the gavel striking once.

McMichaels barely had time to speak before she said, "Be seated."

"The State may proceed," she added.

Hill rose from the prosecution table, files already in hand. "The State calls…"

The fire alarm didn't sound so much as cough. Once. Then again, louder. The bailiff lifted a palm, listening. Judge Lampson frowned, waiting for the system, or the building, to decide whether to panic.

Then the double doors at the back shuddered under pressure from outside, followed by the low, chaotic swell of shouting. The crowd outside wasn't dispersing; it was collapsing inward, a single noise contracting and expanding all at once.

McMichaels turned toward Reddings, and for the briefest moment, his face flickered with relief.

The bailiff's radio crackled. "Dispersal now…smoke…repeat, smoke…."

"Ladies and gentlemen of the jury," Lampson said, already halfway to standing, "you will remain in the box. Bailiff, secure the doors."

Outside the courtroom, shouting. Glass somewhere. A smell…. not fire, but the bitter chemical of a cheap smoke device pushed past its ambition. The bailiff and two Marshals moved to the hallway, a practiced flex of muscle and calm.

Jackson looked at Lucas. Lucas looked at Otis Black and

Cane Walls in the gallery. Without exchanging a word, they all stood.

"Counsel will remain," Lampson said, but she didn't bark. Her gaze had moved to the jury again, a mother hen with a gavel.

The marshal returned and closed the doors behind him. "It's a smoke bomb," he told the judge softly. "Someone tossed it into the crowd. Patrol is clearing the steps. No fire."

"Very well," Lampson said. "We will recess for the day. Jury, you will be escorted to the room and then dismissed. The same admonitions apply. Court is adjourned."

The gavel fell. The room exhaled all at once and then tried to inhale too much.

The corridor was chaos governed by badge and habit. Reporters surged, asking questions that started with "Is it true?" and ended with "on background." Protestors shook signs, voices hoarse from chanting, faces streaked with cold and anger. Someone had stepped on the canister; a gray smear marked the floor, acrid at the edges. Outside the glass, blue lights pulsed.

"Inside," Cane told Jackson and Lucas. He didn't ask. He put a hand on Jackson's arm and steered him back through the courtroom doors as if tidal currents could be reversed with a palm.

Across the hall, Jasper and Wyatt didn't head for the elevators as usual. They moved in the other direction, toward Otis Black and Cane, as the detectives turned to re-enter.

"Detectives," Jasper said, stopping them with a word he didn't like to use. "We need to speak. Now."

Cane's eyebrows lifted a millimeter. "About?"

Wyatt's hand shook holding out the phone. The message glowed. *Some people need to learn to keep quiet...*

Cane read it once. Otis read it twice. Neither of them asked who the "some people" were. They didn't need to.

"Let's go," Otis said. "Downstairs. Back way."

Chapter 9: Unknown Threat

They cut through a service corridor, past a bulletin board that hadn't been updated since last year's flu clinic, into a stairwell that smelled like old paint. At the bottom, a side door opened onto a loading lane where a patrol car idled. Cane waved; the driver nodded, pulled forward.

"Station," Otis said. "We'll have tech look at it." Jasper hesitated. "Detective… we have a client…." "You have a problem," Cane said. "Bring it."

They piled into unmarked cars, the kind that only didn't look like a police car to people who never looked at police cars and slid out onto the side street where the city pretended not to be watching.

Red Leaf PD's tech room had low ceilings, humming towers, and a whiteboard with a smear of numbers that meant more than most testimony did. Amaya, she wore her hair in a bun that threatened to win a fight with gravity and rolled her chair over when Otis held up the phone.

"Unknown sender?" she asked. "Unknown, likely a VoIP hop," Otis said.

"Uh-huh," Amaya said, fingers already playing the keyboard. "Text came from a relay…yep, third-party app, burned within a minute of send. Disposable routing. Whoever sent it paid two dollars to be a ghost. I can slap a subpoena on three companies and be told to go talk to the fourth."

Wyatt sank into a chair. The fabric squeaked. "Anything?" Jasper asked.

Amaya tilted the monitor, scrolled. "If I'm lucky, I'll get a time zone and a shrug. But watch this…. whoever sent it used the same route as three other messages in the last forty-eight hours. Same header shape, same clock drift. All went to different recipients, all unknown numbers attached, all burned on impact."

"Recipients?" Cane said.

Amaya's eyes flicked. "Two of them are local. One went to a reporter. One to a burner phone the lab saw on a case last month. The third is a number registered to a nonprofit's info line." She looked up. "Red Leaf Community Resource Center."

Jasper felt his mouth go dry. "You're telling me the same sender hit a reporter, a burner, and the Center?"

"I'm telling you the same tool did," Amaya said. "Whoever is behind it knows how to make a message float without a return address."

Wyatt rubbed a hand over his jaw. "Can you…Can you protect us? I mean, our homes…"

Otis looked at him, and for once, there was no adversary in it. "Chief can put units on you tonight. But understand something, Counselor. People who send messages like this aren't warning you for your safety. They're measuring your fear."

Chief Ezra Lightening stepped into the doorway then, his tie loosened, his eyes like someone had rung his bell three times too many today. "Counselors," he said with a nod. "Detectives. Update?"

Amaya spun her chair. "Untraceable relay. Pattern matches three other messages, one pinged the community center's line."

Lightening's mouth pressed into a line. "We'll assign escorts for counsel this evening," he said, looking at Jasper and Wyatt. "You'll have a car to your homes and a drive-by on the hour until morning."

"Chief," Jasper said, equal parts rattled and offended by the existence of rattling, "we are not the State."

"Today you are all in the same city," Lightening said. "And the city is jumpy." He looked to Otis and Cane. "Keep the

Marshals looped. I don't want Ruby Keys walking out of that building without a uniformed shadow until we get her back tomorrow."

"Yes, Chief," Cane said.

Lightening's gaze returned to the defense. "If you receive another message, you send it to Detective Black immediately. Don't reply. Don't posture. Don't assume you understand who it's for."

Wyatt nodded too fast. Jasper nodded once, slowly, as if agreement had to be earned by his own mouth.

Lightening's phone buzzed. He checked it, grimaced. "Protest got spicy," he said. "Smoke device, two minor injuries, a half-dozen detained. No one with a brain is talking. We'll clear the steps by nightfall. In the meantime, leave by the south exit."

He left like a gust.

Amaya handed the phone back to Wyatt with two fingers, like returning a lab specimen. "If they're smart, they'll go dormant. If they're cocky, they'll ping you again. Either way, leave your ringer on."

Wyatt pocketed the device. "Detective Black," he said, voice lower now, "what do you think this is? Grove's enemies? Grove's… friends?"

Otis looked at him for a long beat. "This is what it feels like when someone behind bars wants to move the furniture and can't reach the room."

"You mean Waters," Wyatt said, not a question.

Otis didn't confirm. He didn't need to. He looked at Cane, then at the clock.

"Let's move," he said. "We'll take you back through the secure entrance. Press is still outside. They smell blood but don't know where it's coming from."

Back at the courthouse, the day had bruised into evening.

The red trees along the avenue appeared darker, almost brown, in the fading light. A chalky residue clung to the steps where the smoke had been; officers, wearing gloves, swept it into bags. Protest signs leaned against the barricades like exhausted sentries.

The main doors were shut. The south entrance…rarely used, always locked, opened to Otis's badge. He led Jasper and Wyatt down a short hall where cinderblock paint met bulletin board, and into the shadowed lobby where Jackson Hill and Lucas O'Hell were waiting with two Marshals. Jackson's tie was loose; his face read no comment even when he wasn't speaking.

Reporters hovered outside the glass like moths, cameras ready. One spotted the movement and slapped the pane with a palm.

"Mr. Hill…. did the State receive threats today?" "Is the wife going to testify?"

"Did Social Services collude?"

Jackson kept his eyes forward. Lucas's hand closed on the handle. "Not this way," Otis said quietly. "Back hall. Then cars."

They turned and passed the witness's room. The door was shut; a marshal sat on a folding chair outside it, looking not at his phone but at the opposite wall, the way men look when they don't trust distractions. Inside, Ruby Keys sat with her purse in her lap and her phone face-down on the table, staring at the seam where two floor tiles met.

In the stairwell, breath and footsteps echoed. At the bottom, a side door opened to a narrow strip of pavement bordered by hedges. Two patrol units idled to take them to their cars.

"Counsel first," Cane said. "Then the State."

Wyatt climbed into the back seat of the first car. Jasper paused, hand on the door. "Detective," he said to Otis, so low it might have been to himself, "if this is Waters… why threaten us?"

Otis met his eyes. "Because fear is a blunt instrument. And because sometimes the easiest way to keep a witness quiet is to make everyone else wonder what happens if they speak."

Jasper's throat worked. He got in.

The cars pulled away with that slow, deliberate creep that says we are not running, even when we are. The hedges shivered in the evening wind. Otis watched them go until the taillights turned the corner and slipped into traffic.

Behind him, Jackson exhaled. "Tomorrow," he said, like a promise and a problem. "Tomorrow," Lucas echoed.

"Tomorrow," Cane said, but his eyes were on the witness room door.

Otis's phone buzzed. He checked it. A patrol unit had parked on Francine Grove's block. Another had taken a lazy loop past the Community Resource Center. He texted back: Hold. Quiet. Report any unknown vehicles. He thought of the boy who had lined up his pencils, of a woman on a jail phone talking to an inmate.

The night settled, thin and watchful. Somewhere in the next county, Hudson Waters lay on a metal cot and stared at the ceiling, a man calculating the value of other people's fear. Somewhere in a holding cell in Red Leaf county jail, Benjamin Grove sat with his hands folded exactly the way he had told donors to fold theirs at prayer breakfasts and listened to the sound a city makes when it begins to understand the price of silence.

Back at the precinct, Detective Otis Black was the last one in the station that night. The hum of the vending machine in the corner was louder than it should have been. Paperwork was stacked on his desk, but his mind was still on the message Wyatt Reddings had slid to McMichaels during Ruby Keys' testimony.

He pinched the bridge of his nose, exhaled, and reached for

his jacket when his cell phone rang. At 10:37 p.m., calls weren't casual.

"Detective Black," he said, voice gravel.

"Detective, this is Prosecutor Angela Valintino, federal task force." The voice was clipped, professional. "I was briefed that Ruby Keys testified today about payments from Grove in exchange for child access. That's… new to us. I'll need contact information to set a meeting. This could strengthen our case against Hudson Waters."

Black hesitated. "That testimony was sealed until the transcript's processed."

"We got ears in the room, Detective," Valintino said quickly. "I'm not here to debate procedure. I need Keys' information before the trail goes cold. Waters' case hinges on every link in that chain."

Black stared at the paperwork scattered across his desk, a dozen names. Half a dozen lives are already ruined. What harm could come from passing a number along?

He read it to her slowly, careful to pronounce each digit. She thanked him briskly and ended the call.

He shut the light off at 10:58 p.m., walked down the corridor, the echo of his own shoes following him.

Outside, the parking lot was too empty, the sodium lamps buzzing. He unlocked his car and slid his hand toward the door handle. That's when the roar of an engine cut through the silence. A sedan flew down the street, windows open. A voice spat into the night: "Too many witnesses! They need to shut up!"

Black froze, hand still on his sidearm. He spun, eyes searching the dark, but the car was already gone, taillights disappearing around the bend.

"What the heck is going on?" he muttered. His pulse rattled in his throat.

For a moment, he considered dialing Chief Lightening, but the hour, the fatigue, the futility stopped him. Instead, he slipped into his own car cautiously, checked his mirrors twice, and drove home with one hand resting on his weapon the entire way. At home, he locked every door and window. Usually, his pistol went in the safe at night, but not tonight. Tonight, he laid it on the nightstand, staring at it longer than he should have, before letting sleep drag him under.

Chapter 10: No One Is Safe

The buzz of his phone woke him at 6:30 a.m. Detective Cane Walls' voice was low, urgent. "Otis, you need to get to 5462 Cherry Lane. It's Ruby Keys. She's dead."

Black sat up, heart snapping awake before his mind. "Say that again."

"Neighbor found her this morning. The dog was sitting on the porch, whining. The door was ajar. She went in, found Ruby face down in the tub. We're holding the scene. You'd better get here."

"I'm on my way."

Black threw on yesterday's clothes, holstered his gun, and was out the door before the coffee maker even clicked on. The streets of Red Leaf City looked innocent under the morning sun …. school buses, joggers, and commuters sipping drive-thru cups. But every shadow felt heavier than it had last night.

When he pulled up to Cherry Lane, squad cars blocked the street. Yellow tape flapped in the breeze. Neighbors stood in clumps, whispering, their faces pale. A neighbor's dog barked somewhere behind a fence, frantic.

Cane met him at the curb, jaw tight. "It's bad."

Inside, the air smelled wrong. Not of blood, but of intrusion…. overturned furniture, drawers yanked out, papers scattered. A lamp lay shattered near the couch. The television was still on, volume low, a children's cartoon laughing over the scene.

"This wasn't a burglary," Black said flatly. "No," Cane replied. "This was a message."

They walked down the hallway. The bathroom door was half-open. The tub was half-filled, the water tinged faintly pink. Ruby Keys floated face down, hair fanned like black seaweed, one arm twisted unnaturally against the porcelain.

Black swallowed hard, the image searing. "Jesus."

Cane lowered his voice. "Neighbor says the dog wouldn't stop barking. That's why she checked. Said she thought Ruby must've overslept. Found the front door cracked."

They stepped back into the hall. Both men stood in silence, listening to the sound of uniforms moving around the house, snapping photographs, bagging evidence.

Black finally spoke. "I gave Valintino her contact info last night. Fed prosecutor. She called, asking for it."

Cane turned. "You think that's how they found her?"

"I don't know," Black admitted, anger chewing at his words. "But somebody knew Ruby had testified. And they didn't wait twenty-four hours to shut her up."

Cane exhaled through his nose. "If Valintino's clean, someone on her staff isn't. If she's dirty, she just fed Keys to the wolves."

Black stared at the ransacked living room, his fists curling. "Either way, we can't trust anyone anymore."

For the first time since the trial began, both detectives felt it in their bones … this wasn't about justice anymore. It was about survival. Detective Otis Black had seen death in all its shapes, but something about Ruby Keys sitting face down in a half-drawn tub gnawed at him. Maybe it was the pink tint of the water, perhaps the way her hair had spread like dark seaweed, maybe it was that he had handed her phone number to a federal prosecutor less than twelve hours earlier.

He and Detective Cane Walls stood shoulder to shoulder in the hallway, letting the crime scene techs work the bathroom. They were looking around the house once more, it was a mess.

They left the house once the photos were taken and the scene secured. The morning air felt colder than it should have been, like the city itself was recoiling. Neighbors whispered from their porches, clutching bathrobes around their shoulders. A woman held Ruby's dog on a leash, the animal still whining, ears back, as if it had seen more than anyone should.

At the curb, Walls exhaled a curse. "I'll meet you back at the precinct. Chief needs to hear this straight."

By the time they reached the station, the clock over the bullpen read 8:12 a.m. The building buzzed with early shift chatter…. phones ringing, keyboards tapping, coffee cups clinking. None of it sounded normal anymore.

Chief Ezra Lightening's office door was open, the man himself pacing inside. He was tall and broad-shouldered, but his constant movement shaved away authority, leaving him looking jittery instead of commanding. His tie was loosened, his jacket tossed on a chair. He stopped pacing only long enough to glance at his watch.

"Detectives," he said as they stepped in. "You've been at the scene?"

"Yes, sir," Black said. "Ruby Keys is dead. A neighbor found her this morning. House looks staged as a burglary, but…"

Walls finished it. "But it isn't. Someone wanted her gone."

Lightening rubbed a hand down his face. "Darn it. She just testified yesterday."

"That's the problem," Black said carefully. "And last night, a federal prosecutor called me. Said she'd heard Ruby testified in the Grove's case, and she asked for her contact info, so I gave it.

This morning, Ruby's dead."

Lightening stopped pacing, but his eyes flicked to his watch again. "Prosecutor's name?" "Angela Valintino. She said she's on the task force, tied to Waters' case."

Lightening pressed his lips together, then nodded. "All right. I'll make some calls, see if she checks out. In the meantime, this doesn't leave this office. Understood?"

Black and Walls both nodded.

Lightening grabbed his jacket, then set it back down again, restless. "We'll lock down Ruby's files, notify the DA, and keep this out of the press as long as possible. The last thing we need is protestors adding a martyr to their chants."

He looked at his watch again, frowned, and waved them off. "Go. Be at the courthouse. Keep the trial moving. I'll handle this end."

The detectives exchanged a glance but said nothing.

They left the office in silence, walking side by side through the bullpen. When they reached the lot and slid into Black's car, Walls finally spoke.

"Did something feel off to you about the Chief?"

Black turned the key. "He's always pacing. He's a nervous guy. It's how he's wired." "Yeah," Walls said slowly, "but did you notice how he kept looking at his watch?" Black frowned, thinking back. "Yeah... maybe it's something, maybe it's not."

"It's 8:38 a.m.," Walls said, checking his own watch. "He just got in, and already he's wearing out the numbers. That's not nerves. That's timing."

Black shot him a sideways look. "Forget about it, Walls. You might be overthinking it."

"Maybe," Walls said, staring out the windshield. "But I'd rather trust my gut and be wrong than ignore it and bury another witness."

Black drummed his fingers on the wheel. After a long pause, he nodded once. "Copy that. But until we have facts, we keep everything between us."

"Deal," Walls said. "We don't even speak assumptions out loud unless we can back them up."

They pulled up to the courthouse twenty minutes later. Protestors already lined the steps, their signs like a forest of accusation: JUSTICE FOR JONAH, FRANNIE IS INNOCENT, GROVE LIED TO US. Police kept a barricade between the crowd and the doors, but the chants still bled through the glass.

Inside, the corridors hummed with tension. Reporters loitered, jurors shuffled, attorneys whispered in huddles. But something was off; there was no movement toward the courtroom.

Black and Walls pushed through a knot of people gathered near the double doors. "What's going on?" Black asked.

The bailiff looked worried, his hand gripping his belt like it was the only thing holding him upright. "Court's delayed. The court reporter's machine is missing. Can't proceed without it."

From somewhere down the hall, they heard Henry Printerson's voice, sharp with frustration. "They're blaming me for the delay! I don't take the machine home, for goodness' sake. I leave it locked in the cabinet every night. Somebody took it."

Black and Walls didn't comment. They just looked at each other, two men who'd seen too many coincidences pile into patterns.

They sat on the wooden bench near the doors, watching the hallway swirl with rumors and irritation. The trial was paused, but the tension wasn't. If anything, it was louder now.

Walls leaned back, his arms crossed. "First Ruby. Now this."

Black didn't reply. His eyes stayed fixed on the courtroom doors, waiting, listening, every instinct screaming that the silence was being sharpened into a weapon.

And for the first time since the trial began, he wondered how many more voices would be erased before justice ever spoke.

Chapter 11: Fractures

The bailiff's voice cracked over the chatter in the corridor:

"Court will now resume. All parties to the courtroom."

The announcement sent a ripple through the crowd. People straightened coats, folded newspapers, and capped coffee cups. For three hours, they had sat restlessly on benches or wandered the halls, irritation simmering just beneath the surface. Now, as the doors opened, they poured in like passengers boarding a delayed train —exhausted, resigned, but needing to see where it would take them.

Detectives Otis Black and Cane Walls slipped into their usual place along the side rail. The jury filed in, eyes glassy with fatigue. Even the protestors outside had grown quieter, their chants reduced to hoarse murmurs that bled faintly through the walls.

When Judge Nancy Lampson took the bench, she carried the weight of the wasted morning in her expression. She adjusted her glasses, glanced at the clock, and exhaled audibly before speaking.

"Due to the unfortunate delay this morning," she said, "today's session will be shortened. Counsel, we will adjourn early. Mr. Hill, hold all vital testimonies and key witnesses until tomorrow, when the court can give them due time. Understood?"

Jackson Hill, the prosecutor, nodded, jaw tight. "Yes, Your Honor." "Very well. Defense may proceed."

Jasper McMichaels rose with studied calm, though Black noticed the tension in his shoulders. "Your Honor, the defense calls Evan Gills, staff director to long-time Red Leaf politician Benjamin Grove."

Evan Gills was a broad-shouldered man in his forties, the kind of aide who looked like he had spent his adult life catching papers before they fell off a desk. He swore the oath, sat, and folded his hands neatly on the stand.

"Mr. Gills," Jasper began, "you have worked with Benjamin Grove for how long?" "Twelve years," Gills said proudly. "Since his city council days."

"And in those years, how would you describe his influence on Red Leaf City?"

Gills smiled at the jury. "Transformative. He was always the first to arrive and the last to leave. He pushed tirelessly to reduce crime rates, open community centers, and connect with families. I've seen him personally pay for kids' school supplies, make late-night hospital visits, and sponsor after-school programs. He's a man of integrity."

Black glanced at Walls. Neither detective moved a muscle.

Jasper's questions rolled on, painting Grove as the model citizen, the public servant betrayed by circumstance. Gills affirmed them all, his voice steady, his tone almost pastoral.

When Jasper finally said, "No further questions," Judge Lampson gestured to the prosecutor. "Cross?"

Jackson Hill stood but kept his voice even. "Mr. Gills, you testified that Mr. Grove sponsored community centers. Did you personally oversee the funding for those centers?"

"I facilitated them, yes."

"Did you track where every dollar came from and went?" "I… no, not directly. That was the accounting office." Hill nodded once. "We'll return to that tomorrow. No further questions."

"Witness dismissed," Lampson said.

Jasper rose again. "Your Honor, the defense calls Betty Williams."

Betty Williams was smaller and older, with her silver hair tucked into a bun. She carried a ledger into the witness stand like a shield. After swearing in, Jasper began with a smile.

"Ms. Williams, what is your occupation?"

"I'm an accountant. I've handled Mr. Grove's campaign finances and personal books for fifteen years."

"And have you ever uncovered evidence of illegal transactions in those books?"

"Never," Betty said firmly. She held the ledger up slightly. "Everything has always been clean. No off-the-record transfers, no suspicious wires. If Mr. Grove were laundering money, I would have seen it."

The defense table nodded like a choir hearing its hymn.

But across the aisle, Jackson Hill's expression darkened. He had not expected this witness. He shuffled his notes quickly, but the clock betrayed him. Lampson leaned forward.

"Mr. Hill, it is nearly four o'clock. Do you wish to begin cross now or reserve for the morning?" Hill hesitated, then exhaled through his nose. "The morning, Your Honor."

"So ordered," Lampson said. "Court is adjourned until nine a.m. tomorrow." Her gavel struck once, and just like that, the day was done.

The corridor was filled with noise again, as reporters called out questions, attorneys whispered, and protesters pressed against the barricades outside. Black and Walls moved against the flow until they reached Henry Printerson, the court reporter. He stood red-faced near the door, his arms crossed, a storm under his breath.

"They're blaming me for the delay," Henry snapped before they even asked. "You believe that? I don't take that machine home. It stays locked in the cabinet behind the judge's chambers every night. Someone lifted it, and it wasn't me."

"Show us," Black said.

Henry led them through a narrow hall to the back chamber area. He opened a tall metal locker, empty except for a dust mark shaped like the missing machine.

"Right there," he said, stabbing the space with a finger. "Locked it at five last night. Came in at eight this morning, gone."

"Anyone else have access?" Walls asked.

"Clerks. Bailiffs. Maybe janitorial." Henry's voice hardened. "But not me." "You get any strange notes or texts lately?" Black pressed.

Henry frowned. "No. Why would I? What are you asking me these questions for?"

The detectives didn't answer. They thanked him curtly and left, his indignation following them out the door.

Back at the precinct, the fluorescent lights hummed a little too loudly. Black and Walls sat at adjoining desks, typing their report with deliberate care. They wanted a paper trail…something clean, something no one could twist later.

When the report was filed, Black stared at the phone on his desk. His gut told him to leave it. His instincts told him otherwise. Finally, he dialed.

Valintino answered on the first ring. No hello, no greeting. "Who killed my witness?" she snapped.

Black froze. "What?"

"Don't play dumb," she said, her tone like a whip. "Ruby Keys. She was mine. She could've tied Waters to Grove, and now she's gone. Who killed her?"

Black closed his eyes, pinched the bridge of his nose. "Lower your voice, Prosecutor. How do you even know she's dead?"

"Word gets around," Valintino shot back. "I didn't even get to talk to her. Do you think I enjoy hearing about it secondhand? Black, what the heck is going on in your city?"

The silence stretched. He could feel her anger buzzing through the line like electricity. Finally, he sighed heavily. "That's what I'd like to know."

He ended the call, dropped the receiver back in its cradle, and stared at the desk. Walls looked over. "Well?"

"She knew," Black said quietly. "Knew before I said a word. Angry, but clean. If she didn't feed Ruby to the wolves, then who did?"

Walls leaned back, arms folded. "You think it's inside?"

Black's jaw tightened. "Absolutely. I think I'm done trusting anyone with a badge until we find out."

The two detectives sat in silence, the hum of the station louder than it should have been, both men carrying the same thought: the real danger wasn't only outside the courthouse, it might already be sitting inside their walls.

Chapter 12: Above Our Pay Grade

The station clock bled its way toward five in the late afternoon, the kind of hour when adrenaline collapses into coffee and stubbornness. Detective Otis Black stared at his monitor but saw only the ripples from this morning: Ruby face down, pink water, the neighbor's shaking hands. Across the desk, Cane Walls clicked his pen open and closed, the tiny snap serving as a metronome for his impatience.

Walls broke it. "We should go see him." Black didn't look up. "See who?"

"Waters," Walls said. "Federal holding. We keep circling the shadows. Let's put a name back in a chair and see what his mouth does when it thinks it's safe."

Black felt the automatic no-rise and choke mechanism. "We're not on his case."

"But it's our city," Walls said. "And the city's bleeding from a hundred paper cuts. We ask, we listen, we don't tip. If he's behind the scare tactics, it'll itch him to show it." Black pushed away from the desk, the old chair protesting. "Fine. We go together. We ask nothing we can't deny later."

"Music to my ears," Walls said, already standing.

Forty-five minutes later, crossing into Brand County, they passed through the checkpoint at the federal holding facility… a concrete hymn to procedure. Bad lighting, polished floors, and a receptionist with the eyes of a woman who had taught four teenagers to drive.

They were buzzed through two doors and a metal detector that breathed and beeped like an asthmatic robot. A guard checked their badges twice and their expressions once.

"You're here for Waters," the guard said without needing to ask. "Just a chat," Walls replied.

"Nothing is 'just' with that one," the guard muttered and signaled to another. "Heavy watch."

They walked the corridor past doors with numbers and no names. At the end, a room waited with a table bolted to the floor and a camera eye winking in the corner. Two more guards took up posts, hands comfortably near their hips. The air carried a faint tang of bleach and stale coffee. Hudson Waters came in with the slow swagger of a man determined to make shackles look like jewelry. Orange jumpsuit, cuffs at wrist and ankle, hair cut short enough to deny vanity. He sat, leaned back until the restraints made their argument, then leaned forward with a smile that never reached his eyes.

"Detective Black," he said, rolling the name like a wine he didn't plan to swallow. "Detective Walls. To what do I owe the pleasure?"

"Have we met before?" Walls asked.

"No, but word gets around about smart, witty detectives who think they're smarter than most people," Waters said.

"Yes, we are," Walls replied, taking a seat.

Black remained standing just long enough to remind everyone he could. Then he sat too, folding his hands loosely, the way men do when they want a liar to underestimate them.

"We want to talk about the weather," Black said. "A lot of smoke around town. People coughing." Waters chuckled. "Boys, if we're going to do metaphors, at least bring me a thesaurus."

Walls's pen lay on the table. He didn't touch it. "You know Ruby Keys?"

Waters leaned his head against the cinderblock, like a man thinking through ceiling tiles. "Name doesn't jingle any bells."

"She works at Social Services," Black said. "Worked."

Waters's eyes flicked back to him. "Past tense?" He shook his head, a sham sympathy. "Shame she's dead."

The room tilted. Black did not move. Walls did not blink. Neither detective let their faces register the slip. They stared back the way officers stare at a night road: alert, expressionless, the deer moving only in peripheral vision.

Black let a beat pass as if choosing the next card in a deck. "We asked if you knew her," he repeated mildly. "We didn't ask you to read the obituaries."

Waters smiled wider. "Relax, Detective. I watch the news." "There's been no bulletin," Walls said. It wasn't a question.

"Then maybe my TV gets better reception from your side of town," Waters said, and his smile thinned to something that showed wire beneath.

Black switched lanes. "Your case is stacked," he said. "Trafficking, RICO, money laundering. You'll need to live the rest of your life very quietly to outlast it."

"I don't do quiet well," Waters said, and the guards straightened almost imperceptibly. "So, we'll do it for you," Walls said. "In a box."

Waters rocked his cuffed wrists, the chain whispering against itself. "You want to know a secret?" He leaned in. "This little empire you think you're storming. You're coming in through the gift shop. You're not even in the lobby yet."

"We're here about your lobby," Black said. "Names. Deskers. Coaster. Williams. Task. The State has two that flipped. One almost died. One did die. Men positioned to testify have a strange habit of going mute around you."

"If I had men," Waters said, feigning boredom, "I'd teach them manners. I'm a people person."

"Then prove it," Walls said. "Start caring about a woman you don't know. Ruby Keys. We've got questions about who wanted to scare her. And now she's gone... dead."

Waters tilted his head. "You hear yourselves? You walk into federal holding and ask me to flip on a woman I've never met about a thing I didn't do, because it suits your narrative? Gentlemen, I deny the premise. I deny the conclusion. I deny the accusation."

"Deny all you want," Black said. "People are breathing smoke because somebody lit a match. From where I sit, there are only two arsonists with access to gasoline: you and Benjamin Grove."

Waters laughed then, not big, but sincere. "Grove," he said, savoring it. "The politician with the stained halo. He thought he could wade into my ocean without getting his shoes wet." He looked past them at the camera, then back. "If he drowns, it's because he never learned to swim."

"Who taught him to wade?" Walls asked.

"Everyone who wanted to be dry," Waters said. "Including your city's best and brightest. Don't look at me like I'm the only one who discovered thirst."

Black felt the urge to snarl and swallowed it. "You're on federal charges," he said. "You'll have your day. Until then, know this: people in my jurisdiction are dying. If I find out one of your whispers turned into action, I'll make sure the only voice you hear again is a parole board telling you no."

Waters stood. The guards didn't move, but their attention narrowed like a camera lens.

"This has been fun," Waters said. "But I'm due back at my regularly scheduled cage. I'll leave you with a little wisdom for free." He leaned forward, close enough that Black could count pores and bad choices. "It's above your pay grade."

He flicked his chin at the guard, a small gesture like a man signaling a waiter that he was finished. They unlatched the chain, turned him, and escorted him out. At the door, Waters looked back once, just enough to slide oil across the words. "Gentlemen."

The door clicked behind him, and the room inhaled.

Walls did not reach for his pen. Black did not lose his temper. They sat in the slow hum, both listening to the same silent thing: their instincts, battling each other.

"I hate him," Walls said simply.

"Get in line," Black said. He stood, the chair legs scraping against the floor. "Let's go."

They didn't speak until they were both in the car. Walls put the key in the ignition and didn't turn it. Outside, a skinny tree threw a mean shadow across the windshield. Somewhere, a siren did its long, flat cry and gave up.

Black stared at the dashboard. "He said she was dead." "Yeah," Walls said.

"Before we did." Walls nodded.

Black's fingers drummed once against his thigh. "And then he said it's above our pay grade."

Walls turned the key halfway. The instrument panel lit up like a small, obedient city. He didn't finish the turn. "We should stay quiet, Black."

Black's head snapped, just a fraction. "What?"

Walls still didn't look at him. "He's right. Whatever this is, it's not just Grove, and it's not just Waters. We push without a plan, we'll get flattened. We talk in halls we shouldn't, our words will be in someone else's mouth by morning. We keep it tight. We keep it small. And for now, we stay quiet."

Black felt something cold slide behind his ribs. He didn't know whether it was fear, or agreement, or the sudden awareness that the air in the car had thinned.

"Yeah," he said, forcing his voice to level ground. "Maybe we should just stay quiet. See how it plays."

Walls turned the key the rest of the way. The engine caught, the car shuddered, then smoothed out.

As they pulled away, Black looked at the reflection in the window: his own face, tired enough to look like a stranger's. He told himself he was reading too much into tone and timing. He told himself he had known Cane long enough to know where his fault lines were. He told himself many things, and none of them got rid of the sentence ricocheting inside his skull:

I'm not entirely confident in the person driving.

They arrived at the federal prosecutor's building, which wore its authority like a pressed suit. The lobby lights were low; the security desk logged them in and issued badges with "VISITOR" stickers so bright they felt like loud voices. A young assistant with a nervous ponytail met them at the desk, swiped their badges, and led them down a corridor of glass and carpet to a small conference room, whose table seemed more critical than the chairs surrounding it.

Valentino was already there, back to the window, sleeves rolled up, hair pulled into something practical. When they stepped in, she didn't look up. She checked her watch. "It's almost six p.m., gentlemen... better late than never. I have a life outside this federal building."

"Yeah. We got delayed," Black said. Walls said nothing.

Valentino slammed a file onto the table; the sound landed like a slap. "I don't know what's going on with this investigation," she said, breath clipped, "but I am not dropping it. I don't care if I have to take the entire city down to get it done."

Black closed the door behind them gently. Cane took a seat because someone should, and because he knew what chairs could do for tempers.

"Prosecutor," Black began.

"No," Valintino said, pointing at him, the finger not rude so much as surgical. "Don't 'Prosecutor' me. Who killed my witness?"

"We're working...." Black started.

"Who leaked her testimony? Who put her address in the wind? And why wasn't she under protection the minute she left the stand?" She was furious in a way that didn't look performative. It looked like the kind of anger you get when you ask for help and the universe says it is busy.

Walls opened his palms. "Anyone could have leaked her testimony," he said. "It was said in open court. You know how fast a hallway rumor becomes a headline, even when the press can't print it. Don't aim your muzzle at the department because we're the only target not wearing a federal badge."

Valintino blinked once, hard, like the word federal had become a dare. "You want targets? I can draw you a constellation. Your Chief. Your ADA. Your court clerks. Your janitorial staff. This isn't a leak, Detective. This is a pipe burst. Keys was a link in the chain to Waters, and now the link is snapped. You know what that does to my case?"

Black kept his voice steady. "We didn't know she was in immediate danger. She wasn't slated to flip. She was a supervisor who handed schedules to the wrong inbox. We could not have known the clock on her life was hours."

"You could have assumed it," Valintino said, and there was a crack in the fury where grief was trying to get out. "You could have assumed every person who opens their mouth is a target in Red Leaf City until they prove they're not."

Black felt his own temper rise and forced it back down like a man holding a door against the wind. "Why not work with us?" he said, each word placed like a brick. "Share what you can, and we share what we can. We nail them both instead of slapping each other in a conference room."

Valintino let out a disbelieving breath that almost became a laugh. "I don't trust you," she said and picked up the file. "Not yet. Maybe not ever. Find me the source for her leak and the sender of those messages, and maybe we start borrowing each other's sugar."

She moved to leave. Black stepped aside. "Valintino," he

said, and she paused in the doorway, profile carved out of anger. "Waters knew before we said it. About Keys."

She turned. "Because he ordered it." "He's in a box," Walls said.

"Boxes have phones," she said. "Boxes have lawyers. Boxes have cracks." She looked like a woman who hadn't slept much and didn't plan to. "You don't even realize what you're up against...." She cut herself off like she'd remembered a rule. "Do your job, Detectives. I'll do mine."

She left the room, the air she vacated rushing in as if to fill a vacuum.

Walls stood, smoothing a wrinkle from his jacket that wasn't there. "Well. That was productive."

"It was," Black said.

Walls shot him a look. "She just told us she doesn't trust us and might blow up the city."

"She also told us her anger is honest, not staged," Black said. "And honest anger isn't the hand that set Ruby up. It's the hand that wants the hand that did to burn."

"And in the meantime?" Walls asked.

"In the meantime," Black said, "we let her cool. We don't give her our insides. And we start looking at our own hallways."

Walls's eyes narrowed. "Inside the department."

Black didn't answer. He didn't need to. He opened the door, nodded to the ponytailed assistant, and they walked out without making the kind of eye contact that turns into rumor.

They didn't speak much on the drive back. The day outside the windshield looked normal: a delivery truck double-parked in front of a bakery, a man walking a dog that insisted on sniffing the same square of grass twice, a couple arguing quietly at a crosswalk. Normal was an obscenity today.

Traffic slowed two blocks from the precinct. A city bus sighed, pulled away, and left behind a smear of diesel breath. Black watched the exhaust and thought about smoke again, how it travels faster than flame and convinces people that there's nothing they can do but cough.

"Above our pay grade," he said aloud, surprising himself.

"Yeah," Walls said without turning his head. "What does that mean, Cane?"

Walls tapped the wheel with his thumb. "It means there are people with titles and money and habits way older than your badge who have more to lose than a job. It means if we try to pull everyone into the light at once, the room goes dark. It means we pick our spots and stay alive long enough to see them fall."

Black studied the lines at the corners of Walls's eyes. He had seen those lines pleased, angry, tired. He'd never seen them this still. "And who do you think flips the main breaker?" he asked gently. "Chief? ADA? Somebody in Records?"

Walls worked his jaw, the silence like a coin you flip and never catch. "We talk facts when we have them," he said finally. "Until then, we keep our circle small."

Black nodded as if that settled anything. It didn't. The knot between his shoulders refused to loosen. He stared out his window again and saw, reflected, his partner at the wheel: a good cop, a stubborn man, a friend who had just told him to be quiet.

He thought of Francine at the community center, of children laughing at each other's jokes, of a boy lining up pencils. He thought of Ruby in a tub and a court reporter's machine that had gone on a walk, no machine taking itself by itself. He thought of Hudson Waters in orange with his smirk and his sentence, and of a Chief who checked his watch like it owed him money.

He thought of a city choking on silence.

By the time they pulled into the precinct lot, he had made a decision he didn't write in any report: he would stop saying out loud the names that floated across his mind at night. He would listen more, speak less, and move only when what he moved couldn't be pushed back.

He also slid his hand to his phone and typed a note he didn't send: Pull access logs, judge's chamber locker…. Printerson cabinet, after-hours entries. He saved it. He locked the screen.

Walls turned off the engine. "You coming in?" "In a minute," Black said. "I need… air."

Walls nodded, climbed out, shut the door, and walked toward the entrance with a gait Black had matched a thousand times. Today, he watched it like a man watching a stranger walk into his house.

In the quiet hum of the cooling engine, Black rested his forehead on the dashboard for a beat, then sat back upright, and watched a flock of birds jolt into the air from the precinct's roofline in the distance, startle, re-form, and head somewhere else in a hurry.

He whispered, because there was no one in the car to hear him, but the truth: "I couldn't trust the Chief. I couldn't trust Red Leaf politicians."

He looked at the closed door the detectives always used and felt that old, cold thing slide behind his ribs again.

"And now, God help me," he said to the dashboard, "I'm not sure I can trust Walls, either." He got out, locked the car by habit, and walked into a building that still claimed to be safe.

Chapter 13: Shadows in the Halls

The precinct always smelled faintly of burnt coffee, a mix of colognes, and something heavier no cleaning crew could ever scrub away. Walls pushed through the front doors just after seven; Black followed ten minutes later, the federal building's air still clinging to them. Officers moved past with case files tucked under their arms, but too many eyes slid away too quickly. Black caught it, the kind of silence that happens when everyone knows something, but no one dares to say it aloud.

"Feels like a morgue," Black muttered. He didn't get two steps toward his desk before the phone on the duty sergeant's counter lit up. Walls was already seated. The sergeant glanced at the caller ID, then at them. "Chief wants you in his office."

Walls shot Black a look. Black only nodded.

Chief Ezra Lightening's office was always too neat, as if he spent more time polishing the brass lamp on his desk than handling the weight of a city's rot. He was already pacing when they entered, his tall frame moving between the blinds and the wall clock that ticked too loudly.

"Detectives," Lightening said, forcing a smile that died before it reached his eyes. "Sit."

They did.

"I want a clear update," he said. "On… the complications of this morning." He never said "Ruby." He didn't say "murder" either… just "complications," as though her death were a scheduling error.

Walls shifted in his chair. "Her testimony put Grove's people on edge. That's obvious. Now she's gone, and we're treating it as…."

"Treat it however you want," Lightening interrupted, eyes

flicking to his watch again. "Just don't let it derail the trial. The city needs this over quickly."

Black watched him, silent, cataloging the deflections. The Chief kept checking the time as if he were waiting for someone.

"Anything else?" Walls asked.

"That's it." Lightening stopped pacing and dropped back into his chair. "File everything by the book. No freelancing. Dismissed."

They rose. As Black turned toward the door, it opened. Jasper McMichaels, Grove's lead defense attorney, stepped out of the side corridor. He froze when he saw them, then forced a grin.

"Gentlemen," he said smoothly. "Wrong hallway, I suppose." He tucked a file against his side and brushed past, his cologne trailing like arrogance.

Walls whispered, "Wrong hallway, my butt." Black didn't answer, but his jaw tightened.

They hadn't made it ten feet back to their desks before another voice chased them down. "Detectives!"

They turned to see Eddie Harmon, the youngest tech in the lab, jogging down the corridor with a clipboard pressed to his chest. His glasses were crooked, his shirt wrinkled, but his urgency was sharp.

"You need to come with me. Now. It's about the machine." Walls frowned. "What machine?"

"The court reporter's. Printerson's." That stopped them from getting irritated.

The lab smelled of solvent and static, the hum of machines filling the sterile air. On one of the metal tables sat a clear evidence bag containing what looked like a small wreck... gray casing cracked, wires dangling like veins, keys smashed inward.

Eddie pulled on the gloves and lifted them carefully. "This

is what was found in a dumpster three blocks from the courthouse. Sanitation crew spotted the case before it went to the compactor."

Walls swore under his breath. "So, it wasn't misplaced."

"Not even close," Eddie said. He laid the wreck down gently and tapped the fractured interior. "The drive unit's been deliberately shattered. Whoever did this knew exactly what they were destroying. The shorthand logs are gone. Wires clipped, not torn. This was sabotage, Detectives."

Black leaned closer. His mind replayed Henry Printerson's weary voice from earlier: *I don't take the machine home. I lock it behind the judge's chambers. They're blaming me for something I never had control over.*

"Printerson said he keeps it locked in a cabinet behind the judge's chambers," Black murmured. "If it ended up here…" Walls finished the thought. "Then someone inside the courthouse took it. Someone with access." Eddie nodded. "Exactly. It wasn't random. It was targeted."

The weight of the room shifted, like even the fluorescent lights wanted to dim.

Walls rubbed the back of his neck. "Sabotaging testimony. Killing witnesses. Next, they'll come for the jury."

Black's eyes stayed fixed on the twisted machine. He didn't say anything, but his silence was louder than anger.

They left the lab with the evidence bag sealed, walking the long corridor back toward the squad room. Every footstep echoed too sharply.

Walls spoke first. "If the trial's being dismantled from the inside…"

Black cut him off, voice low. "Then it's not just Grove. Waters still has his fingers on the strings."

They stopped in the dim squad conference room, the broken machine resting between them on the table. For a long moment, neither moved.

Finally, Black spoke, quiet but confident: "Somebody inside wants Grove free. And they don't care how many bodies fall before he walks."

The room swallowed the words, and the city outside kept roaring, unaware that justice was bleeding out on the floorboards of its own courthouse.

Chapter 14: Guarding the Record

The morning light poured into the courthouse as if it didn't know the city was breaking apart. Protestors were already gathering, voices echoing off the stone steps, signs lifted high: JUSTICE FOR THE CHILDREN on one side, STAND WITH FRANCINE on the other. The air was tense, as if the entire building was holding its breath.

Inside, Detectives Black and Walls moved with purpose down the hallway lined with portraits of judges long gone. They had no time for reporters shouting questions or clerks whispering rumors. They were headed straight for Judge Nancy Lampson.

The bailiff at her door stiffened when they approached. "Court doesn't resume until nine," he said.

Walls showed his badge. "This can't wait." After a short pause, the bailiff let them through.

Judge Lampson was at her desk, black robe folded neatly over the chair, reading glasses perched low as she scanned a file. She looked up, frown deepening. "Gentlemen? What's so urgent you're pounding on my chambers before dawn?"

Black stepped forward, placing the sealed evidence bag on her desk. Inside, the shattered remains of Henry Printerson's stenograph machine looked like the corpse of a language.

"This was found in a dumpster three blocks from here," Black said evenly. "It didn't walk there on its own."

Lampson set her pen down, eyes narrowing. "You're telling me someone sabotaged the record of my courtroom?"

Walls nodded grimly. "Not someone. Someone with access. Printerson swears he locked it in the cabinet. That means whoever took it wanted to silence the record. No testimony, no appeal-proof evidence.”

For a long moment, the only sound was the soft hum of jazz playing in the background. Lampson leaned back, the weight of twenty-five years on the bench pressing harder than ever.

“And your solution?” she asked.

Black didn’t hesitate. “Keep the next machine in here. Your chambers. Locked. No one gets near it without your direct authorization. It’s the only way to guarantee this trial doesn’t collapse from inside.” Lampson’s gaze shifted from Black to Walls, searching for cracks. “You’re asking me to believe my own courthouse has been compromised.”

Walls leaned in. “We’re not asking. We’re telling you. Ruby Keys is dead. Witnesses are rattled. Now this. If the record keeps disappearing, Grove walks.”

The judge froze, her hand halfway to the stack of files. “What did you just say?” she whispered. “Ruby Keys is dead?” The color drained from her face, and for a heartbeat, the room went utterly still.

“Yes,” said Walls.

She exhaled slowly, composure sliding back into place like a practiced robe. Her finger began to tap the desk, deliberate and sharp, “Do you realize the firestorm this will cause if word gets out about tampered court records and a missing stenograph? I’m... I’m sorry to hear about Ms. Keys.”

“That’s why it stays between us about the missing stenograph,” Black said. “But you need to act now.”

Lampson finally nodded, sharp and decisive. “Fine. From this morning forward, the machine stays with me. If anyone wants access, they’ll have to walk through fire first.”

She stood, slipping on her robe, eyes flint-hard. “But hear me, Detectives, if you’re wrong, and this is just another scare tactic without teeth, I’ll have your badges.”

Black inclined his head. "Understood."

The bailiff cracked open the door. "Judge, it's nearly time."

Lampson straightened, the robe settling over her shoulders like armor. "Then let's go remind the city that justice still has a voice."

She swept past them, gavel in hand. Black and Walls followed into the hall, knowing the trial would resume, but that the walls themselves were listening. The hallway had become a vein of motion…. clerks, Marshals, attorneys, the slow pulse of a city's judgment inching toward the chambers where words were transmuted into law. Judge Lampson cut through it in her robe, and the corridor straightened itself as if to attention. The doors swung wide.

Inside, the gallery rose. Reporters stilled their pens, then lifted them again. The jury filed in, weary but attentive, the three-hour silence of yesterday still clinging to their collars. Black and Walls took their place along the far wall beneath the painted stare of a long-dead judge. Above the frieze, the clock moved with deliberate certainty, as if time itself had sworn an oath.

"Be seated," the bailiff said.

The murmur subsided. Judge Lampson surveyed the room, absorbed the weight of expectation, and nodded once to the court reporter, whose replacement machine will now remain locked inside her chambers at night. "Yesterday," she said, "we were delayed. Today, we proceed. Mr. Hill, you indicated you had cross-examination for the defense's witnesses."

Jackson Hill rose. His tie had loosened a fraction, but his eyes were flint. "Yes, Your Honor. The State requests that Evan Gills be recalled to the stand for cross."

A low breath moved through the room. Gills, who'd sat in the back row to watch, looked briefly to the defense table for permission. Jasper McMichaels gave a comforting spread of his hand….. You'll be fine…and Gills stepped forward.

He retook the stand. The oath was not repeated; the truth already sat beside him.

Hill approached with a thin folder. "Mr. Gills, yesterday you testified to politician Grove's community service, his routine presence at charitable functions, and his consistent leadership in Red Leaf City. Do you stand by that testimony?"

"I do," Gills said, shoulders squared.

"Good." Hill slid a page from his folder. "Let's talk about consistency. On the night of March 14, what did Mr. Grove do between 8:30 p.m. and 10:15 p.m.?"

Gills blinked. "I'd have to consult a calendar."

"I brought one." Hill held up a printed agenda and placed it on the evidence tray. "Defense Exhibit Twelve, admitted yesterday.... your own office's schedule. The event is listed as 'Donor Roundtable, Foster Care Initiative,' set for 8:00–10:00 p.m. at the Civic Trust Building. Yes?"

"Yes," Gills said.

"Excellent. Would you please review State's Exhibit K, a certified parking log from the Civic Trust Building? We subpoenaed it last night." Hill handed the paper to the clerk, who passed it up to the judge. "It shows the Grove staff SUV...plate ending -2F7.... entering at 7:58 p.m. and exiting at 8:41 p.m.. Not 10:00 p.m. Not 10:15 p.m. It was 8:41 p.m. Does that refresh your recollection?"

A beat. "We... stepped out. The politician had another obligation."

"So, the donor event was not attended for its full duration." Hill's voice was mild. "Where did you go, Mr. Gills?"

"I don't recall."

"Then perhaps State's Exhibit L can assist." Hill produced a printout. "A security list from Red Leaf Logistics, a small warehouse on Ambrose Street, you know it?"

"No."

"It logs a visitor entry at 9:02 p.m., name left blank, but the guard typed in 'Grove's car.' The plate matches the Grove staff SUV. The log also notes a second entry that night, two minutes later: 'C. Deskers.' You testified you don't know Charlie Deskers."

"I don't," Gills said, but the word wobbled.

"Do you know Red Leaf Logistics is controlled by a shell entity tied to Hudson Waters?" Hill asked.

"Objection," Jasper snapped. "Assumes facts not in evidence…. compound…prejudicial."

"Withdrawn," Hill said smoothly. "Mr. Gills, you drove a city official's vehicle from a donor event you claim lasted until ten, left at 8:41 p.m., and parked at a warehouse whose entry log shows your arrival at 9:02 p.m. The same log shows C. Deskers arriving at 9:04 p.m. Care to name the other obligation?"

Gills exhaled slowly. "The politician asked me to drop him off at a private meeting. I parked." "With whom?"

"I wasn't in the room."

"So, you can't deny it was Deskers."

"I can deny I saw Deskers," Gills said, his lawyerly hedge not quite fitting.

Hill flipped a page. "Let's try another inconsistency. On May 2, you scheduled 'Youth Center Photo Op…. Red Leaf Resource Center for 4:30 p.m. Do you see that?"

"Yes."

"The center's guest log shows Mr. Grove arrived at 5:18 p.m. and left at 5:31 p.m., thirteen minutes, not forty-five. Meanwhile, cell tower pings put Grove's phone near an industrial strip by the river at 4:52 p.m. Between 4:52 p.m. and 5:16 p.m., three calls were placed from his phone to a number attributed to Levi Coaster, one of Waters' associates. Why was Mr. Grove calling Coaster on his way to a photo op with schoolchildren?"

"Objection...foundation," Jasper said, rising. "We haven't stipulated that those numbers belong to Mr. Coaster."

"We will stipulate to the tower data and the dialed number," Hill replied. "Identification of the subscriber can be established in a subsequent witness."

"Sustained as to the attribution," Lampson said. "The jury will disregard the characterization tying the number to Mr. Coaster at this time. The question may stand regarding the calls themselves."

Hill nodded. "Mr. Gills...why was the politician making three calls on the way to pose with kids?"

"Politicians make calls," Gills said, the line clearly prepared.

"Of course." Hill's smile was thin. "Final area. Internal emails from your account to Betty Williams.... 'Flag any transfers over $50,000, code as consulting; do not route to public-facing ledger.' Did you write that?"

Gills swallowed. "There are contextual reasons for internal coding...." "It's a yes or no question."

"Yes," he said, too quietly for confidence. "And who told you to code them that way?"

Gills' gaze slid toward the defense table. Benjamin Grove, hands folded, looked down at his cuffed wrists as if reading scripture.

"I was following instructions," Gills said. "From whom?"

A long silence. The gallery leaned into it. "From the politician," Gills said at last.

A whisper rippled. Jasper stood. "Move to strike...speculation as to intent."

"Denied," Lampson said. "The answer stands."

"No further questions," Hill said, stepping back.

Gills gripped the rail tighter as if it had been holding him upright. He glanced once at Grove, who didn't return the look. He remained seated. "The defense may re-direct," Lampson said.

Jasper rose, the picture of smooth reassurance. "Mr. Gills, when you said 'consulting,' could those funds have covered legitimate policy research? Economic development consulting? Legal work?"

"They… could," Gills said, grabbing the rope thrown.

"And when the politician asked to be dropped off at a private meeting, is it possible he met with donors? Business owners?"

"It's possible."

"Thank you. No re-direct beyond that."

Gills was dismissed. He left the stand with the gait of a man who'd learned how quickly a staircase could turn into a slope.

"Next witness," Lampson said.

Chapter 15: The State Calls Betty Williams

"The State calls Betty Williams for cross," Hill replied.

Betty approached as if she had done so all her life, chin up, ledger clutched. She sat. The court reporter's keys whispered.

"Ms. Williams," Hill began, "yesterday you testified that Mr. Grove's books were clean, that you have been his accountant for fifteen years, and that no illicit funds passed through his accounts. Correct?"

"That is correct," she said, each syllable precise.

"Wonderful. You're familiar with Red Leaf Forward PAC, yes?"

"Yes."

"And the Grove Renewal Initiative?"

"Yes."

"Are you also familiar with the entity Future Path Consulting, LLC?" Betty hesitated, almost imperceptibly. "I've heard of it."

"Is it true Future Path Consulting bills the PAC for 'strategy' and 'issue research'?" "I don't manage the PAC's internal invoices."

"Do you manage Red Leaf Progress Fund?"

"Yes."

Hill lifted another document. "State's Exhibit M. A cluster of ACH transfers from Red Leaf Progress Fund to Future Path Consulting totaling $235,000 over eight months. Do you see those?"

Betty adjusted her glasses. "Yes. Line items coded as consulting." "Which you testified you would have seen."

"Yes."

"And you testified you saw nothing illegal."

"Correct."

Hill nodded, almost kindly. "Let's put a pin in those transfers and meet Future Path Consulting. We pulled bank registrations and vendor addresses. FUTURE PATH lists a suite at 1460 Ransom, Suite B. When our investigator went to Suite B, he found... a mailbox room. No staff. No office. In fact, Suite B is a shelf of rented boxes. Did you know that?"

Betty's lips pressed thin. "Not specifically."

"So, to your knowledge, FUTURE PATH is a mailbox."

"Plenty of legitimate firms use mail drops," Betty said, finding a patch of ground.

"Certainly. But plenty of shells use them too." He turned a page. "Do you know who owns Future Path Consulting?"

"No," she said.

"Hudson Waters' sister-in-law," Hill said. "Through a Delaware trust." The gallery rustled; Jasper was already up.

"Objection...facts not in evidence, and this is deliberately inflammatory, Your Honor." "Mr. Hill?" Lampson said, "level."

"We will put on the registrar," Hill replied. "For now, I'll withdraw the familial link and move on with the structure. The point is that the entity is effectively opaque. Ms. Williams...would you, as an accountant, typically advise a public official to route six-figure 'consulting' payments to a mail drop company with no staff and no office?"

"I don't give political advice. I classify expenses," she said.

"Then classify this." Hill placed a printout on the rail. "$75,000 on June 3 to Future Path. The memo field reads

'Event logistics…. Ambrose'. On June 3, a 'pop-up donor event' took place at a warehouse on Ambrose Street, the same warehouse we saw in the parking log for March 14.

That evening, two children went missing from the neighborhood and were recovered forty-eight hours later in a safehouse linked to Levi Coaster. We're not arguing causation at this second. We are asking why a civic account paid a shell for 'logistics' connected to a warehouse that keeps intersecting with your client's calendar."

"I don't plan events," Betty said, her voice smaller now. "I reconcile them."

"Then reconcile these." Hill clicked his pen and read rapidly: "$42,500 to Clearwater Assets…. registered to a P.O. box, memo 'community research'; $31,900 to Briar Lane Media…no physical office, memo 'youth outreach'; $18,200 to Greenleaf Solutions, memo 'consult schedules.' Notice that last one, Ms. Williams? Schedules."

Betty's hand went to her ledger as if it could shield her. "We often hire outside firms to manage calendars for public events," she said. "It happens…"

"Did any of those outside firms correspond with Ruby Keys?" Hill asked, and the name landed like a nail.

"Objection," Jasper said at once. "Assumes facts, he's smuggling in a narrative."

"Sustained," Judge Lampson said. "Rephrase, Mr. Hill."

"I'll rephrase," Hill said. "Ms. Williams, do you know about any payments made for program schedules, the names of children, their times, their presence at the Resource Center… being shared or sold?"

"No," she said, but it came out too fast.

"You testified you would have seen illegal transactions," Hill said gently. "But what if the illegality was coded as legitimacy? What if the ledger said consulting and meant access?

What if you were the last person who wanted to see what those words really bought?"

Her jaw tightened. "I am not a cop, Mr. Hill. I keep numbers. I am not responsible for what other people do with them."

"Numbers are choices," Hill said softly. "Who told you to route consulting off the public-facing ledger?"

Betty swallowed. "It's standard to split campaign funds from civic funds…" "Not what I asked. Who told you?"

Betty's eyes slid toward the defense table. Grove did not look up.

"Evan Gills," she said at last, barely audible. "He said Grove preferred not to confuse donors."

Hill let the quiet sit until it grew teeth. Then he lifted a final document. "State's Exhibit N. An email from your account…. June 1, to Gills: 'Will do…FUTURE PATH and Greenleaf off public ledger; will note as internal consulting.' Do you deny writing this?"

"No," she whispered. "No further questions."

Betty's breath stuttered as if the room had thinned. She clutched her ledger again, but it no longer looked like a shield. It looked like a record of a road she hadn't bothered to see.

Judge Lampson glanced toward the defense table. "Mr. Jasper, redirect?"

"Yes, Your Honor."

"Briefly," she said.

Jasper stood carefully, like a man measuring the angle of a bridge before stepping on. "Ms. Williams, to be clear—you never saw a line item that read 'purchase of schedules' or 'payment for children,' correct?"

"Of course not," she said, indignant, returning as a lifeline.

"And you have no personal knowledge that any of these vendors were criminal."

"I do not."

"And you understand that political entities often hire consultants for perfectly legitimate logistics."

"Yes."

"Then your testimony is simply that you coded expenses in good faith."

"I did," she said, a touch of steel in it now.

"No further questions," Jasper said, relief flickering under his practiced calm. "Ms. Williams, you may step down," Lampson said.

Betty left the stand, passing close to the jury box. One juror tracked her with a troubled frown, another with careful neutrality; a third stared at the floor like it might offer better answers.

Lampson glanced at the clock. "Counsel, it is nearly four-thirty. We will break for the day. Tomorrow at nine a.m., we will continue with the State's case-in-chief."

"Yes, Your Honor," Hill said.

"Your Honor," Jasper said, rising, "given the State's last-minute filings, the defense requests…."

"You will receive the same consideration you were granted yesterday," Lampson said crisply. "Nothing further today."

Her gavel touched the block like a final period. "Court is adjourned."

The room uncoiled. The bailiff shepherded out the jury, their faces drawn tight to conceal what the day had placed there. Reporters stood on tiptoes to catch a glimpse of the exhibits as they were gathered. Lucas O'Hell stacked the State's folders into ranked columns, a general packing map after a raid. Across the aisle, Jasper spoke in low tones to Grove, who listened with that stone stillness that had stopped meaning control and started meaning fear.

Black and Walls did not move until most of the pews had emptied. When they finally stepped into the aisle, the courthouse sound changed…less echo, more breath. They threaded toward the rear doors and paused as Henry Printerson crossed to the side entrance leading to the judge's chambers to secure the new machine. He caught Black's eye and gave a grim nod…the case disappeared through the doorway, and a moment later, the click of a lock echoed faintly. Lampson's bailiff turned the key. Outside the courtroom, the corridor was its usual tunnel of half-heard questions and shoe squeaks. But from beyond the glass doors at the front of the courthouse, the protest had swollen. Two currents collided, Justice for the Children folding into Stand with Francine, like voices fighting for the same breath. A chant lifted, was swallowed, lifted again.

Lucas brushed past the detectives with a tight smile. "Not a bad day," he said softly, which in prosecutor meant the walls held. Hill was already on the phone, pacing in a small rectangle, the rhythm of a man threading his way through a minefield of tomorrow's witnesses.

Jasper and Wyatt Reddings turned down the side hallway that led…coincidentally, they would say, to the corridor outside heading to the precinct. Black watched them go. He felt the urge to follow and let it pass. Three steps forward, one back. He could feel the city's arithmetic in his bones.

Walls leaned close. "Gills cracked. Betty bled. It's movement." "And motion attracts fire," Black said.

A reporter spotted them and started forward, but a uniform eased a forearm across her path: "Not now." Through the doors, a smear of smoke, not a bomb this time, just the smoky breath of too many bodies in too little space, of street food and street fury… blurred the late sun.

"Detectives," the bailiff said from behind them, almost sotto voce. "The judge asked me to tell you that we'll post an extra deputy in the hall."

"Post two," Walls said. Black nodded.

The man didn't argue. He headed back down the corridor with the gait of someone who had just learned a new meaning for guard duty.

They stood a moment longer, letting the building's hum press around them. Behind the doors, the chants bucked and softened like surf. Somewhere a child laughed, a sound that didn't belong and therefore mattered more.

"Tomorrow," Walls said.

"Tomorrow," Black echoed.

They pushed into the evening. The courthouse steps held their heat even as the air cooled. Protest signs knocked softly against one another in the breeze with cardboard clapping for a show none of them wanted tickets to. On the far curb, a man with a camera zoomed in on the doors as if he could photograph justice itself if he only caught it leaving at the right second.

Black paused at the top step and looked back through the glass. In the dim rectangle of the courtroom, he could make out the bench, the rail, the place where a record lived or died by inches. The new machine was a dark shape in the judge's chambers locked. They descended into the crowd and the cameras, into a city that had begun to understand that silence, like smoke, finds every open window.

Chapter 16: The State Calls Daniel Gray

"All rise."

The jurors stood stiffly, notebooks clutched, their eyes a little heavier than the day before. The gallery buzzed with anticipation, the undercurrent of protestors' chants seeping through the tall courthouse windows. Judge Nancy Lampson entered with practiced authority, but this time there was a flicker of weariness in her face. She had spent much of her career deciding the fates of hardened criminals, but never had her bench been so crowded with reporters, cameras, and a city's hunger for justice.

"You may be seated," she said. The benches groaned as everyone sat, the weight of bodies matched only by the weight of expectation.

Lampson's gaze cut across the room. "The court will now resume the trial of the State versus Benjamin Grove. Mr. Hill, you may call your next witness."

Jackson Hill rose, buttoning his jacket with steady hands. His tie was a shade of blue softer than usual, chosen intentionally. He wanted no sharpness to intimidate the boy they were about to call. He glanced briefly at his second chair, Lucas O'Hell, then fixed his attention on the jury.

"Your Honor, the State calls Daniel Gray."

A ripple ran through the courtroom. The boy. The survivor.

From the front pew, a small figure rose hesitantly. Daniel Gray, twelve years old, with a mop of brown hair and thin shoulders beneath a borrowed dress shirt, walked carefully toward the stand. His foster parents, Eva and John Billings, followed him with their eyes, Eva's hand covering her mouth, John's jaw locked tight.

The bailiff held out a Bible. Daniel's voice quivered as he raised one hand, his other hand pressed against the book.

"Do you swear to tell the truth, the whole truth, and nothing but the truth, so help you God?"

"I do," Daniel whispered, almost inaudible.

Judge Lampson leaned forward, softening her voice. "You may be seated, young man. Take your time."

Daniel slid into the witness chair, his feet swinging just above the floor. His small hands gripped the armrests until his knuckles turned pale. He glanced once at Eva and John, who both nodded firmly, then looked back at the prosecutor.

Hill stepped forward, but carefully, no towering, no sharpness. His voice lowered as though he were talking in a school library.

"Daniel, can you tell us about your day, the one when this all began?"

Daniel licked his lips, nervous. "I went to school. It was just…regular. We had a math test. I had lunch in the cafeteria. I walked home after."

"What happened when you got home?"

"I asked Ms. Eva if I could go to the community center. I go there a lot. My friends were gonna be there. I like it there. It feels…safe."

Daniel's eyes flicked toward Francine Grove. She sat stiffly at the gallery's edge, her hands trembling slightly as she clutched a folded handkerchief.

Hill nodded gently. "What did you do when you arrived at the center?"

"I went to the café. I got a bag of chips, a turkey sandwich, and an orange soda." "Did you pay for it?"

Daniel shook his head, a small smile breaking through the nerves. "No. It's free. Ms. Frannie makes sure kids can eat for free. I like Ms. Frannie."

His voice cracked on the last word. He rubbed his eyes with the back of his hand, embarrassed. Hill softened his tone even more. "Take your time, Daniel. You're doing just fine."

After a shaky breath, Daniel went on. "After I ate, I played video games with my friends in the game room. It was almost five, and I was supposed to be home by five-thirty."

"What happened then?"

"A man from the resource room asked if we could help carry boxes to the dumpster out back." Hill tilted his head. "Had you seen him before?"

"Once, maybe. He always stayed in the back. Like, the storage area. Cleaning stuff." "What did you and your friends do?"

"We carried the boxes. But when we turned around, the back door was closed. It locks from the outside."

"What did you do then?"

"We had to walk through the alley to get to the front. That's when a van pulled in. Men jumped out. They grabbed us."

Gasps erupted from the gallery. Reporters scribbled furiously. One juror's pen slipped from her hand and clattered to the floor.

Hill's voice was steady. "How many children were taken that day?" "Three. Including me."

"Did you know the other two?"

Daniel's eyes darted down. "I'd seen them around. But I didn't know their names." Hill kept his voice even. "Daniel, after the men grabbed you... Where did they take you first?"

Daniel swallowed. "We were put in the van. It smelled like

oil and old fries. They tied our hands with duct tape and put tape on our mouths. Then they covered our eyes with something scratchy… maybe a towel.”

“Could you see anything?”

He shook his head. “Only little pieces of light near the floor.” “How long were you in the van?”

“A long time.” He lifted his chin, gathering courage. “I didn’t fall asleep. I wanted to know where we were going. I counted by… by songs. In my head. And by… how often the van stopped and went.”

Hill nodded, not leading him, letting the boy own the moment. “Did you notice anything else?”

“I heard… birds.” Daniel’s brow furrowed, searching for the right word. “Seagulls. And a big metal clanking sound. Like chains.”

“Objection,” Jasper McMichaels said, on his feet. “Speculation. He can’t know what birds sound like with a towel over his face.”

“Overruled,” Judge Lampson said, without looking up from the bench. “The witness is describing what he perceived. The jury will weigh credibility.”

Daniel glanced at the judge as if reassured by the sound of an adult drawing a clear line.

Hill took a small step closer, careful not to crowd him. “Daniel, do you like geography?”

“Yes.”

“How did that help you?”

He straightened a little. “My foster dad and I go fishing. It takes almost two hours to get to the lake. I counted the bumps in the road and turns, and… time felt the same. So, I thought… we went that far. And when I heard the birds and the water… I thought we weren’t in Red Leaf City anymore.”

"Why did you think that?"

"Because our city isn't by water," Daniel said, as if this were the most obvious thing in the world. "And the lake's far."

"Thank you," Hill said gently. "What happened when the van stopped?"

"The doors opened. The air was cold. Wet." He shivered at the memory. "Someone pulled the towel off and ripped the tape off my face. It hurt. There was a dock… and big metal boxes stacked up. Like giant toy blocks, but rusty. We were pushed into one."

Hill kept his tone soft. "A shipping container?"

Daniel nodded. "There were other kids already inside. Fifteen, maybe more. Some were little. One girl kept saying the alphabet because she didn't know what else to do." He swallowed. "It smelled bad. Pee… and… people. We only got a little water. And crackers sometimes. We had to take turns lying down and using the bathroom in a bucket."

A juror dabbed at her eye. Another stared fixedly at his legal pad, jaw tight. "Did you hear anything outside the container?" Hill asked.

"Footsteps. A radio. Sometimes men laugh." He blinked hard, then pushed on. "They took the older kids out after three days. We thought we were next. They never came back."

"Objection," McMichaels said quickly. Assumes facts not in evidence. The witness cannot testify about the fate of unknown parties."

"Sustained," Lampson said. "The last phrase is stricken. The jury will disregard the conclusion. Mr. Hill, proceed."

Hill inclined his head. "Daniel, without guessing what happened to the others, just tell us what you saw and heard."

"We… didn't see them again," Daniel said.

He rubbed his wrist where the duct tape had been, a child's

absent gesture with an adult's gravity. "A man came sometimes. He had a scar on his hand. He called someone on the phone and said, 'Mark says the truck's late.' Another time he said, 'Levi's got the east side handled.'" Daniel's gaze flicked to the counsel tables and then down again. "I remember because those are easy names."

"Objection, hearsay," Clair Winston said from the defense table. "And highly prejudicial name-drops."

Lampson looked at Hill. "Response?"

"State offers not for the truth of the assertions, Your Honor, but to explain the witness's subsequent identification and to show the operation's continuity," Hill said, careful, crisp.

"Limited purpose only," Lampson ruled. "The jury will not consider the statements as proof of the matters asserted, merely as part of the witness's experience. Move on, Mr. Hill."

"Yes, Your Honor." Hill softened again. "Daniel, did you see the faces of the men clearly?"

"Only sometimes. They kept their hoods up. One had a tattoo on his neck that looked like a…" He made a shape with his finger in the air. "Like a hook with a line."

Hill held a page up for identification. "Your Honor, we'll address that in a later witness. No further details with this child."

Lampson's chin dipped once: approved.

Hill's voice thinned to a whisper. "Daniel… how long were you there?" "Eight days."

"How do you know?"

"I counted. I… I made a calendar in my head. Morning was when the birds screamed. Night was when my stomach hurt." Tears fell quickly down his cheeks.

A sound escaped someone in the gallery, too raw to be language. The bailiff turned his head, scanning, but Lampson didn't gavel. Her mouth had set into a line that anyone who had watched her career would recognize: the line she got when facts, not volume, demanded order.

Hill stepped back half a pace. "Do you need a break?"

Daniel shook his head, quick and fiercely. He wiped his eyes. "No. I want to finish."

"Okay." Hill nodded. "What happened on the eighth day?"

"The door opened again. We thought... we thought it was time." His breathing quickened. "Everyone was crying. I held the little boy's hand next to me. He was six. Then the light changed. It was brighter. And someone yelled, 'Police! Hands where I can see them!'

The courtroom went very still.

Daniel dragged in a breath. "Two men ran away. We heard them. Boots on the dock. Another fell. I heard the splash. Then a woman's voice said, 'It's okay. You're okay. We've got you.' She had... she had a radio voice. Like the people at the center who talk kindly even when everything's bad."

Hill's throat worked once. "Do you remember her name?"

He thought hard. "Officer... Turner? No, that's Ms. Luna. A different one." He shook his head. "I just remember she said my name after I told her. Daniel. It sounded like it belonged to me again."

"Objection to narrative," McMichaels said, softer now, as if even he heard what everyone else heard. "Move to strike anything beyond what happened in sequence."

"Overruled," Lampson said. "The witness is describing his perception of being rescued."

Hill took a breath. He let the quiet lie over the court like a blanket, then folded it back gently. "Daniel, are you safe now?"

He looked at the Billings. Eva had stopped breathing for the answer. John's hand pressed white into the pew.

"Yes, I love my foster parents," Daniel said. "But sometimes I dream I'm still in the metal box. And I can't tell if the door is opening or closing."

Several jurors blinked, hard. Francine…Frannie…. Grove pressed her knuckles to her mouth. Benjamin Grove stared down at the defense table as if the wood could answer for him.

Hill's voice was barely there. "No further questions."

He turned, glancing at Lucas O'Hell. Lucas's jaw was tight, the look of a man who knew there would be no victory laps today…. only the work of holding a line.

"Cross?" Lampson asked, eyes shifting to the defense.

Jasper stood, smoothing his tie. He approached with a softened cadence, a practiced "kindness" reserved for child witnesses, calculated to seem human.

"Daniel," he said, hands open, palms visible. "My name is Mr. McMichaels. I'm going to ask you just a few questions, and if you don't understand, you tell me, okay?"

Daniel nodded, watching him like he watched the van door in his memory. "You said you heard seagulls. You didn't see them, correct?"

"Not with my ,eyes," Daniel said.

"And this towel…could have been something else across your face?" "Maybe," Daniel said. "Scratchy."

"You testified you were in the van a long time. But you don't wear a watch, do you?"

"No."

"So, you were guessing."

"I was… counting," Daniel said, and there was a small stubbornness in it, the kind that builds forts out of blankets and refuses to come out.

Jasper smiled a careful smile. "Of course. And when you say

you heard the names 'Mark' and 'Levi,' you don't know who those men are, personally, correct?"

"No," Daniel said. "I just heard the names."

"And you didn't see Mr. Grove in that container, did you?" The room tightened.

"No," Daniel said.

"Thank you," Jasper said, turning slightly toward the jury as if to share a reasonable man's relief. "No further questions."

He returned to the counsel table, and if he allowed himself a breath of satisfaction, it was small and hidden.

Hill rose. "Brief redirect, Your Honor."

"Proceed."

"Daniel," Hill said, voice steady, "is there anything about your testimony today that you made up?"

"No."

"Is there anything you're unsure of that you told us as if you were sure?"

"No."

"And when you heard a woman say your name at the end, did you feel like you were safe again?"

Daniel's chin trembled, then steadied. "Yes."

"Nothing further."

Lampson leaned forward. "Thank you, Daniel. You may step down."

He slid off the chair. His shoes hit the floor with a small thud. Eva rose instinctively, arms out, but stopped herself with a glance at the judge. The bailiff nodded. Daniel ran the last two steps and folded into her, his face vanishing against her shoulder. John wrapped both of them in a broad, shaking embrace.

For a handful of seconds, no one moved. Even the court reporter's keys rested.

Lampson cleared her throat, not to break the moment, but to give it edges. "Ladies and gentlemen of the jury," she said, voice even, "you will disregard counsel's tone and focus only on the witness's words. We will take a fifteen-minute recess."

Her gavel tapped, delicate as a teacup set on a saucer.

The room exhaled and then immediately tried to inhale more than it could. Reporters leaned out of the pews toward the aisle, reaching for their phones. A marshal appeared at the side door like a conjured shadow and gestured the Billings family toward a quiet corridor.

Hill gathered his files, but his hands didn't move for a moment. Lucas touched his sleeve. "You did right."

Across the aisle, Jasper said something low to Grove. Grove did not answer. He kept staring at his hands as if the cuffs might, if he looked long enough, become decorative rather than functional.

Black and Walls lingered near the back rail. Black stared at the empty jury box, his mind still somewhere inside the last testimony. Walls' whisper broke through the fog.

"Names."

Black blinked. "What?"

"Mark and Levi."

His mouth thinned. "We'll thread them tomorrow." The recess ended. The jury returned with tissues tucked discreetly into sleeves and pockets. Lampson retook the bench, her gaze sweeping the room.

"Mr. Hill," she said, "your next witness?"

Hill stood. He glanced at the second row of benches, where two federal Marshals had taken positions that suggested they were waiting for someone, not guarding anyone. He weighed the time, the room, the beating heart of the day.

"Your Honor," he said, "given the time and the sensitivity of our next witness, the State requests that we adjourn for the afternoon and resume first thing tomorrow."

Jasper was up before the sentence finished. "Objection…. trial by ambush. The State cannot repeatedly dangle mystery witnesses."

"It's not a mystery," Hill said, voice cool now. "It's a matter of security." A murmur ran through the gallery. Security meant risk. Risk meant danger with a name.

Lampson considered, then nodded once. "Granted. Jury admonitions remain in full effect. Speak to no one about this case. Court will reconvene tomorrow at nine a.m."

The gavel fell with authority this time, a clean strike that promised order whether the city wanted it or not.

As benches emptied, a marshal brushed past Hill. "Your escort's ready," she said, clipped.

Hill nodded, then looked up to find Francine Grove watching him from the end of a pew. Their eyes met for a fraction. She gave the slightest, almost invisible shake of her head, not yet, then turned away, folding into the anonymous flow toward the doors. Hill and Lucas exited with the Marshall.

On the courthouse steps, the protest chants rose again, competing rhythms colliding into one: Justice for the children. Stand with Frannie. Cardboard signs thumped in the breeze. Somewhere, a can rattled across concrete.

Black and Walls stepped into the lobby together. "He held," Walls said softly.

"For now," Black answered. His gaze drifted to the side corridor leading to the judge's chambers…. the new stenograph machine locked in chambers, keys limited, a narrow moat around a fragile castle.

"Tomorrow we call someone who once stood beside

Grove," Lucas said as he passed, a line meant for no microphone and every ear that could hear.

"Tomorrow," Black echoed, and the word sounded less like a calendar and more like a cliff.

Outside, the city roared. Inside, the record waited… chain locked, plug sleeved, ready to catch the next voice before someone could silence it.

Chapter 17: Inside the Walls

Court had barely cleared when Jackson Hill told Lucas O'Hell, "We're not done for today."

Reporters swarmed the courthouse steps, shouting questions, shoving microphones toward their faces. Hill kept walking, his eyes fixed straight ahead. O'Hell followed, clutching his leather briefcase tighter than usual. A marshal cleared a path to the black government sedan idling at the curb.

"Where to?" the driver asked.

"The jail," Hill said. "We've got someone to see."

The ride was silent, the city flashing by in streaks of red protest signs and blue police tape. The chants outside the courthouse still rang in their ears: Justice for the children. Stand with Frannie. Two voices pulling at the same wound.

By the time they reached the county jail, the sun was low, throwing long bars of gold across the razor-wire fences. Inside, the smell of disinfectant hit like a slap.

The guard at the desk checked their credentials, then led them through two heavy doors and into a visitation room. The fluorescent lights buzzed overhead, painting everything a sickly white.

Levi Coaster was already waiting, wrists shackled to the table, a bruise darkening under his eye. His leg bounced uncontrollably under the table.

Hill and O'Hell sat across from him. "You wanted to talk," Hill began.

Levi's voice was hoarse. "Charlie Deskers is dead."

The words dropped like a gavel. O'Hell straightened. "When?"

"This morning. They said suicide." Levi leaned forward,

chains rattling. "But I knew Charlie. He was scared, yeah, but not in that way. Somebody wanted him quiet."

Hill exchanged a quick look with O'Hell, then leaned in. "You're saying it was a hit."

"I'm saying I'm next if I open my mouth," Levi whispered. His eyes darted toward the guards posted near the door. "But I can't keep it in anymore. I'll testify tomorrow. I don't care what happens. Grove ordered things no man should ever order."

"Then you'll be under federal protection from tonight on," Hill said firmly. "You won't be left alone."

Levi let out a bitter laugh. "Protection didn't help Charlie."

The silence that followed was thick. Even the buzzing lights seemed louder.

"Tell us what you're prepared to say tomorrow," O'Hell pressed. "We need to know how far you'll go."

Levi looked down at his chained hands. "Everything I saw. Everything I did. Grove's meetings with Waters. The shipments. The kids. All of it." His voice cracked. "I'm not clean, but I'm not carrying this anymore."

Hill nodded once, sharp and certain. "Good. Then tomorrow, the jury hears you."

An hour later, they were escorted to another holding wing. Henry Task sat slouched at the table, tattoos crawling up his arms.

"Henry," Hill said, "you have the chance to cooperate. Tell the truth, and we can talk about leniency."

Henry didn't even look at him. "No." He pushed back from the table and jerked his chin at the guard. "Take me back."

"Henry...." O'Hell tried.

"No," Henry repeated, eyes flat. "I'm not your witness." The guard led him out without another word.

They tried Mark Williams next. Mark entered with a smirk, his cuffed hands loose as if he were wearing jewelry, not chains.

Hill cut straight to it. "You want to save yourself? Testify against Grove. Help us stop this."

Mark leaned back in the chair, considering. Then he shook his head slowly. "No, Counselor. You don't want this case. Stop pushing it."

"Why?" O'Hell asked.

Mark leaned forward, lowering his voice. "Because the paper trail runs deep. Deeper than Grove. Deeper than Waters. You don't want to know what's under it."

O'Hell frowned. "Then tell us."

Mark smiled without warmth. "No." He rapped twice on the table. "Guard."

The door buzzed, the guard stepped in, and Mark stood, stretching his shoulders like a man leaving a bar, not a jail cell. He glanced once over his shoulder at Hill and O'Hell. "Walk away while you can."

Then he was gone.

Hill sat back, exhaling slowly. "Two no's. One maybe. One dead."

O'Hell rubbed the bridge of his nose. "And tomorrow Levi walks into a courtroom where half the city thinks Grove is a saint."

Hill's jaw tightened. "Then we make sure Levi's voice is louder than their chants."

They rose, their footsteps echoing down the corridor. Outside the jail, the night had entirely fallen. The city lights blinked in the distance, restless and alive.

For Hill, the case had never felt heavier. Tomorrow, Levi Coaster would put his life on the line….and if the threats against witnesses kept coming true, tomorrow might also be his last chance to speak. The ride back from the jail was thick with silence. Neither Hill nor O'Hell spoke, though the air between them carried the words neither dared to say: If Levi doesn't make it through the night, this case collapses.

When they finally reached the prosecutor's office, the building was nearly empty. The fluorescent lights hummed over abandoned desks, and the janitor's cart sat idle in the hallway. Hill unlocked his office, tossed his briefcase on the desk, and sank into his chair with a groan.

"We can't roll into tomorrow blind," Hill muttered, reaching for the phone. "Levi's scared, and I don't blame him. Let's see how serious this protective custody really is."

O'Hell leaned against the file cabinet, arms crossed, eyes tired but sharp. "Call the warden. Push him."

Hill dialed, waited through two rings, then a gruff voice answered. "Warden Fields."

"This is Jackson Hill. We need to talk about Levi Coaster's safety."

A pause. "Coaster's already in protective custody. Nothing's going to happen to him." Fields' tone was dismissive, almost bored.

Hill's jaw tightened. "With all due respect, you said the same thing about Charlie Deskers. He's dead now… under your watch."

The line went sharply silent before the warden snapped, voice raised. "Watch yourself, Hill. I run a corruption-free jail."

"I wasn't implying corruption," Hill said evenly, though his grip on the receiver whitened his knuckles. "I'm implying negligence. And negligence kills witnesses."

"Careful," Fields barked. "You want me to cooperate, not bury your calls."

Hill's voice dropped into steel. "What I want is Coaster

alive tomorrow morning. He's testifying, and if anything happens to him, it's on you."

"Watch yourself," Fields repeated, then slammed the phone down.

The deadline buzzed in Hill's ear. Slowly, he set the receiver back in its cradle. From across the room, O'Hell raised an eyebrow. "What was that?"

Hill leaned back, exhaling hard. "Fields is on edge. Real defensive." "He sounded more than defensive," O'Hell said. "He sounded scared."

"Yeah," Hill muttered, staring at the ceiling. "And if I were under investigation, I'd be scared too."

O'Hell straightened. "You think he's dirty?"

"I think Charlie's death wasn't random. Somebody knew he was about to testify. That kind of information doesn't leak from the streets; it leaks from inside."

The room fell quiet again. Outside, the streets were thinning with traffic, the city settling into evening. But inside the office, the weight of tomorrow pressed heavier than the night itself.

Hill rubbed his face. "If Levi dies tonight, the jury never hears the truth. We can't let that happen. His testimony is the thread that ties Grove's orders directly to the trafficking. Without it, Grove walks."

O'Hell nodded grimly. "Then tomorrow's everything."

Hill began filling out the protective orders, his pen scratching across the page with urgency. O'Hell gathered the case files into a neat stack, though his eyes kept drifting to the window, as if half-expecting to see shadows moving in the dark.

Finally, Hill shut the file and said, "Let's pray the night lets him survive."

Chapter 18: A Devil in a Suit

The hum of the courthouse had long faded. At eight o'clock, the halls were empty, just the echo of their shoes as Jackson Hill and Lucas O'Hell waited at the elevator.

The doors slid open, and a hand shot out, stopping them, a janitor they didn't recognize leaned in with a stiff smile.

"Have a good night," he said flatly.

Hill nodded cautiously, the words sticking in his throat. "Yeah... you too."

The doors closed. O'Hell exhaled sharply. "Does he even work here? I've never seen him before."

Hill shrugged, but his jaw tightened. "We don't know every night shift guy." "Yeah, but something about him felt... off."

The elevator chimed, carrying them down. Both men fell into silence. At the lobby doors, Hill asked, "You locked up the files?"

O'Hell tapped his briefcase. "Better than locked...they're right here."

Hill gave him a look of relief. "Good. Things are getting uneasy these days." They parted in the garage, both muttering the exact words: "Be careful."

Later that night, Lucas O'Hell pulled into his driveway, talking to his wife on the phone. The garage door hummed shut behind him, but not before he noticed a black sedan idling at the curb. He froze, staring into the dark glass. By the time he ran to the door, the car was gone.

"Lucas?" his wife's voice snapped him back.

"Nothing, honey," he muttered, forcing calm. "Just... nothing." But when he went to bed, his mind wouldn't let it go.

The next morning, a black SUV sat three houses down, with tinted windows impossible to read. O'Hell swallowed his unease. I'm paranoid. It's nothing.

On the freeway, his hands tightened on the wheel when the same SUV cut in front of him, forcing him onto the guardrail. Metal screeched, tires spat gravel. His chest slammed against the belt.

The SUV slowed just enough for him to see a hand jutted out of the window, middle finger raised. Then it roared off, leaving O'Hell trembling behind the wheel.

By the time he reached the prosecutor's office, his hands were still shaking. He sat in the car, debating whether to call Hill. At last, he walked in.

"You look pale," Hill said, frowning.

O'Hell told him everything. Hill listened in silence, then spoke quietly: "This isn't a coincidence. They're planning moves around us. We tell Black today. No more waiting."

In court, the jury filed in, restless after yesterday's chaos. Judge Lampson called for order. Hill rose.

"Your Honor, the State calls Levi Coaster."

The side door opened, and Levi shuffled in under guard. Shackles clinked against the floor, but it was his face that stopped the room cold. His left eye was swollen shut, his lip split, and purple bruises were spreading across his jaw.

Hill's chest clenched. He shot to his feet. "Your Honor…what happened to my witness?"

Judge Lampson's gavel struck hard. "Mr. Coaster, take the stand. Counselors, approach."

At the bench, Hill's voice was low but burning. "I spoke to Warden Fields last night. He promised Coaster's safety. This…this isn't a jail fight. This was to silence him."

Defense attorney Jasper McMichaels smirked. "Speculation.

No evidence my client…" "No one accused your client, Counselor," Lampson cut him off, eyes sharp.

Hill stepped back, fists clenched at his sides. He turned to Levi. "Mr. Coaster… can you tell us what happened last night in custody?"

Levi raised his head slowly. For a beat, the courtroom held its breath. Then he lifted a trembling finger and pointed directly at Benjamin Grove.

"You set me up." His voice cracked but carried. "You're a devil in a suit."

Gasps rippled through the gallery. Grove's mask cracked. He surged to his feet, voice a snarl. "Shut your mouth, Levi! You don't know what you're talking about!"

Levi stood too, chains rattling. "I know enough! You think you can kill us off one by one? You're going to pay, Grove!"

Marshals rushed in, hands on both men. The jury gawked as the shouting spilled into chaos.

"Remember Deskers!" Grove barked over the noise, his voice venomous.

Levi lunged forward against the shackles. "Don't you dare threaten me, Grove!"

The courtroom erupted, spectators shouting, reporters scribbling, the jury frozen in disbelief. Judge Lampson slammed her gavel again and again, her voice cutting through:

"ORDER! ORDER IN THIS COURTROOM!"

Finally, the Marshals dragged both men back down. The jury was hurried out. Breathing hard, Lampson glared down from the bench, her voice steel. "Counsel, chambers. Fifteen minutes. Now."

The gavel cracked like thunder.

And for the first time, it felt like the walls of the courthouse might not hold. Inside the judge's chambers, the heavy oak door slammed shut behind the bailiff. The noise of the courthouse faded, replaced by a suffocating silence broken only by Judge Nancy Lampson's heels as she paced.

Her robe still clung to her shoulders like armor, but her face carried the strain of what she'd just witnessed. She stopped, turned sharply, and fixed her eyes on Jasper McMichaels.

"Counsel," she said, voice clipped, "control your client."

McMichaels lifted his hands, trying for calm. "Your Honor, Mr. Grove was provoked. Mr. Coaster directly…"

"Don't insult this bench." Lampson's voice cut like a whip. "I heard the words with my own ears. Remember Deskers." She leaned forward, palms pressing hard into the desk. "That was not self-control breaking. That was a threat, plain and direct, in my courtroom."

McMichaels' jaw twitched. Wyatt Reddings and Clair Winston exchanged nervous glances behind him, but no one spoke.

Lampson turned next to the prosecution table, eyes narrowing at Jackson Hill. "Mr. Hill, I understand the State's frustration. But if this trial descends into theatrics, you'll lose the jury's faith. Do you want that?"

"No, Your Honor," Hill said tightly. His hands were still balled into fists. "But I'll also say this, I warned the Warden last night that Levi Coaster's life was in danger. And today, he shows up looking like he fought for it. This isn't theatrics. This is intimidation bleeding into my case."

Lampson studied him, then glanced back at the defense. "And as for your client, Counselor, you will tell Mr. Grove that if he so much as twitches in my courtroom again, I will have him gagged and shackled. Do you understand me?"

McMichaels swallowed hard. "Yes, Your Honor."

"Good." Lampson exhaled slowly, the weight of her years

on the bench pressing through her shoulders. "Because what I saw today was not the behavior of a man fighting for his reputation. It was the behavior of a man with something to hide."

The room froze at her words. Grove's attorneys stiffened, their faces drained.

Hill and O'Hell traded a look…they hadn't expected Lampson to speak so bluntly.

The judge's eyes flicked to the bailiff. "Bring the jury back in after recess. But for now…" She tapped her desk with the gavel in her hand… not to bang it, but to remind everyone she still held it. "This court is not a stage for threats. If there are any more outbursts, I will not hesitate to treat them as contempt and beyond.

"Levi Coaster will resume his testimony, but due to today's disruption, he may need to return for further questioning in a day or two. Counsel, keep your questioning short. This court needs to readjust after today's circus."

She straightened. "Do I make myself clear?"

"Yes, Your Honor," both tables answered, though unease rippled through every word.

As the attorneys filed out, Lampson remained still, eyes lingering on the empty chairs across from her desk. Her lips pressed into a hard line. If even half of what Coaster says is true, she thought, this city is standing on the edge of a cliff. Back in court, the jury filed back into the box, some whispering nervously, others stealing glances at Benjamin Grove as if he were a caged animal who had just rattled the bars. Judge Lampson's gavel struck once, sharp and final.

"This court will come to order. Ladies and gentlemen of the jury, you are reminded to disregard any outbursts that occurred before recess. What matters is sworn testimony, not theatrics. Mr. Hill, proceed."

Hill rose, his voice steadier now, though his jaw was still

tight with anger. "Mr. Coaster, thank you for your patience. I want to return to the record and ask you about your involvement with Mr. Grove."

Levi shifted in the chair, wincing from the bruises on his ribs. The chains clinked when he leaned forward. His voice was raw, but it carried weight.

"I wasn't always in this life," he began. "But Grove... he had a way of finding men like me. Men who needed quick money, no questions asked. At first, it was errands. Pick up this. Drop off that. Then it turned into kids."

The jury stiffened. "Kids?" Hill asked.

Levi nodded. "Children. From the community center, mostly. Grove gave orders through his people, but it always came back to him. We'd wait outside, sometimes use the back exit.

Sometimes a kid would be lured to help with boxes or errands. Once they were outside, it was quick: they were shoved into a van and driven to holding spots. We didn't ask where they went after. Some came back. Most didn't."

Gasps filled the gallery. A reporter's pen clattered to the floor.

Hill let the silence hang, then asked softly, "Mr. Coaster, did Mr. Grove ever speak to you directly about these children?"

Levi lifted his swollen face, locking eyes with Grove. "Yes. He told me once, plain as day: 'They're not kids, they're money.'"

Grove shifted in his seat, whispering furiously to McMichaels. The defense table looked rattled. Hill took a step closer. "Did you receive money for these jobs?"

Levi's eyes dropped. "Yeah. Cash. Sometimes, it is funneled through companies that Grove's people set up. I didn't know all the names, but the one that stuck was Future Path Consulting. That's where envelopes came from."

Judge Lampson's eyes flicked to the defense table, noting the reaction. "Mr. Coaster," Hill pressed, "why are you testifying today?"

Levi hesitated. His chained hands trembled. "Because I can't sleep at night anymore. Because every time I close my eyes, I see those kids crying in the back of the van. I hear them begging for their moms." His voice cracked, thick with shame. "I know I don't deserve forgiveness. But maybe telling the truth will stop Grove from hurting anyone else."

The courtroom was silent. Even the protestors outside seemed muted, their chants faint through the walls.

Hill's voice softened. "Thank you, Mr. Coaster." He turned to the judge. "Your Honor, no further questions."

Judge Lampson looked to the defense. McMichaels rose slowly, but even he looked wary, as if cross-examining might backfire. "Mr. Coaster, isn't it true you're only testifying now to save yourself from a harsher sentence?"

Levi gave a broken laugh. "Save myself? Lady Justice already has her scales tipped against me. I'll die in prison for what I've done. This isn't about saving me. This is about making sure Grove doesn't walk out and shake your hand on the courthouse steps."

McMichaels froze. A murmur rippled through the jury. Lampson's gavel cracked once. "Order."

But the damage was done. Levi Coaster's words had landed. The jury was dismissed for the afternoon break; their faces were pale, and their eyes darted away from Benjamin Grove. Lampson's gavel echoed one last time before she swept out of the courtroom, robes trailing like storm clouds.

The defense team huddled at their table, papers scattered, whispers harsh. Jasper McMichaels rubbed his temples as though trying to press the headache out of his skull. Wyatt Reddings leaned back in his chair, eyes darting toward the gallery doors as if escape might be an option. Clair Winston sat stiff, pen tapping against her legal pad in rapid bursts.

"Future Path Consulting," McMichaels muttered, voice sharp as broken glass. "How the heck did he know about that? That wasn't in discovery."

Reddings hissed back, "Doesn't matter. He said it under oath. The jury heard it. That's enough."

Across the table, Grove leaned in, his cuffed wrists rattling. His voice was low, venom dripping from every syllable.

"Fix it. That man is lying through his teeth, and you're letting him bury me alive. Do your jobs."

Clair swallowed hard. "Benjamin, listen…this jury isn't blind. They saw you stand up, shout at him, threaten him. That's on the record now."

"You think I care about optics?" Grove snarled, eyes blazing. "If that snake Levi Coaster keeps talking, I'm finished."

McMichaels snapped back before he could stop himself. "You might already be finished. You should've kept your mouth shut."

For a moment, the table went dead silent. Even Grove blinked, caught off guard by his own counsel's candor.

Reddings leaned forward, lowering his voice. "Listen, we need to pivot. Tomorrow, we push hard on credibility. Levi's a convicted criminal; remind the jury of that. Undermine him. Show he's only doing this to cut a deal."

Clair added quickly, almost desperate: "And we hammer that 'no bodies, no proof' line. They've got accusations, not evidence. If we let them paint Grove as the mastermind without hard proof, we lose."

McMichaels adjusted his tie, trying to compose himself. "Fine. Tomorrow, we cut Coaster apart. But for now, keep Grove under control. If he so much as twitches, Lampson will bury us in contempt citations."

Grove leaned back, chains rattling. His lips curled into a smile that didn't reach his eyes. "Don't worry," he said softly. "The courtroom isn't the only battlefield."

The three attorneys exchanged uneasy glances, none willing to ask what he meant.

Across the aisle, Hill and O'Hell watched the huddle from their table. Hill whispered, "They're bleeding. Levi just landed the first real blow."

O'Hell nodded, eyes still on Grove. "Yeah. But something tells me Grove isn't the kind of man who goes down quietly."

The recess bell chimed, calling everyone back. The jury would return soon. The fight was far from over. The court adjourned under a cloud. The jury was released for the day, whispering as they shuffled past reporters waiting like wolves in the hall. Judge Lampson had left the bench looking grim, her gavel still echoing in everyone's ears. Grove had to be restrained as he was led out, his glare fixed on Levi Coaster as though his eyes alone could finish what the bruises hadn't.

Hill and O'Hell didn't linger. They gathered their files and headed straight to the precinct.

At the station, Detectives Black and Walls were bent over paperwork when the prosecutors arrived. Black rubbed his eyes, looking up with an apology.

"Sorry, we missed court. Paperwork's stacked a mile high. What happened?"

O'Hell didn't sit down. His voice carried too much weight for that. "Levi Coaster happened. He came in beaten to an inferno and left eye swollen shut. Lip busted. And Grove threatened him in open court."

Walls froze mid-pen stroke. "He what?"

"Word for word," Hill said grimly. "Remember, Deskers. He practically confessed to ordering a hit in front of the jury."

Black swore under his breath. "And the judge?"

"She's furious. But we're hanging by threads here." O'Hell finally dropped into the chair across from them. He ran a hand over his face, then leaned forward. "That's not all. Last night, a car tailed me home. "This morning, I hit a guardrail after a black SUV ran me off the freeway. I need to take my car to a body shop to have it assessed. I didn't call it in, but it wasn't a coincidence." Walls sat up straighter. "Darn it, Lucas, you should've called."

"I wasn't sure if I was imagining it," O'Hell admitted. "But after today in court? I'm not imagining anything."

Black nodded once. "We'll put a squad car outside your house tonight. No questions asked." Relief flickered over O'Hell's face.

Hill tapped the desk, voice low and pointed. "And I want a call made to the Chief—Grove's pulling strings from inside. Coaster barely survived last night. If he dies before finishing testimony, we lose our best chance at conviction. Someone in custody is failing, maybe intentionally."

Black and Walls exchanged a look, then rose to their feet. "Come on. Let's see Chief Lightening. If he won't put pressure on the Warden and the commissioner, then we'll know where his loyalties really are."

The four of them left the squad area together, their footsteps heavy with unease. And for the first time, all of them wondered if justice was still stronger than the shadows moving against it. They walked towards Chief Lightening's office. "He'll have to lean on the Warden," said Walls.

Hill nodded, his notes in hand. O'Hell rubbed at his temple, still rattled from the SUV.

As the four of them were walking down the hall, Walls slowed his step. He glanced sideways at Hill.

"Hey, Jackson…ever thought about asking Francine Grove to testify? As a backup, just in case Coaster doesn't make it through this trial?"

The words hung heavily in the stale precinct air. Hill stopped cold, his jaw tight. "Francine?"

"Yeah," Walls said. "She's loved in this city. Respected. If she takes the stand against him, the jury won't forget it."

Hill didn't answer right away. He just stared at the floor, the thought turning in his mind like a knife.

Finally, he muttered, "That's not a card you play lightly." Walls shrugged. "Might be the card that wins the game."

The silence stretched between them until Hill exhaled and kept walking, his expression unreadable.

Chapter 19: The Chief's Watch

Chief Ezra Lightening's office smelled faintly of clean linen and old musk cologne. The blinds were drawn tight, slivers of streetlight cutting the room into stripes. His desk was neat, too neat. Papers stacked with military precision, a framed commendation centered just so, and on the left sat a photo of his wife and daughter.

But the man behind the desk paced, restless, one hand on his hip, the other tugging at the cuff of his sleeve.

Detectives Black and Walls stepped in first, with Hill and O'Hell just behind them. The room was silent except for the measured thud of footsteps crossing the floor.

"Gentlemen," Lightening said, voice flat, "this better be urgent. My phone's been ringing all day with reporters asking why this city looks like it's on fire."

Black didn't flinch. He dropped a file onto the Chief's desk. "Coaster came into court this morning, beaten half to death. Protective custody, my butt. You need to call the Warden. And the commissioner."

Lightening paused mid-stride, his jaw tightening. "And what exactly do you want me to say? That I've lost control of my own jail system?"

Hill cut in, sharp. "I don't care how you spin it. But the fact is, one witness is already dead, another nearly killed, and if Levi Coaster doesn't make it through this trial, Grove walks. That'll be on all of us…including you."

The Chief stopped pacing and turned, eyes narrowing. "Careful, Counselor. You don't get to threaten me."

"It's not a threat," Hill shot back. "It's reality."

For a long moment, the room was taut as a drawn bowstring. Then Lightening reached for the phone on his desk, punching in numbers with deliberate force. He turned his back, speaking low but clipped.

"This is Chief Lightening. I want Levi Coaster moved. Double guard rotation, no exceptions. And put it in writing that this order comes from me."

He hung up, exhaling through his nose, then turned back. "There. Done. You satisfied?" Black folded his arms. "We'll be satisfied when Coaster makes it to the stand tomorrow."

Lightening's eyes flicked to his watch…. a nervous tick the detectives didn't miss. "Then pray he does. Because if this city loses another witness, it won't just be the trial collapsing. It'll be everything."

The room fell into silence. The Chief sat down heavily, as though the weight of the city itself had just landed on his shoulders.

Hill finally broke the quiet. "Tomorrow's testimony decides everything. Levi is going to retake the stand. If Grove doesn't go down in that chair, we're all finished."

No one argued. The team drifted off from Lightening's office in different directions, O'Hell toward the parking lot, Black and Walls back at their desk.

Back in his office, Hill hung up the phone, the line with Francine Grove gone quiet. She had agreed to meet him after court the next day. He stared at the receiver in his hand a moment longer, then set it down gently. The silence of the office pressed in, filled only by the echo of the day, Coaster's bruised face, Grove's threats, Lampson's fury.

If Levi didn't survive, Francine's voice might be their only hope.

Across the city, in a narrow cell, Levi Coaster sat on his cot, staring at the fiberglass slit of a window. A guard stood outside his door, arms crossed, face unreadable. Levi exhaled and muttered, "At least Hill came through. Extra protection."

He sat back, stretching sore muscles, whispering to himself. "Grove's dirty. Always has been. But he won't bury me that easily."

Forty-five minutes later, just as sleep was pulling him under, the lock clicked. The door swung open.

Two men slipped inside like shadows. One smirked, pulling something from his waistband. "Boss said to finish it."

Levi shot to his feet, blood pounding in his ears. "Round two."

The cell erupted. Levi swung first, landing a fist on the taller man's jaw. The other slammed him against the wall. Fists flew, chains rattled. Then the sharp scrape of plastic against concrete. A sharpened toothbrush.

Pain ripped through Levi's back as the blade drove in. He gasped, knees buckling. "Snitches get stitches," the attacker hissed in his ear. "But you? You get a box."

The second stab was worse. The men slipped out as quickly as they'd come. The guard glanced up, then back down at his watch. Five long minutes ticked by before he touched his radio.

"Medical to Block C. Inmate down."

Blood pooled beneath the cot as Levi Coaster drifted in and out of consciousness, dragged onto a stretcher. The corridor swallowed him, the flicker of the infirmary lights the last thing he saw.

Chapter 20: Clinical Truths

The next morning, Hill woke early, as usual, coffee in hand. The bitterness didn't ease the weight in his chest. Something about Levi Coaster gnawed at him, a premonition he couldn't shake. At 6:00 a.m., he dialed the Warden's office, knowing Fields wouldn't be in yet. The line rang until a voicemail clicked. He left a short, tense message: "Checking status on Levi Coaster. Call me back."

By the time Hill reached the courthouse, the halls hummed with clerks and officers. He set his briefcase on the chair outside Judge Lampson's chambers, flipping through notes, when his phone buzzed. Fields.

Hill pressed it to his ear. "Warden, I wanted to confirm…"

Fields cut him off, voice flat. "Coaster's fine. He'll make it to court. Nothing happened overnight."

Hill frowned. "You checked the report yourself?"

Silence. Then: "He'll be there. That's all you need to know." The line went dead. Hill stared at the phone, muttering under his breath, "What a jerk."

He barely had time to stew before court began. The bailiff called, "All rise." The room shuffled to its feet as Judge Lampson took her bench. Just as Hill stood to announce his first witness, a paralegal burst in. Lisa, red-faced, nearly stumbled down the aisle.

She tugged his sleeve and whispered, "Levi's in the infirmary. Attacked last night. Alive, but won't testify today."

Hill froze. Fury climbed his throat, but he masked it and addressed Lampson. "Your Honor, I must inform the court that our scheduled witness, Levi Coaster, is currently hospitalized following an attack in protective custody. He cannot appear this morning."

Lampson's face iced over. "Mr. Hill, this court is not in the business of delays. Move on to your next witness. Now."

Hill opened his mouth to request a recess, but she slammed her gavel once. "Denied."

McMichaels leaned back with a smirk, the kind of grin that begged to be wiped off his face. Hill's jaw tightened. He would not give them the satisfaction.

He shuffled through his notes, pulse racing. He needed a witness… solid, unimpeachable. Then his eyes landed on the name.

Hill swallowed the fire rising in his throat and steadied himself. He couldn't give Grove's defense team the satisfaction of seeing him unravel. He straightened his notes and, with a firm voice, said,

"The State calls Dr. Savannah Houser."

The courtroom doors opened, and a tall woman in her mid-sixties stepped forward, white lab coat traded for a conservative brown suit. Her glasses caught the overhead lights as she walked with quiet authority to the stand. She placed her right hand on the Bible, swore her oath, and took her seat.

Hill approached, his tone was sharper than usual. "Dr. Houser, could you please state your name and profession for the record?"

"Savannah Denise Houser. I am the Chief Medical Examiner for Red Leaf County."

"Dr. Houser, were you the examiner assigned to conduct the autopsy on Jonah Carter, the minor found deceased earlier this year?"

She nodded. "Yes, I was."

"Please share with the court your findings."

Dr. Houser opened her folder with deliberate calm, the room going still. "Jonah Carter's cause of death was manual strangulation. There were clear petechial hemorrhages in the eyes, deep bruising along the neck, and fractures to the hyoid bone, all consistent with strangulation by human hands. His death was not accidental. It was a homicide."

A ripple moved across the jury box. Even Grove's defense table shifted uneasily. Hill's voice hardened. "And where was Jonah's body recovered?"

Dr. Houser didn't look away from her notes. "On property registered to Mr. Benjamin and Francine Grove. Specifically, on the south side of the property by the pool and retaining wall. He died in a shed but later buried."

The words hit like a hammer. Hill let them linger, watching the jurors write furiously.

"Dr. Houser," Hill said, lowering his voice, "was there any evidence to suggest Jonah died elsewhere and was simply placed there after the fact?"

She shook her head. "No. Blood patterns, soil samples, and decomposition state all confirmed he died on that property."

McMichaels sprang to his feet. "Objection, Your Honor. Speculative without full chain-of-custody context."

Judge Lampson leaned forward, eyes sharp. "Overruled. The medical examiner may answer."

Dr. Houser continued without missing a beat. "The condition of the body, the lividity patterns, they all indicate Jonah Carter died in that shed later buried. He was not transported postmortem."

The silence that followed was heavy, broken only by Hill's next question:

"In your professional opinion, Dr. Houser, could Jonah Carter's death have been anything other than homicide?"

Her reply was firm, clinical, and final: "No. Jonah Carter was murdered."

Gasps rippled again, this time from the gallery. Grove shifted in his chair, jaw tightening. Hill caught it. So did the jury.

He closed his folder with purpose. "No further questions, Your Honor."

Judge Lampson nodded. "Mr. McMichaels, you may proceed with cross."

As Hill walked back to his table, he could feel the energy shift; the jury had just been handed a cold, clinical truth. And in a trial full of smoke and threats, truth had weight.

McMichaels rose slowly, buttoning his jacket with that same smug confidence. He paced toward the witness stand and let his voice drip with mock courtesy.

"Dr. Houser, you've given us a very vivid account. But let's get something straight. You cannot tell this jury with absolute certainty who placed their hands on Jonah Carter's throat, can you?"

Dr. Houser kept her tone steady. "No, sir. That determination is outside the scope of medical examination. My role is to establish the cause and manner of death."

"Exactly," McMichaels said, turning to the jury as if he'd landed a blow. "Cause and manner. You deal in bodies, not suspects. So, your testimony here today doesn't actually link my client, Benjamin Grove, to this child's death, does it?"

Her reply cut through the air with precision. "What my testimony establishes is that Jonah Carter was strangled to death on Mr. Grove's property. That is a fact. Whose hands did it…that is for this court to determine."

A ripple moved through the jury box. McMichaels leaned harder. "But you don't know when the strangulation occurred, do you? Could have been hours, days, even weeks before his body was found?"

"The lividity, rigor mortis, and insect activity were consistent with death occurring approximately twenty-four to thirty-six hours before discovery," Houser replied calmly. "That's not weeks, Counselor."

She paused before continuing. "The evidence also indicates the victim was alive for some time after he went missing. The scene of death and the scene of recovery aren't necessarily the same."

A few muffled laughs slipped out from the gallery until Judge Lampson's gavel cracked down.

McMichaels flushed but pressed on. "And isn't it true that strangulation can occur in many ways? Hands, rope, a belt. Perhaps the boy… tragically… accidentally hung himself while playing?"

Gasps swept through the room.

Houser's eyes narrowed. "No. The fingermark contusions on the neck were distinct, consistent with manual strangulation. The bruising pattern, depth, and associated hemorrhaging are inconsistent with ligature or accidental asphyxiation. This was not a game. It was a homicide."

The word homicide echoed through the courtroom like a gavel of its own.

McMichaels stammered. "But you can't say it was my client, can you?"

"I can say Jonah Carter was murdered," Houser said firmly. "And he was found buried on your client's land."

The silence that followed was deafening. McMichaels fumbled his notes, muttered something about no further questions, and slumped back into his seat.

Houser straightened, steady under the weight of the room.

A ripple of unease moved through the gallery. Lampson thanked the witness and dismissed her, gaveling the court into adjournment for the day.

As the jury filed out, Hill's jaw was tight, his eyes already on the clock. He gathered his files with quick, jerky motions, stuffing them into his briefcase. O'Hell caught the shift, the urgency rising off him like static.

"What's going on?" O'Hell asked quietly as they pushed through the courthouse doors.

Hill didn't answer right away. His mind was already ahead, already in his office, already dialing Francine Grove.

Finally, he muttered, "We're out of time. She needs to decide tonight if she's ready to take the stand."

O'Hell exhaled, sensing the storm building. "Then we'd better be ready too."

Together, they disappeared into the afternoon shadows, both knowing tomorrow would either break their case wide open.... or bury it.

Chapter 21: The Weight of Silence

Hill pushed through the courthouse double doors with O'Hell right on his heels, both of them cutting a path through the thinning crowd of reporters and clerks. Neither man spoke as they strode across the marble floor, the silence between them humming with everything that had happened in court. Levi Coaster's brutal beating. McMichaels' smirk. Lampson's hard stare.

They needed Francine Grove. And they needed her now.

Hill's jaw was set tight as they reached the prosecutor's office. "She'll be here," he muttered, more to himself than to O'Hell.

"You sound like you're trying to convince yourself," O'Hell said quietly. "Maybe I am."

Hill yanked open the office door, the smell of French vanilla coffee and air fresher hitting him as he stepped inside. The clock on the wall read just past four. He tossed his briefcase onto the desk, the leather landing with a thud that seemed too loud in the stillness.

"She said after court," O'Hell reminded him, loosening his tie, but his eyes stayed sharp. "She'll come."

Hill didn't answer. He was pacing, already feeling the weight of the jury's eyes, the judge's expectations, the city's chants outside the courthouse. If Francine walked through that door and told the truth, the case against Grove would have flesh and bone, not just files and suspicion. If she didn't…

The doorknob rattled. Both men turned. Francine Grove stepped inside.

She looked composed at first glance, with a tailored blazer, neat hair, and a purse clutched tightly, but her eyes betrayed the storm underneath. They darted from Hill to O'Hell, then down to the floor as she shut the door behind her. For a long moment, she didn't move further in.

Hill's voice softened. "Mrs. Grove. Thank you for coming."

Francine finally raised her gaze. "Don't thank me yet." Her voice was steady, but it carried the weight of someone standing at a cliff's edge. Francine Grove stepped into the prosecutor's office.

"Please sit down, Francine," Hill said.

"Please call me Frannie," she replied softly as she lowered into the chair, smoothing her skirt as though to steady herself.

"What can I help you with?" she asked.

"Well, Frannie…" Hill's voice wavered, the nerves showing. "I wanted to speak with you about taking the stand against Benjamin Grove, your husband. I know that it's difficult. You don't have to decide right now, but I wanted you to think about it. About the severity of the case…"

Frannie cut him off, lifting her hand slightly. "With all due respect, I know the severity of the case. And he is still my husband." Her voice caught, and she blinked quickly. "I know he used my non-profit to funnel children into human trafficking, which I can't stomach. Those children are my heart and soul." Tears brimmed, and she looked down at her clasped hands. "As a child, I promised myself I'd build a safe place for children like me, kids shuffled through the system, tossed around until someone cared enough to stop the cycle. The center was supposed to be a second home."

Her throat tightened. "He almost destroyed my dream. Some of my contributors have already pulled funding. The center is still open, but I'm left rebuilding trust one brick at a time. I don't think I want to get involved on the legal side. Benjamin has already begged me not to testify."

Hill's jaw tightened. O'Hell shifted uncomfortably in his chair, but neither man interrupted.

"Please, Frannie," Hill finally said, leaning forward, voice low. "If you could just think it over and look at the evidence."

O'Hell slid a photo across the desk.... Jonah's picture. His tone was quiet, careful. "You heard Daniel's testimony. You know what's at stake."

Her breath hitched, and she shook her head quickly, pushing the photo away with trembling fingers. "Please don't remind me. I relive it every day. Do you think I don't see their faces when I close my eyes? I'm trying not to let that cruelty define my center."

She stood abruptly, chair scraping the floor. "I will think it over. But I don't need to be railroaded into guilt. What happened... it happened right under my nose. I trusted Benjamin. He was my husband. But wrong is wrong."

Her hand lingered on the doorknob for a fraction too long...a moment that looked like hesitation, like maybe she wanted to turn back. Then she pulled the door open and walked out without another word.

"Frannie...." Hill started, but the door clicked shut. The room sank into silence.

"Well, that went well," O'Hell muttered, forcing a grim half-smile.

Hill dragged both hands down his face, exhaling hard. "If Coaster survives, we'll need every word of his testimony. We still don't know how many kids disappeared from that dock." Frannie stood in the elevator, her reflection in the chrome doors blurring through tears she couldn't hold back. She pressed the heel of her palm against her eyes, furious with herself. Why didn't I say yes? The prosecutors' words rang in her ears, heavy with guilt. She had promised her community a safe haven, and yet children had been betrayed under her own banner of hope.

As the elevator slowed, she quickly wiped her face, forcing her expression into composure. "Stay strong. The community can't see me fall."

The doors slid open. She walked with purpose across the lobby, heels clicking a rhythm of determination, but inside her chest, her heart was still breaking. She headed to her car, slid into the driver's seat, and sat for a moment gripping the wheel.

Her voice slipped out in a whisper, then louder: "It's my choice. I don't need to be told to do it. And I won't be forced, either."

With that defiance still stinging her tongue, she drove to the community center, her refuge, her peace. Pulling into the lot, she let the sight of children streaming in and out of the glass doors soften her tension. This was still the place where laughter healed broken days.

Inside, she spotted Olivia at the front desk, kneeling to press a band-aid on a little girl's finger. "What happened?" Frannie asked, crouching slightly.

The child looked up, her eyes bright even through the sting. "I got a paper cut turning my book. It stings like a bee. But I'm okay, Ms. Frannie."

Frannie smiled, brushing the girl's shoulder gently. "That's my brave reader."

She turned toward her office, but Manny appeared suddenly, his expression tight, unreadable. He touched her elbow firmly. "Frannie, in here. Please."

She followed him into his office. He closed the door quickly, almost too quickly, and handed her a sealed envelope.

Her pulse quickened as she tore it open. The paper trembled in her hands as she read:

Your center is mine. Your children are mine. If you speak, your voice will be the last sound you make. Stay Quiet.

Frannie's knees weakened. The words blurred as tears

welled again. She pressed the letter against her chest, as though trying to shield her heart from it.

Manny's voice cracked. "What are we going to do? We can't feed the children to a monster. But we can't risk you either. I'm scared, Frannie."

Her heart pounded in her ears. For the first time, she wondered what Benjamin had truly promised, how deep the roots of his corruption went, and whether her beloved center had already been poisoned beyond saving.

After a long silence, she lifted her chin, though her voice trembled. "I need to fix this. I will not be used."

Manny's eyes filled. "If the center isn't safe... then where can they go?"

Frannie looked past him at the sound of children laughing down the hall. Her tears fell silently this time. I have to protect them. Whatever it takes. Manny's office felt too small, the air heavy with fear after Frannie read the letter aloud. Her hands still shook as she folded the paper, pressing it flat against the desk.

Manny was pacing in tight circles, running a hand through his hair so many times it stood on end. "We can't ignore this, Frannie. We can't. Whoever wrote this knows our doors, knows our kids. What if...." His voice cracked, and he stopped, pressing his palms into the desk like he needed it to hold him up. "What if the center isn't safe anymore?"

Frannie steadied her breathing, even though her heart was hammering. "Then we make it safe," she said firmly.

Manny looked at her eyes wide. "How?"

She forced herself into problem-solving mode, her voice low but steady. "Starting tomorrow, every staff member must show ID when they enter. No exceptions. I will also consider adjusting the hours of operation. And no outside volunteers unless they go through me personally."

Manny nodded quickly, scribbling notes on a pad, though his hand shook.

"Deliveries," Frannie continued, her voice sharper now. "No boxes left at the back door. Every package, every food drop, every supply order gets opened and signed for under supervision.

We'll double-check every back door lock, every window latch."

"I'll call maintenance tonight," Manny said. "We'll get extra bolts put on."

"I'll purchase more security cameras," Frannie added. "Not just at the doors. Inside the hallways, outside by the playground, and down by the alley."

Manny swallowed hard. "And the kids, Frannie. Some of them come and go alone. I don't… I don't want another incident. I can't." His voice cracked again.

She softened, but only slightly. "Then we assign staff to walk the children home if their parents don't show up. Even if it's just a few blocks. No one leaves alone."

Manny's pencil snapped between his fingers. He didn't even notice until the pieces dropped to the floor. "I'm scared, Frannie."

Her throat tightened, but she reached across the desk, resting her hand over his. "So am I. But we can't show it. If the children see us falter, they'll lose the one place they trust."

For a moment, silence settled. Only the muffled sound of children laughing in the gym filtered through the walls. It made the letter on the desk feel like poison.

Frannie stood, pulling her shoulders back. "We'll make this center stronger than ever. He doesn't own us. He doesn't own these children."

But as she crossed to the window, a chill ran through her. A dark van idled across the street, engine humming, no driver visible through the tinted glass. Her pulse spiked, but she forced her face to remain calm for Manny's sake. She pulled the blinds down slowly.

When she turned back, she gave him a tight smile. "Start drafting the new rules tonight. Tomorrow morning, we lock this place down."

Manny nodded, but his fear still bled through. "I'll do it. But Frannie… whoever sent that letter… they're already watching." She didn't deny it. She couldn't. A sharp knock rattled Manny's office door. Both of them jumped.

Frannie's heart skipped until she heard Olivia's voice.

"Frannie? Manny? Sorry to interrupt, but the kids are asking for you."

Frannie and Manny exchanged a look, both silently agreeing to tuck the fear away. Manny stuffed the broken pencil into the trash. Frannie slid the threatening letter back into the envelope and tucked it under a stack of papers.

"Come in," Frannie called.

Olivia poked her head inside, smiling gently, but her eyes flicked to their tense faces. "Two boys want to play ping pong with you, Manny. They won't stop arguing about who gets you as a partner."

Manny exhaled, forcing a grin. "Tell them I'll take them both on."

"And you, Ms. Frannie," Olivia added, looking her way. "There's a little girl in the game room who insists she'll only play pool if you're her teammate."

Frannie's throat tightened. The children still look at me like I can fix everything.

She stood, smoothing her skirt, slipping her mask back on. "Then I guess I'd better not keep her waiting."

Manny followed her out, trying to shake off the weight that

had crushed the office minutes earlier.

In the hallway, the sound of laughter floated to them.… ping pong balls bouncing, sneakers squeaking against the tile, kids calling each other's names. It was the kind of noise that used to soothe Frannie. But tonight, every sound felt fragile, like it could shatter if the wrong shadow stepped into the room.

Two boys spotted Manny and raced over, practically dragging him toward the table. He let them pull him, laughing half-heartedly, but when his eyes caught Frannie's, the fear behind the smile was still there.

Frannie stepped into the game room. A girl of maybe ten waved wildly from the pool table, her cue stick too big for her hands. "Ms. Frannie! You're on my team!"

Frannie forced a warm smile and crossed the room, crouching to the child's level. "You've got yourself a partner. But fair warning.… I'm terrible at this game."

The girl giggled. "That's okay. We'll still win."

Frannie laughed softly, though her eyes flicked to the window at the far end of the room. For the briefest second, she thought she saw the reflection of headlights sweep across the glass.

Her chest tightened. She steadied her voice for the little girl beside her. "Alright, champ. Let's show them what we've got."

The clatter of balls breaking filled the air, but Frannie couldn't stop glancing toward the blinds. Every laugh, every cheer from the kids felt precious and fragile. The evening wound down with laughter still echoing through the halls, but Frannie's smile never reached her eyes. She stayed a little longer than usual, helping Olivia tidy the front desk, waiting until the last child was picked up. The building finally grew quiet.

She gathered her purse and keys, then walked to the front doors. Her reflection stared back at her in the glass. She unlocked the door, stepped out, and pulled it shut behind her.

That's when she saw it, a figure across the street, half-hidden in the shadows. They weren't moving, just standing there, watching.

Frannie's breath caught. Her hand trembled on the key as she turned the lock quickly, double-checking it. Click. Secure.

She forced herself to keep her pace even as she crossed to her car. Sliding into the driver's seat, she locked the doors and started the engine. Her hands were clammy on the steering wheel.

One last glance in the rearview mirror. The shadowed figure was gone.

Frannie's chest tightened, her pulse roaring in her ears. She gripped the wheel and whispered to herself, "Stay strong. They can't see you break."

She drove off, but the unease clung to her like smoke. As she headed home, she knew she had to decide whether to tell Hill and O'Hell about the threats at tomorrow's hearing, but for now, she would remain silent.

Chapter 22: A Weakness on the Bench

Judge Nancy Lampson gripped the edges of the porcelain sink, her black robe hanging loose over her shoulders. Another wave hit her, and she bent forward, retching into the toilet. Her stomach churned like acid fire.

She wiped her mouth with the back of her hand, sweat beading across her forehead. Coffee. It has to be the coffee. She tried to replay her morning, wondering who had come into her chambers and who might have touched her cup, but her thoughts were jumbled.

Her administrative assistant, Megan, hovered in the doorway, nervously wringing her hands. "Go to the vending machine," Lampson whispered hoarsely. "Get me a ginger ale."

Megan darted out, heels clicking across the marble hallway. She nearly collided with Bailiff Young, who was making his morning rounds.

"Megan, what's wrong?"

"It's Judge Lampson," she blurted. "She's sick. She's been vomiting...."

Young didn't wait for more. He hurried to the judge's chambers and pushed open the heavy oak door. Lampson was back at her desk now, hunched over, her skin pale and clammy.

"Judge? Judge, are you alright?"

She waved a hand, slow and weak. "I'll be fine. Megan went to get something for my stomach." "Are you sure you can preside today?" Young pressed, concern sharpening his voice.

"Yes." Her voice was raspy but firm. "I have an hour to get myself together, Young. That's enough."

He nodded reluctantly and stepped back into the hallway just as Megan returned, ginger ale in hand.

For the next hour, Lampson sat in silence, sipping slowly, breathing through the nausea, trying to steady herself. She told herself she could shake it off. She had to.

But as the clock struck nine and Young called the courtroom to order, Lampson's stomach turned again. She rose to take the bench, the robe heavy on her frame. She gripped the gavel to hide the trembling in her hand.

"All rise," Young announced.

The sea of people stood, reporters scribbling, jurors shifting, the air thick with expectation.

Lampson forced herself into the chair, lips pressed tight. "You can do this. You're in control," she said.

But as Hill gathered his papers and McMichaels rose at the defense table, Lampson's vision blurred at the edges. Her body betrayed her with another twist of nausea.

She slammed the gavel once. "Court... court will recess." Her voice cracked. A stunned murmur swept the room.

"Judge...?" Hill started.

"Recess until further notice," Lampson snapped, pushing back from the bench. She could barely stand.

Young was already moving toward her, steadying her arm. The courtroom erupted in whispers. The trial, already plagued by sabotage, missing machines, and witness attacks, had another delay.

And this time, the weakness was at the very top. Judge Lampson slumped back in her chambers chair, her face pale, her breathing shallow. "I'm so weak... exhausted," she murmured. She rummaged in her purse with trembling hands until her fingers brushed a small pack of ginger chews. "If this doesn't settle me, Megan, I may need to postpone until tomorrow."

"You only had coffee and a muffin this morning," Megan said gently, hovering by the desk. Lampson's eyes narrowed.

"Who was in my chambers?"

"No one," Megan replied quickly. "Just me. You poured your own coffee, and Bailiff Young brewed the pot. You brought the muffin with you."

Lampson chewed slowly, trying to calm the storm in her stomach. But an hour later, the courtroom was restless. Reporters whispered, jurors fidgeted, and the defense table leaned toward the bailiff.

"What's going on?" McMichaels asked, his tone edged with impatience.

Hill exchanged a look with O'Hell. "Something's not right with Judge Lampson," he muttered.

At last, the doors opened. "Court will continue," Bailiff Young announced. The crowd shuffled quickly back inside, relief and curiosity buzzing in the air.

"All rise."

Lampson entered, walking slower than usual but wearing her robe like armor. She lowered herself carefully into the chair and gripped the gavel.

"Defense," she said, her voice thin but steady. "Call your first witness." McMichaels rose smoothly, adjusting his jacket. "The defense calls…"

The words cut short as Lampson suddenly lurched forward. The gavel clattered from her hand. She tumbled from the bench, collapsing onto the hardwood floor with a sickening thud.

The courtroom erupted in gasps and screams. Jurors stumbled back, reporters leapt to their feet, cameras flashing wildly.

"Judge!" Bailiff Young shouted, sprinting forward. Several sheriffs rushed to the bench, kneeling beside her pale form.

"Call 911!" someone barked into a radio.

"Clear the courtroom!" Marshals ordered, shoving open the doors as chaos exploded. Attorneys grabbed their files, jurors hurried out wide-eyed, the gallery pressing against each other in a frantic tide.

Hill stood frozen for a moment, heart pounding. McMichaels pressed a hand to his chest, muttering something about her health, but Hill caught the glint in his eyes, too controlled, too calculated.

As the Marshals forced them all into the hallway, the sound of protestors outside bled through the walls. Shouts rose: "What happened? What's going on in there?"

Red Leaf City was about to learn that its trial, and its judge, were no longer secure.

The courthouse parking garage was chaotic, with sirens wailing, reporters shouting questions, and officers rushing to block off the exits. Black gripped the steering wheel hard enough for his knuckles to pale as Walls slid into the passenger seat.

"Never seen anything like that," Walls muttered, still half turned toward the flashing lights in the rearview.

Black eased the car into traffic, tires squealing against the ramp. "Yeah, well, we've seen plenty these past weeks. I didn't expect Lampson to be the one hitting the floor."

Walls rubbed the back of his neck. "What if it wasn't just nerves or bad timing? What if someone got to her?"

"You think she was poisoned?" Black shot him a glance as the cruiser weaved through late-morning traffic.

Walls didn't answer right away. He stared out the window at the blur of sirens and cars pulling aside. "Ruby's dead. Charlie Deskers is dead. Levi is barely hanging on. Now Lampson drops in the middle of the court? You tell me that's a coincidence."

Black blew out a breath. "Or it's stress. Or a bug. Everyone wants this case to feel bigger than it is."

Walls turned, his voice flat. "This case is bigger than it is. And somebody knows we're close."

The rest of the drive settled into heavy silence, only the wail of their escort clearing a path toward the hospital. When they finally pulled up to the emergency entrance, both men climbed out without another word, carrying the weight of suspicion with them through the sliding glass doors. The ER waiting room smelled faintly of antiseptic and disinfectant spray. Black and Walls stood near the double doors, watching as paramedics wheeled Judge Lampson into a curtained bay.

Reporters were already crowding the hospital entrance, flashes sparking against the glass.

Nearly an hour later, a harried doctor finally emerged, clipboard in hand. "She's stable. We've run preliminary tests, it looks like a mild case of salmonella poisoning."

"Salmonella?" Black repeated, his brows knitting.

"Yes. Likely something she ate last night. Bad meat and undercooked poultry don't take much. She'll be fine in a few days." The doctor shrugged, already moving down the hall.

Black exhaled, shoulders slumping with relief. "So that's it. No poison, no conspiracy. Just foodborne illness."

Walls didn't move. He stared at the waiting room floor. "You buy that?"

"It makes sense," Black said firmly. "Everyone's been on edge, expecting shadows behind every corner. Maybe this is the one thing that isn't connected."

Walls finally looked up, his expression taut. "Or maybe that's exactly what someone wants us to think. Judges don't just collapse in the middle of the most high-profile trial in the city."

"Come on, Walls," Black muttered. "Sometimes a bad meal is just a bad meal."

Walls folded his arms, voice low and steady. "Then let's ask her ourselves. What did she eat last night? Who was with her? Who knew what she'd had for breakfast?"

Black rubbed his jaw, irritation flickering across his face. But he didn't dismiss it. Not entirely.

They stood in silence, the hum of the hospital machines filling the air. Somewhere down the corridor, Lampson groaned softly in bed.

Outside, the media was already spinning their story. Inside, the detectives had to decide whether to dig deeper or let it go. Lampson shifted against the crisp white sheets, her face still pale but steadier now. Black stood at the foot of the bed, Walls near the IV stand.

"Judge, we just need to ask," Black said gently. "Do you remember what you ate before this morning?"

She sighed, rubbing her temple. "Dinner last night. My husband grilled two steaks from the freezer…. Medium-well, like always. Our two adult kids came over afterward for coffee and dessert. Nothing out of the ordinary."

Walls scribbled in his notebook, eyes flicking up once. "No visitors in chambers this morning besides your clerk?"

"Just Megan," Lampson said firmly. "And I poured my own coffee. Honestly, detectives, this feels like food poisoning, not foul play."

Black nodded. "We had to ask."

When they stepped out into the sterile hallway, the heavy door closing behind them, Black loosened his tie.

Walls shook his head. "Maybe it was bad meat, but the timing couldn't be worse. The court's down for days. That won't stop other incidents from brewing."

Black gave him a sideways look. "Yeah, you're right. Let's go check on Coaster."

They walked toward the elevators, each carrying the weight of too many fires burning at once.

Chapter 23: In the Shadow of Custody

The day pressed heavily as Detectives Black and Walls pulled out of the hospital parking lot. The glow of red and blue emergency lights still washed across their rearview mirrors, fading as they turned onto the main road. Neither man spoke for the first few blocks; the hum of the engine and the rhythmic click of the turn signal were the only sounds filling the silence.

Black finally broke it. "Food poisoning, I can't believe it," he muttered, shaking his head. "That's what the doc said."

Walls kept his eyes on the windshield. "You buying that?"

"I don't know. Maybe. But if it's true, then it was lousy timing." Black's jaw tightened. "And timing's never just a coincidence in this case."

The tires hit a stretch of uneven pavement, jolting the car. Walls leaned back in his seat. "Poison or not, Lampson's out for a few days. That gives Grove's people breathing room and makes our job harder."

Black grunted in agreement. "Which means our focus shifts. If Levi Coaster's still alive, he's our next card to play. If they manage to silence him…"

"…then the whole house of cards collapses," Walls finished, his voice grim.

They drove the rest of the way in silence, headlights cutting through the light until the looming walls of the jail came into view. Floodlights bathed the perimeter in stark white, and the air around the facility seemed to hum with tension. Black parked, killed the engine, and both men sat for a moment, staring at the building that held too many secrets.

"Let's see if Coaster made it through the night," Black said finally, his tone low, steady.

They pushed open their doors, the sound of them shutting echoing sharply in the still afternoon, and headed toward the entrance. The air inside the jail's infirmary was sharp with disinfectant, the hum of fluorescent lights buzzing overhead. Black and Walls exchanged a glance as they stepped through the double doors. The guards posted at the entrance stiffened, clearly surprised to see them.

"Detectives?" one said, shifting his weight. "This isn't on the schedule."

"We're not here for a schedule," Black replied coolly, flashing his badge. "We're here to see Coaster."

The guards hesitated, exchanging nervous looks. For a moment, it seemed they might try to stall. Then Sergeant Harris emerged from behind the nurse's station, his arms folded. "Make it quick," he said gruffly. "He's stable, but he doesn't need to be worked over."

The detectives pushed past, their footsteps echoing down the narrow corridor. Inside the last room on the right, Levi Coaster lay propped against thin pillows, an IV line running into his arm. His face was still bruised, one eye swollen nearly shut, but when he spotted them, he smirked.

"Look who came to check if I'm still breathing," he rasped. His voice was rough but laced with cocky bravado. "Don't worry, Detectives…. I'm tough. I wasn't going down without a fight."

Walls stepped closer. "You're lucky you're still here, Levi. What happened?"

Coaster chuckled, then winced as the movement tugged at his ribs. "Those punks thought they had me. Two against one, shank in hand, and I still made them bleed. Took more than a toothbrush to put me down."

Black's eyes narrowed. "You know who they were?"

Coaster's grin faded, and for the first time, his tone sharpened. "Yeah. I know exactly who they were. And they weren't Grove's boys."

Walls leaned in. "What do you mean? If not Grove, then who?"

"I mean what I said," Coaster replied, his voice low but steady. "This hit didn't come from Grove's payroll."

A heavy silence hung between them. Black and Walls exchanged a glance, both thinking the same thing.

"Waters?" Walls pressed.

Coaster didn't answer right away. He looked down at the IV running into his arm, then back up at them. The silence stretched until the tension was nearly unbearable.

Finally, with a sly smile tugging at his swollen lip, he said, "No need to worry about me. I'm still testifying. And when I do, I've got information that'll bring both sides down for good."

The words landed like a hammer in the sterile room, leaving Black and Walls staring at a man who was suddenly more than just a witness.... he was a loaded weapon pointed at every power player in the city. Black and Walls left the infirmary in silence, their boots heavy against the concrete floor. Behind them, Levi Coaster's cocky grin lingered in their minds like a sour taste. The guard closed the door and locked it, muttering something under his breath, but neither detective caught it. They were too busy replaying Coaster's words.

Out in the parking lot, the afternoon air was damp, heavy with the smell of rain-soaked asphalt. They slid into Black's unmarked sedan, both men staring straight ahead for a long beat before anyone spoke.

"Both sides," Walls finally said, shaking his head. "What the heck does that even mean? If Grove didn't call that hit..."

"…then Waters did," Black finished, his tone clipped. "Or someone bigger. Someone neither of us has eyes on yet."

Walls rubbed the back of his neck, uneasy. "If Coaster really has information that ties them both together, then this case is about to explode. Jury delays, witness attacks…this isn't just intimidation anymore. It's a war."

Black gripped the wheel but didn't start the car. His voice dropped, firm and low. "And Coaster just made himself the spark."

For a moment, they sat in silence, the weight of it pressing down on them. Then Black pulled out his phone and dialed Hill's number. No answer. He left a message instead, keeping his words tight.

"Hill, it's Black. We need to meet as soon as possible. Coaster just gave us something you need to hear before the court resumes. Don't wait. Call us back tonight if you can."

He ended the call, tossed the phone onto the dashboard, and started the engine. The headlights cut through the mid-afternoon lot as they pulled away from the jail.

Walls exhaled heavily, as if releasing the last of his doubt. "Tomorrow's going to be a nightmare." Black's jaw tightened, his eyes on the road. "Then we'd better be ready."

Chapter 24: The Message

Dawn was beginning to thin the edges of night. A pale gray light crept across the quiet downtown, brushing rooftops and catching the faint shimmer of dew on small patches of grass. The streets were empty, except for the distant hum of a garbage truck and the soft rustle of leaves in the breeze. Inside the prosecutor's office, the air still carried the scent of fresh coffee. A half-empty pot sat forgotten on the warmer. Hill had started early. He sat forward, tie loosened, staring at his phone as if it might answer for him.

"Did you listen to Black's message from last night yet?" O'Hell asked, his voice low. He leaned against the file cabinet, scrolling through his phone.

Hill shook his head. "Yeah. It came through this morning, my phone died last night, and I forgot to charge it. I didn't see it until now."

Hill pressed play again, the gruff voice of Detective Black filling the room: "Hill, it's Black. We need to meet urgently first thing in the morning. Coaster just gave us something you need to hear before the court resumes. Don't wait. Call us back tonight if you can."

The message ended. Silence stretched.

O'Hell crossed his arms. "That doesn't sound like routine police chatter. He was rattled."

Hill rubbed his temples. "Coaster's alive, but barely. If he said something strong enough to push Black to leave this message, then it's big. Maybe bigger than Grove alone."

"Waters," O'Hell muttered, pacing now. "Or worse. Remember what Levi shouted in court? 'Devil in a suit.' What if he wasn't just grandstanding? What if he knows who's pulling the strings above Grove?"

Hill pushed back from his desk, standing. His voice carried a quiet urgency. "Then we don't wait. I want Black and Walls in here before noon. No excuses. If Coaster has the key to connect both Grove and Waters, it changes everything…our strategy, our risk, maybe even our witness list."

O'Hell looked uneasy. "Unless Coaster's just baiting us. He's arrogant enough to play games."

"Arrogant or not," Hill said firmly, "he's still breathing, and right now he's the only one giving us a line straight into the heart of this operation. We can't afford to ignore him."

The phone on Hill's desk buzzed, breaking the tension. He and O'Hell exchanged a look before he picked it up. The secretary's voice came through: "Detectives Black and Walls are in the lobby. Should I send them up?"

Hill locked eyes with O'Hell. "Send them up." Moments later, the door swung open and Detectives Black and Walls stepped in, their coats still damp from the morning rain. Both men looked like they hadn't slept much.

Hill motioned to the chairs across from his desk. "Sit. No small talk…what did Coaster tell you?"

Walls leaned forward first, his jaw tight. "He's alive, still beat up, but talking. And not just talking…boasting. He said the two men who came at him weren't Grove's."

O'Hell frowned. "Not Grove's? You sure?"

Black nodded, voice clipped. "Dead sure. Coaster said it himself… 'this hit didn't come from Grove's payroll.' He was confident, almost cocky about it. Like he knew exactly who was moving the pieces."

Hill's fingers tapped the edge of his desk, slow and deliberate. "Then whose payroll was it?"

A heavy pause stretched across the room before Walls answered. "He didn't name Waters outright. But when I asked, Coaster went silent. Didn't deny it. Didn't confirm it. Just let the air hang thick."

O'Hell shook his head. "That silence is confirmation enough. Waters is locked up in federal holding, but he's still calling shots."

Hill exhaled through his nose, thinking fast. "And then?"

Black's eyes darkened. "Coaster leaned in, told us not to worry…. because he's still going to testify. Said he has information that will 'bring both sides down for good.' Those were his exact words."

The room went still. Even the old clock on the wall seemed to hold its tick. O'Hell broke it first. "Both sides. Grove and Waters."

Hill's voice was low, steady, but there was steel beneath it. "If he's telling the truth, then Levi Coaster is about to hand us the entire map of this operation. But it also makes him a bigger target than ever."

Walls nodded grimly. "That's why we wanted to meet now. You need to understand, we're past local politics. If Coaster spills what he claims to know, it could crack open a network bigger than Red Leaf City."

Hill stepped away from the desk, pacing toward the window. Outside, the gray clouds pressed low against the skyline. He spoke without turning back. "Then we don't waste time. We lock Coaster down tight, tighter than ever before. And when Lampson brings court back, we make sure his testimony is the one that sets this city on fire."

Black exchanged a look with Walls. "That's exactly why we came to you. But you need to be ready, Hill. Because if Coaster's right, the storm that's coming will make everything we've seen so far look like a drizzle."

Hill finally turned, eyes sharp. "Then let it rain." Hill's pacing slowed. He stopped at the edge of his desk, voice steady but laced with urgency.

"If we can get Francine Grove to testify, if she's willing to say that her husband used her community center to funnel those children, we seal this case shut."

Across town, Francine Grove's house still held the hush of sleep. In her bedroom, only a sliver of morning light slipped through the curtains, cutting a faint line across the quilt. Frannie sat propped against her headboard, knees drawn close, a journal open but untouched in her lap. She had been awake for hours, replaying Hill's request over and over, trying to convince herself that silence was safer than staying quiet meant staying alive.

But guilt has a way of whispering louder than reason.

She told herself she'd stop by the center before six, yet the clock on the nightstand blinked 6:47 a.m. She exhaled, rubbed her temples, and muttered to herself, "Get up, Frannie. You're running late. Go start your day."

Then came the sound.

A sharp, brittle crash from downstairs. The shatter of glass slicing through the calm.

Her dog sprang from the foot of the bed, barking wildly, claws skidding on the hardwood as he bolted toward the stairs.

Frannie froze…. heart hammering, listening as the house that had felt too quiet moments ago now held a new, dangerous sound.

Her scream broke free before she could stop it. She stumbled from the bed, slammed the lock on her bedroom door, then darted into the closet, hands trembling. The darkness swallowed her as she crouched low, the phone slick in her palms.

With a shaking finger, she dialed 911. Her whisper was ragged, urgent:

"This is Francine Grove. Someone's in my house…please, send help!"

The operator's calm response blurred in her ears as the

sound of heavy boots creaked on the floorboards below.

Frannie clutched the phone tighter, heart hammering so loud she feared whoever had broken in could hear it.

And then…silence.

Only the dog's growl, low and unyielding, vibrated through the walls.

Chapter 25: The Home Invasion

The dog's furious barking grew sharper, closer, until the intruder yanked open the back door. With a swift boot, he shoved the animal outside, slamming the door before it could turn back. The dog's frantic scratching on the other side of the wood only seemed to amuse them.

"Clear," one of the men muttered, stalking down the hallway.

They moved with brutal efficiency, boots hammering across the hardwood. They headed straight for Benjamin Grove's study, yanking open drawers, scattering files across the carpet. Papers floated like fallen leaves.

"There has to be a safe," the tallest one growled, dragging a bookcase aside. His eyes caught the black steel hidden in the wall. "Found it."

He spun the dial twice, cursed under his breath, then slammed his fist against the metal. "Locked tight."

Frustration boiled over. They tore through the shelves, flipping framed pictures and splintering the desk. Then the crash of her bedroom door. Hinges screamed, the lock snapping loose.

Francine barely had time to scream before a rough hand grabbed her hair, yanking her from the closet. She kicked, clawed, shrieked. Her feet scraped against the floor as they dragged her toward the study.

"Open it!" one snarled, shoving her in front of the safe.

"I don't know the code!" Her voice cracked, raw with terror.

A fist snapped across her cheek, white-hot pain exploding through her jaw. She crumpled, but they yanked her up again.

"Don't play with us, lady. You live here. You know the code."

Another punch came swiftly, cracking against her cheekbone. Her body fell sideways, hands clawing at the carpet to keep herself upright. She stayed on her knees.

"I don't know the code!" she shouted.

Blood filled her mouth; she spat onto the carpet, trembling but defiant. "I called the police. You need to leave."

"Wrong answer." Cold metal pressed against her temple.

The third man shifted nervously, glancing toward the window. "Forget it, sirens."

In the distance, the wail of police cruisers grew louder, swelling toward the house.

"Darn it!" The leader shoved her hard against the floor, hovering over her. "You're gonna get what's coming to you."

A final punch landed squarely against her jaw. Frannie hit the carpet hard, her head snapping against the floor. Dazed, she curled in on herself, bracing for another blow....

But when she looked up, they were gone.

Minutes later, they bolted.... shoving through the back door and kicking the dog against the fence. The animal yelped but couldn't retaliate before the men vaulted over and vanished into the early morning. The gray sky swallowed them just as red-and-blue lights flashed across the Groves' house, turning it into a scene from a crime report.

Francine lay on the floor amid shattered frames and scattered papers, shaking, her hand pressed to her bruised face. She had survived the break-in, but she knew now...silence would not protect her anymore.

The next sound she heard was the door crashing open under the weight of police boots. "Red Leaf PD!" voices shouted, sharp and commanding. Two officers swept through the hall, weapons drawn, clearing the rooms.

"Victim is in here!" one of them called.

An officer knelt beside her. "Ma'am, can you hear me?"

She nodded weakly, tears streaking her cheeks. "They're gone."

Moments later, Detectives Black and Walls pushed through the crowd of uniforms.

Walls helped Frannie from the floor and guided her to the living room, draping a blanket around her shoulders. Her cheek throbbed where the punches had landed, her lip split.

Detective Walls crouched in front of her, notebook in hand. "Mrs. Grove, did you recognize any of the intruders?"

She shook her head. "Masks. Hoodies. All I saw were their eyes…angry, wild. The leader had hazel eyes. He was the one who punched me three times and shoved a pistol against my head. He gave orders to the others."

Black leaned against the mantle, arms folded, his voice steady but probing. "Did they say anything? Anything that might connect them to Grove? Or Waters?"

Francine hesitated. The safe. They wanted the safe. She swallowed, forcing the thought down. "They just kept yelling for me to give them something. I told them to get out, that the police were coming."

Black's eyes narrowed. He sensed she was holding something back, but didn't press. Not at this hour.

Walls closed his notebook. "We'll have units seal the back door for now, but you can't stay here alone. Do you have somewhere safe you can go?"

Francine nodded slowly. "My foster sister, Jessica Carpenter. She lives across town. I will call her."

"Good," Black said. "Pack a bag for a day or two. We'll

escort you there."

A sudden scratching at the front porch pulled Francine's head up. She jumped to her feet, rushing to the door. "Mouse!"

The golden retriever bounded in as soon as she opened it, tail whipping like a flag, whining as he pressed against her legs. Francine sank to her knees, burying her face in his fur, finally letting the sobs come.

Walls looked at Black over her shoulder. "We'll post a patrol car out front for the remainder of the day." Black nodded, his jaw tight. "And we'll find out who sent those men."

But as Francine clutched Mouse and trembled on the living room floor, one thought burned in her mind: the safe. Francine packed slowly, her hands shaking as she stuffed clothes into a bag. Mouse followed her every step, whining as if he understood. An hour later, she stood on Jessica Carpenter's porch.

The door opened, and Jessica didn't hesitate. She pulled Francine into her arms, holding her tight. "Oh, sweetheart.

Francine broke down, sobs muffled against her foster sister's shoulder. For the first time, she let herself feel how close she had come to breaking.

Inside, Jessica fixed a cup of warm tea, the steam curling between them at the kitchen table. She reached across, her hand covering Francine's.

"This has to stop. Benjamin's dirty work is bleeding straight into your life…. into your center, and into those kids' lives. You have to testify."

Francine shook her head, staring into the tea. "You don't understand… this wasn't the first." Jessica's brows knitted. "What do you mean?"

"The hang-up calls. They started weeks ago. And then… a letter arrived at the center." Francine's voice cracked. "It said if I talked, I'd never speak again."

Jessica gasped, her eyes widening with fury. "And you didn't tell me?"

"I didn't want to worry you. I could handle it. But today…" She shivered, remembering the gun to her head. "This morning proved I can't."

Jessica squeezed her hand harder. "Frannie, listen to me. You can't let him silence you. The community needs the truth. Those children need the truth."

Francine nodded, tears spilling down her cheeks. Deep inside, she kept the safe locked away in her thoughts, but for now, she wasn't in danger.

She sank onto the couch in the living room and called Manny to tell him what had happened. Her voice shook as she said she'd be taking the day off and would come in within a day or two. For now, she planned to spend the day with her sister and stay away from home.

Tomorrow, she told herself, she would return and finally look inside the safe to see what was so important.

The next morning, Mouse barked eagerly as she unlocked her front door. It smelled of cinnamon air freshener and disgust. Francine set her bag down and took a deep breath. "We're home," she whispered to the dog… though she knew the danger had only followed her here. Francine went straight for the study, her pulse drumming in her ears. The safe loomed in the corner, dented from the intruders' failed attempt. She keyed in the familiar code with trembling hands. The lock clicked.

Inside…papers, account books, contracts. At first, nothing unusual. But on the top shelf, half-buried under a stack of envelopes, her fingers brushed a yellow folder. An envelope. She pulled it free, a single flash drive taped to the inside.

Her throat tightened. She hurried to the bedroom, her laptop still intact where the men hadn't searched. Mouse trailed close at her heels, whining. Francine plugged in the drive.

The screen lit up. Folders. Dozens of them. Missing Children Reports.

Dates. Names. Ages. Locations. Each one linked to Red Leaf Community Center, each one a child she had sworn to protect. Her eyes blurred with tears as she scrolled, hand clapped over her mouth. Jonah Carter's name. Daniel Gray's. So many others.

And then…another file. Financials.

She opened it, and the blood drained from her face. Hudson Waters wired $150,000 to an Offshore Account. Purpose: "Extended Use of Red Leaf Community Center."

Francine staggered back, clutching the laptop as if it might burn her. Her dream, the center she had poured her life into…reduced to a ledger for predators.

Tears streamed hot down her cheeks. Fury rose sharper than grief. She snatched her phone from her pocket and dialed Hill's number with shaking hands.

"Please," she whispered to herself as it rang. "Pick up, Pick up." Her hands were shaking so badly she nearly dropped the phone. The line rang once, twice, three times. No answer.

"Come on, Hill…" she whispered, clutching the phone tighter, eyes darting back to the glowing files on her laptop.

The voicemail clicked on. Francine's voice broke as she spoke:

"Jackson, it's Frannie. I…. I found something. It's in Benjamin's safe. Files… records of the children, and money. Money from Waters. I can't believe this. Please call me back immediately. Please. I don't feel safe."

She hung up, chest heaving. For a moment, the only sound was Mouse pacing the room, nails clicking against the floor.

Francine sank onto the bed, laptop open beside her, the damning files glowing like a curse in the bright room.

"I'm not going to be silent anymore," she whispered to herself. "Not this time." The phone stayed silent.

Chapter 26: Why, Benjamin!

Hill hadn't slept well. His desk lamp was still burning when he stirred awake in the prosecutor's office, tie loose around his neck, papers scattered like a storm had blown through. A voicemail notification glowed on his phone.

He rubbed his eyes and pressed play.

Francine's voice came through broken, trembling, desperate:

"Jackson, it's Frannie. I… I found something. It's in Benjamin's safe. Files…records of the children, and money. Money from Waters. I can't believe this. You need to call me back right away. Please. I don't feel safe."

Hill shot up in his chair, pulse hammering in his ears. "O'Hell!" he shouted down the hall.

Lucas O'Hell appeared in the doorway, still balancing a coffee cup. "You slept here all night, Jackson."

"Yes, I did."

"You need to go home and shower. I'm here, I can finish what's needed," Lucas said.

"No need to worry about me. I'll be fine. However, you need to listen to Francine's voicemail, which she left this morning. I missed her call."

"What now?" Lucas asked.

"Frannie left me this message. Just listen." He shoved the phone at him. O'Hell listened, his face tightening with every second.

"She found proof," O'Hell muttered. "This could bury Grove and tie Waters in at the same time."

"Exactly. We need to head to Frannie's house, now."

Hill pulled a travel-size deodorant from his desk drawer, swiped some on, and reached for the mouthwash. He swished it around and spat into an empty plastic cup sitting on his desk. Then he grabbed his coat and hurried out into the cold morning with Lucas.

The drive to Francine's house was taut with silence, both men running through scenarios in their heads, what she'd found, whether she was safe, whether this was the break… or the trap… they'd been waiting for. Thirty-five minutes later, a black sedan pulled into her driveway. Prosecutor Jackson Hill stepped out first, coat collar up, followed by Lucas O'Hell, carrying an evidence satchel. The two men exchanged a look before knocking.

When Francine opened the door, she looked pale, her eyes rimmed with red, her lip split, and her cheekbone bruised. Mouse, her golden retriever, barked protectively at their feet.

"Frannie, are you alright?" Hill asked gently as they stepped inside.

She didn't answer right away as she pressed an icepack against her cheek. Instead, she motioned them toward the study. She reopened the laptop. The spreadsheet blinked back to life. Hill leaned closer, his jaw tightening as he read the headers: Transaction ID, Recipient Account, Future Paths Consulting, Donor: H. Waters / B. Grove.

"My God," O'Hell murmured. "These are six-figure transfers."

"And timestamps that line up with the missing funds from the trafficking task force," Hill added.

Frannie's eyes darted between them. "It's real, isn't it?"

Hill nodded. "Yes. And it changes everything."

He reached into his satchel and pulled out a clear evidence sleeve. "Mrs. Grove, I need you to hand me the drive exactly as it is. We'll log it officially at the precinct."

She slipped the flash drive from the laptop and placed it in his gloved hand like a confession.

"We'll take it from here," Hill said. "Lock your doors. Don't speak to anyone, not even your husband. Do you understand?"

"Jackson… if they know I found it…."

"Then we'll make sure they don't get another chance."

Hill sealed the evidence bag, scribbled his initials across the tape, and nodded once to O'Hell.

"Black and Walls are expecting us as he hung up the phone," O'Hell said.

"Good. Let's move."

They left the house in silence. Frannie stood in the doorway, watching the sedan pull away, the sound of gravel under its tires fading into the distance.

Only then did she realize she was still holding the broken picture frame. Her reflection stared back at her through the crack, splitting Benjamin's face from her own.

You did the right thing, she whispered.

God, please let it be enough.

After forty minutes, Hill and O'Hell pulled into the precinct lot just before noon. The building glowed faintly under the floodlights, quiet, except for the hum of vending machines and the shuffle of morning-shift officers. Hill carried the sealed evidence bag in one hand, as if it might vanish if he let go.

Detectives Black and Walls were waiting upstairs in the conference room, coffee cooling between them, and case files spread across the table.

"What've you got?" Black asked the moment Hill walked in.

Hill dropped the evidence bag onto the table. The flash drive glinted under the fluorescent lights. "From Francine Grove's house. Ledger files, transfers, and names. She found them in Benjamin Grove's safe. The transactions tie back to the Future Paths Consulting…. money from Waters, six-figure amounts."

Walls leaned forward, frowning. "You logged it?"

"Sealed, tagged, and signed," Hill said. "We'll have Property issue the chain-of-custody log first thing. For now, it stays locked in Evidence."

Lucas O'Hell sank into a chair. "We'll need to file a supplemental disclosure with the defense. They're due notice of any new evidence before the morning session."

Black exhaled slowly, rubbing the bridge of his nose. "That's going to blow the case wide open."

"It already has," Hill said. "But we do it by the book. No surprises the defense can use against us later."

He reached for the folder on the table, flipped it open, and began making notes for the disclosure statement. The room hummed with the sound of the copier starting up somewhere down the hall.

Walls stood by the window, watching the city lights blink through the blinds. "What about Francine?"

Hill didn't look up. "She's scared, but she did the right thing. We'll get protection arranged tonight. I'll call Lampson's clerk within the hour."

The flash drive sat between them, small and harmless-looking, yet heavy enough to tilt the balance of everything.

By mid-afternoon, the precinct buzzed with the slow hum of printers and muted voices. Hill stood at the evidence window while a technician sealed the flash drive inside a labeled envelope, heat-pressing the chain-of-custody strip across the top. The label read: Property #7145, USB Drive, Recovered from Francine Grove Residence, 10:50 a.m.

"Receipt for you, Counselor," the tech said, sliding a pink copy across the counter.

Hill took it and nodded. The sound of the locker door closing echoed down the hallway…sharp, final.

Back in the briefing room, O'Hell was already on his laptop, the cursor blinking over a document titled Notice of Additional Discovery. Black leaned against the wall, arms crossed, while Walls reviewed a printed transaction summary from the Future Paths database.

"We're filing this before the clerk's office closes," Hill said, dropping into the chair beside O'Hell. "The defense gets their copy today, Lampson's chambers gets one, and nobody can claim we buried evidence."

Walls looked up. "What if McMichaels calls it fabricated?"

Hill exhaled, rubbing his temple. "Then he can take it up with the state lab once it's verified. The data's time-stamped, the accounts are real, and the money ties straight back to Waters and Grove."

O'Hell finished typing and printed the notice. "Chain of custody logged. Exhibit sealed. I'll run this to the clerk's office now."

"I'll go with you," Hill said.

They left the precinct and drove the few blocks to the county courthouse. The afternoon sun set high, casting amber light through the windshield. The two men said little, just the rhythmic flick of the turn signal and the thrum of Hill's thoughts replaying Francine's voice: I don't feel safe.

Inside the courthouse, the clerk's office smelled faintly of toner and dust. A tired woman behind the counter looked up over her glasses.

"Supplemental filing?" she asked.

"Yes, ma'am," Hill said, sliding the folder forward. "State versus Grove. New evidence recovered this morning."

She stamped it twice… Received, 2:27 p.m., and placed the papers in the outbox marked Judge Lampson – Urgent.

O'Hell handed her the second envelope. "One copy for the defense."

"Delivered to McMichaels's office before close," she said automatically, sealing it with a strip of red tape.

Back in the corridor, Hill exhaled a breath he hadn't realized he'd been holding. "Now the defense can't claim we hid it. Tomorrow, they'll come in swinging."

O'Hell nodded. "Let them. We've got the truth this time."

Hill didn't answer right away. His gaze drifted toward the courthouse doors, sunlight still beaming, "Truth doesn't always save you," he said quietly. "Sometimes it just makes you a target."

They stepped outside as the clock on the tower struck three. The courthouse doors locked behind them with a dull, echoing click.

Somewhere across town, a woman who had risked everything was probably sitting in silence, praying her truth would hold until morning.

Chapter 27: New Evidence

The bailiff's voice rang out. "All rise."

Judge Lampson took the bench, her face still pale from her recent illness, but her gavel hand steady as stone.

"I greatly appreciate everyone's patience and understanding during the delay of court while I was recovering," she said. "Court will now continue in full force moving forward."

"Be seated."

"Court is now in session," she said, settling behind the bench. "Before we resume with witness testimony, I've been advised that the prosecution filed a supplemental disclosure yesterday afternoon."

All eyes turned toward the state's table. Hill rose, buttoning his jacket. O'Hell stood beside him, a thick manila folder in hand.

"Yes, Your Honor," Hill said. "Yesterday, new evidence was recovered from the residence of Francine Grove, material directly relevant to the ongoing investigation and this trial. We immediately logged and filed notice before the close of business."

Across the aisle, Defense Attorney McMichaels pushed back his chair, the legs scraping the tile. "You're telling this court that less than twenty-four hours before we resume, you've suddenly discovered new evidence?" His voice dripped with mock disbelief. "Is this another fishing expedition, Counselor Hill, or just a convenient surprise?"

Judge Lampson's eyes narrowed. "Mr. McMichaels, you'll have your turn. Mr. Hill, describe the nature of this evidence."

"A flash drive recovered from Mrs. Grove's home," Hill

said evenly. "Containing financial records and transaction data connecting Benjamin Grove and Hudson Waters to Future Paths Consulting. The files include names, timestamps, and dollar amounts, consistent with the embezzlement and child trafficking charges before this court."

Murmurs rippled through the gallery. McMichaels's jaw tightened, but he forced a smile. "Your Honor, the defense objects to the timing. We have not had an adequate opportunity to review or verify this supposed evidence. I move for a continuance until such time that we can examine the material independently."

Lampson turned her gaze toward Hill. "Counselor, why was this not found earlier?"

Hill met her eyes. "Because Mrs. Grove risked her safety to come forward. She contacted my office only yesterday morning, and we acted immediately. The evidence has been logged, sealed, and verified for chain of custody."

The judge leaned back, weighing the air that seemed to have thickened between the two tables. Finally, she nodded once.

"Very well. The defense will receive a full copy of the data by noon today. The court will recess for the afternoon to allow review. We will reconvene tomorrow at nine a.m. for an evidentiary argument."

Her gavel struck the bench… sharp, decisive.

Hill exhaled quietly and began gathering his files. McMichaels leaned toward his co-counsel, whispering something with a smirk. O'Hell leaned in. "He's rattled."

Hill nodded. "He should be. This is the first time the truth's walked through his door."

As the courtroom emptied, the gold light shifted higher along the wall, washing everything in pale morning heat. The truth might be in the record now, but by the look on McMichaels's face, the storm hadn't passed. It had only begun.

McMichaels's office smelled of old coffee and new panic. The blinds were half-drawn, cutting the sunlight into sharp lines across the floor. Clair Winston sat at his desk, her laptop open, scrolling through a spreadsheet that looked too clean to be fake.

"These are bank transfers," she said, voice low. "Future Paths Consulting accounts. Routing numbers match the same ones from the Grove's subpoena."

McMichaels leaned over her shoulder, the veins in his temple pulsing. "You're certain?"

"Positive." She clicked open another tab. "Each one's six figures. The dates align with the funds allocated to the trafficking task force. The person who made these logs wasn't sloppy. They're legit."

He stepped back, running a hand over his jaw. "Then we're finished. If the state can prove these links…. Grove, Waters, the Consulting, we've lost control of the narrative."

Clair kept her eyes on the screen. "Unless the narrative disappears."

He looked at her sharply. "You mean the drive."

"I mean access to it," she said. "The moment it's compromised, their whole case collapses."

McMichaels stared at her, the silence stretching. "You didn't hear that from me," he muttered finally, retreating toward the window.

Clair closed the laptop, slid it into her briefcase, and pulled out her phone. Her tone softened as she spoke into it, calm and practiced, the voice of someone accustomed to cleaning up messes.

"Hey. It's me. I need you to check on something for me at the precinct."

A pause.

"Yes, evidence intake. Property number seven-one-four-five. Make sure it's… missing."

She ended the call and slipped the phone into her blazer pocket, her expression unreadable.

Behind her, McMichaels poured a drink he didn't taste. "You realize if this goes sideways, they'll trace it back to us."

Clair turned toward the window, where the city lights were beginning to blink awake. "Not if it's already gone."

They worked late into the evening before finally leaving the office.

"I'll see you in the morning," McMichaels said.

"You too," Clair replied.

The next morning broke gray and thin over Red Leaf City, the courthouse dome catching a dull gleam of light. Hill and O'Hell arrived at the precinct just after seven, both carrying paper cups of coffee and the exhaustion of too many sleepless nights.

The corridors smelled faintly of disinfectant and burnt toast from the breakroom down the hall. Hill's footsteps echoed as he approached the evidence room, the weight of the coming hearing pressing down on him.

"I want to double-check the drive before court," he said. "Chain of custody, signatures…. everything tight."

O'Hell nodded, flipping open his notepad. "Property number seven-one-four-five. Logged yesterday at 11:42 a.m. Tech's name was Mendez."

They exchanged a look, confirming the details O'Hell had just rattled off as they walked down the hallway.

Hill pressed the buzzer beside the security glass. The evidence clerk, a heavyset man with wire-rimmed glasses, looked up from behind the counter.

"Morning, Counselor," he said, swiping his keycard. "You

signing something out?"

"Just confirming a file from yesterday." Hill slid the pink receipt across the counter. "USB drive, Francine Grove case."

The clerk checked the system, frowning slightly. "That's odd. One moment."

He turned to the back room, the sound of metal drawers and sliding locks carrying into the hallway. Seconds passed, too many. Hill's pulse began to climb.

"Everything all right?" O'Hell asked, leaning forward.

The clerk reappeared, pale and uneasy. "It's not here."

Hill blinked. "What do you mean it's not here?"

"The envelope's missing," the clerk said, voice tight. "Log says it's still checked in, seal number matches, no sign-out record."

Hill stepped closer to the counter. "That locker's restricted. Only two authorized access points exist: yours and the evidence technician's. You telling me it vanished overnight?"

"I'm telling you it's gone," the man said. "Seal's been cut clean. Whoever took it knew what they were doing."

Silence filled the corridor. O'Hell's coffee cup sagged in his hand. "This is just wonderful," he muttered.

Hill pressed his hand against his forehead. "Lock this room down. Pull the security footage from yesterday. I want to know who entered this hallway and when."

"Yes, sir."

Hill turned to O'Hell, his voice low. "They knew exactly what they were after. Someone tipped them off."

O'Hell's jaw tightened. "Inside the department?"

Hill didn't answer. His eyes stayed fixed on the empty evidence locker, the torn seal hanging like a wound.

He finally spoke, almost to himself. "Whoever took that drive just turned this case into a war."

They left the precinct in silence, the weight of what was missing following them all the way to the courthouse.

Judge Lampson's clerk ushered them in before the courtroom doors opened for the morning session. The blinds in chambers were half-drawn, slanting pale light across the table where Hill and O'Hell stood opposite McMichaels and Clair Winston. The judge's robe hung open at the collar, coffee cooling beside a stack of motions. She didn't waste time.

"Counselors, I was informed there's an issue with the evidence submitted yesterday."

Hill cleared his throat. "Yes, Your Honor. The flash drive recovered from Francine Grove's residence…. the one disclosed yesterday, has gone missing from the precinct evidence locker."

Lampson's eyes sharpened. "Missing? Explain."

"We logged it, sealed it, and verified the chain of custody yesterday afternoon," Hill said. "When we arrived this morning to prep for the hearing, the locker seal had been cut. No sign-out record has been found, and no security footage has been reviewed yet. Someone removed it overnight."

McMichaels spread his hands, feigning surprise. "Well, that's convenient. Evidence the State claims proves its case vanishes on their watch."

Lampson's gavel tapped once…. warning, not force. "Mr. McMichaels."

Hill continued, steady but tight-voiced. "We've ordered an internal review. Detectives Black and Walls are pulling hallway footage as we speak. Until the item is recovered, the State will rely on the documented metadata and screenshots logged before the handoff."

Clair crossed one leg over the other. "So, the physical drive is gone, but we're to trust whatever the prosecution claims was on it?"

O'Hell met her stare. "Every byte was photographed and logged. You'll receive mirrored copies once our forensic tech rebuilds them."

"Assuming you find something to rebuild," McMichaels said softly."

The judge leaned back, studying all four of them. "Enough. This court will not spiral into accusations without facts. Mr. Hill, file an incident report with the clerk and submit a supplemental affidavit regarding the missing evidence. Mr. McMichaels, you'll refrain from speculation until the investigation concludes. We reconvene tomorrow at nine to review the findings. Understood?"

"Yes, Your Honor," both sides answered.

Lampson rose, her robe rustling like a warning. "Then find my evidence, gentlemen, and do it quickly. I won't have this courtroom turned into a crime scene."

Outside, the hallway felt colder. Hill exhaled, his jaw tight.

O'Hell muttered, "They think we lost it."

Hill shook his head. "No," he said quietly. "Someone wanted us to."

By the time Hill left chambers, the morning had sharpened into a thin, bitter light. His steps echoed down the marble corridor as he dialed the precinct.

"Black," he said when the detective answered. "I need that hallway footage pulled before noon. Every frame from yesterday. Report back the moment you have it, I'll update Judge Lampson personally."

"You got it," Black replied.

Hill ended the call and slipped the phone into his pocket,

unaware that, miles away, the precinct monitors were already looping static.

At the station, Black and Walls stood in the narrow surveillance room, its hum of machines filling the silence. The evidence hallway played across the screen, a timestamp frozen at 23:58. Then, nothing. A hard flicker. Static. Blank gray feed.

"Try the backups," Walls said.

Black's fingers flew across the keyboard, frustration mounting. "It's gone. Everything. Someone wiped it clean, every camera on this floor."

Walls swore under his breath. "Then it's not just about the drive."

Black grabbed his phone and called Hill. "It's all erased," he said, voice low and controlled but edged with anger. "Every file. Whoever took that drive knew how to cover their tracks."

The silence on the other end stretched long enough to say everything.

"Keep this between us for now," Hill said finally. "Write your report, but don't send it through the main system. I'll handle Lampson myself."

When the call ended, Hill sat back in his chair, staring at the blank monitor. He reached for his phone again and dialed Judge Lampson's private line.

She answered on the second ring, her tone brisk and wary.

"Judge, it's Hill," he said. "We have a problem. The security footage tied to the flash drive is gone… completely erased."

There was a pause, followed by the faint rustle of papers. "Then the drive's compromised," Lampson said. "I'll dismiss it first thing in the morning."

"Yes, Your Honor."

"Keep this quiet," she added. "No reason to inflame

speculation before we're in session."

The line clicked dead. Hill exhaled, rubbing the bridge of his nose. The evidence was gone, the clock was ticking, and tomorrow would be worse. Hill stood by the window, staring out at the city. He dialed another number, forcing steadiness into his voice.

"Frannie? It's Jackson. I just wanted to let you know.... your testimony is still confirmed for a couple of days. We'll keep you updated, but continue to stay inside, all right?"

Her voice was small on the other end. "Jackson... is everything okay?"

He looked at the skyline, the gray clouds pressing low against it. "We're working on it," he said quietly. "Just keep your doors locked."

When he hung up, the reflection in the glass stared back at him... tired, uncertain, and angry enough to keep going.

The evidence might be gone, but the truth wasn't. Not yet.

Chapter 28: The State Calls Levi Coaster

The bailiff's voice rang out. "All rise."

"Be seated."

"Before this court proceeds with testimony," she said, "I want the record to reflect that the evidence submitted, the flash drive and associated security footage, has been reviewed and is hereby excluded. Due to a breach in the chain of custody, the material cannot be verified as authentic."

A ripple of murmurs moved through the gallery.

Lampson's gavel struck once. "The State will proceed without it."

Hill rose, jaw tight, eyes sharp. "Yes, Your Honor. The State calls Levi Coaster."

A murmur rippled through the gallery as Levi shuffled into the courtroom. Shackles clinked against the polished floor, his bruised face a testament to the war he'd already survived inside prison walls. Yet his posture was unbroken, his gaze defiant.

The jury leaned forward as he raised his right hand and swore the oath.

Hill approached the stand. "Mr. Coaster, would you tell the jury your role in Benjamin Grove's operation?"

Levi's lips curled into a crooked smile. "My role? I was a runner, a muscle guy. Grove told me and the others what to do, and we did it. Because in this city, Grove was untouchable."

A sharp inhale moved through the courtroom. "Be

specific," Hill pressed. Levi leaned into the microphone, his bruised eye glinting with something close to pride.

"He told us to use the community centers. Said it was the perfect cover. We were to watch for kids who came in without parents. Hungry ones. Lonely ones. Easy targets."

Francine's stomach turned. She gripped the edge of the pew, forcing herself not to cry. "And once you had the children?" Hill asked.

Levi didn't hesitate. "We drove them to the dock, about two hours away, near the old shipping yards. Everyone knew the route. Drop-off was always the same. Containers waiting."

Gasps broke out. The jury scribbled furiously. Reporters shifted in their seats.

Hill's voice was steady. "Mr. Coaster, are you saying Benjamin Grove knew about these drop-offs?"

"Knew?" Levi laughed, bitter. "He ordered them. And he wasn't working alone. He had direct ties to Hudson Waters."

The room erupted in shouts, gasps, and voices rising all at once. The gavel cracked down like thunder. "Order!" Judge Lampson roared. "Order in my courtroom!"

But Levi wasn't finished. He jabbed a finger toward Grove.

"I was there when he met with Waters. Twice. Heard him say it with my own ears… 'It's time to start pulling kids from the center.' Those were his words. Grove gave the green light."

"Liar!" Grove shot up from his chair, his face purple with rage. "Traitor! You're going to die for this!"

The jury recoiled, some covering their mouths in horror. Francine flinched at the venom in her husband's voice…. but then her fear hardened into rage. Her lip still ached from the men Waters sent. Her swollen cheekbone still throbbed. And now, hearing Levi confirm what she had already seen with her own eyes, something inside her snapped.

She didn't look at Benjamin. She wouldn't. But her silence was heavier than a scream.

"Mr. Grove!" Lampson's gavel slammed down once, twice, again. Her voice cut through the uproar. "That's enough! Bailiffs…. remove him from this courtroom!"

The marshals surged forward. Grove jerked against their grasp, his face flushed with rage. "You can't…"

"Now!" Lampson thundered.

They pulled him back from the table, chair scraping hard against the tile. His attorney, McMichaels, stood quickly, hands raised. "Your Honor, please… my client's emotions…"

"Then control them," Lampson snapped. "This court will not be reduced to chaos."

Grove shouted something inaudible as the marshals dragged him through the side door, his voice echoing even after it shut. The silence that followed was thick and heavy, broken only by the judge's final warning.

"Let that be the last interruption I hear today."

Both tables nodded.

"Good. Jury, you will disregard the defendant's threat and any display of hostility. This court is adjourned for a fifteen-minute recess. Mr. McMichaels, your client may return after recess, if he can control himself. Am I clear?"

"Yes, Your Honor."

Her gavel struck one final time, and the bailiff called for order as the jury was ushered out under marshal escort. Reporters were hurried back into the hallway, their voices rising in a frenzy.

The defense team huddled the moment the jury disappeared. Jasper McMichaels wiped sweat from his brow. "That testimony shredded us. And his outburst? The jury saw a monster in cuffs."

Wyatt Reddings rubbed his temple, whispering, "We can still chip away at Coaster. He's a felon, he's bruised up. We paint him, as desperate and exaggerating, trying to cut a deal."

Clair Winston, calmest of the three, leaned closer to McMichaels. "Benjamin needs to sit still and say nothing. If he so much as twitches at the wrong word, the jury will hang him before the verdict is even read."

McMichaels swallowed, eyes flicking nervously toward Hill and O'Hell across the room. "We'll try. But that was a hole straight through our case. The best we can do now is patch it before the whole thing caves in."

Hill leaned into O'Hell, whispering fiercely. "We just hit gold. Waters, the docks, the order…all of it. The jury heard it loud and clear."

O'Hell's fingers tapped a restless rhythm on his legal pad. "Yeah, but they also saw a defendant lose his mind on the record. Lampson can't erase that. This is bigger than a win; it's exposure. And exposure means Waters won't stay in the shadows much longer."

Hill's eyes tracked Francine, sitting stiff-backed in the gallery, her face a mask of fury and pain. He lowered his voice. "And she knows it now. She can't look at him the same."

Francine hadn't moved since the eruption. Her hands were folded tight in her lap, nails digging into her skin. She wouldn't give Benjamin the satisfaction of a glance, not when his words still rang in her ears.

"Traitor. You're going to die," said Grove.

He could threaten Levi all he wanted. But her heart told her the truth: Grove's war wasn't just with Coaster, or with Waters. It was with himself, and he was losing. The courtroom buzzed with nervous energy as the bailiff announced: "Five minutes."

Everyone scattered…. defense scrambling, prosecution strategizing, the gallery alive with rumor. Outside, protestors' chants grew louder, the city itself straining against silence.

Inside, one fact became undeniable: the trial was no longer about whether Grove was guilty. It was about how many others would fall with him. The jury returned from recess, whispers floating like restless moths across the gallery. Judge Lampson gaveled once, sharp and deliberate, and the hum died instantly.

"Before we proceed with cross," she said, "Bailiff Young, please have the defendant escorted back in."

As Grove entered the courtroom, he caught sight of Frannie and the bruises on her face. His expression hardened. Rage flared in his eyes. He opened his mouth to speak, but Clair leaned in quickly. "Say nothing. Sit down."

He obeyed, dropping into his chair. Under his breath, he muttered to her, "Tell Waters he's dead. He hurt my wife… he's dead."

Clair's jaw tightened, but she said nothing.

Lampson noticed the exchange and straightened slightly, prepared to intervene, but Grove stayed silent, his glare locked on the witness stand.

"Mr. McMichaels," she said, fixing the defense attorney with a cool stare. "You may proceed with your cross-examination."

McMichaels rose with measured calm, straightening his jacket as though the gesture alone might lend him credibility. He sauntered toward the witness stand, lips curling into the faintest smirk.

"Mr. Coaster," he began, his voice carrying that rehearsed confidence of a man who had dismantled witnesses a hundred times before, "let's remind this jury who you really are. You're currently serving time, are you not?"

Levi leaned lazily against the microphone. "Yeah. I don't hide from that."

The attorney's brows arched as though the admission was a victory. "And your record is lengthy. Assaults, theft, drug distribution. Would you like me to read the rest?"

Levi's eyes hardened, but his grin stayed. "Read it, sing it, dance it, jury's got ears. I've lived roughly, I won't deny it. But none of that changes what Grove ordered me to do."

A murmur slipped through the benches. McMichaels pressed forward.

"So, we're meant to take the word of a violent criminal over that of a respected community leader? Isn't it true that you cut a deal with the prosecution, a lighter sentence, maybe? Special protection?"

Levi let out a low laugh, then leaned forward, his face catching the courtroom light. "Protection? Look at me." He pointed to the fading bruises and stitched wounds still etched across his skin. "Does that look like protection? I've been stabbed multiple times since I opened my mouth. If I were lying, you think I'd risk my neck for this?"

A ripple passed through the jury box. Even Judge Lampson's stony expression flickered.

McMichaels shifted his footing. "Or maybe," he countered, "you're enjoying the spotlight. Playing the hero."

Levi's grin dropped. His tone sharpened like a blade. "Ain't no hero in me. I'm a man cleaning up what I helped break. Grove gave the orders. Waters backed him. The kids were moved through that dock like cargo. That's the truth. You don't have to like me. But you can't bury it."

For a moment, the courtroom went utterly still. Even McMichaels faltered, his eyes darting to his client.

"You expect us to believe a thug," he snapped at last, "over a man who built a community center?"

Levi swung his head toward Grove, his voice rising with the fury of conviction. "That man's no builder. He's a destroyer. He used his wife's center to sell kids like property. You can dress it up in a suit, put a Bible in his hand, but filth is filth."

Gasps broke out. Grove lunged half out of his chair before his attorney yanked him back.

The gavel cracked down like thunder. "Enough!" Judge Lampson barked. "Mr. Grove, sit down. Mr. McMichaels, wrap it up."

The defense attorney, his smirk long gone, muttered that he had no further questions. Hill stood slowly, adjusting his tie. "Redirect, Your Honor?"

"Keep it brief," Lampson warned. Hill stepped closer to the stand, his tone steady and controlled. "Mr. Coaster, after everything you've endured, why continue your testimony today?"

Levi's gaze shifted to the jury, his eyes unwavering. "Because somebody's got to tell the truth. Even if it costs me everything."

The words hung in the air like a charge. No one moved.

"Thank you. No further questions," Hill said, returning to his seat.

"You may step down and return to protective custody," Judge Lampson said, tapping her gavel once.

"Court is adjourned until tomorrow morning."

The jurors filed out, whispering furiously. The gallery emptied with a buzz of speculation. At the prosecution's table, Hill sank into his chair, the weight of Levi's words pressing against his ribs like a second heartbeat.

Chapter 29: Fault Lines

The courthouse corridors were still pulsing with murmurs, reporters hovering near the exits, jurors whispering to one another as deputies cleared the room. Hill and O'Hell stood off to the side, just out of the stream of bodies, their voices low.

"I didn't expect Coaster to unload all of that," O'Hell muttered, rubbing the back of his neck. "Waters' name, the docks…he practically handed us a map."

Hill exhaled hard, adjusting his tie as if to steady himself. "Between Levi's testimony and Francine's…. if she follows through, this case is close to sealed. It's a slam dunk if the jury holds onto what they just heard."

The shuffle of heels broke their focus. Francine stepped toward them, her composure fragile but holding. The harsh fluorescent light revealed the bruises on her face more clearly now, and for the first time, Hill and O'Hell both noticed. They froze, shame prickling their expressions.

"I'm still testifying," she said, her voice steady though her eyes betrayed the storm behind them. "You don't need to press me anymore. It's my choice, and I'm doing it. For those kids."

Neither man spoke right away. Hill finally nodded. "Thank you, Frannie. It matters more than you know."

"I'll be staying with my sister until this trial is over," she added quickly, as if rehearsed. "Safer that way."

Before they could respond, Black and Walls appeared through the thinning crowd. Both detectives carried the weight of fresh urgency.

"We just got word from the unit we radioed," Black said. "Dock's quiet, but we're on our way to check it ourselves. If there's anything left to find, it'll be there."

Hill gave a sharp nod. "Call me the moment you see something."

The group was still huddled when Francine's phone rang, the shrill tone cutting through the courthouse buzz. She glanced at the screen, her stomach tightening. A collect call. From the jail.

Her hands trembled as she stepped aside. She pressed the phone to her ear. "This is Francine."

"Frannie…." Benjamin's voice was ragged, urgent, and frantic. "What happened to your face? Who did it?"

She shut her eyes, forcing calm into her tone. "I don't know, they broke into our home. I'm fine. Don't worry about it."

"The heck I won't?" he barked, anger flaring. "Someone lays a hand on my wife, I'll take care of it. Do you hear me? I'll…"

"You can't," she cut him off, her words a sharp whisper. "You're already in enough trouble. You're making this worse."

"I don't care," Benjamin spat, his voice low and trembling with fury. "I need to make this right with you. For once."

Her throat tightened. For a fleeting second, the old Benjamin, the man she had trusted, believed in, loved…echoed through the line. But then reality rushed back.

"No more promises, Benjamin," she said softly. "Not now."

And before he could answer, she ended the call, her chest heaving.

Across the hall, Hill and O'Hell waited, observing her. They didn't know what Benjamin had said, but they could see the weight pressing down on her shoulders. Black checked his watch and glanced at Walls. "We need to move. Let's not wait around here."

Walls gave a nod, and the two detectives excused themselves quietly from Hill and O'Hell. Francine was still off to the side, phone pressed to her ear, her face a storm of conflict, but Black and Walls didn't linger. They pushed through the courthouse doors into the cool afternoon air.

The city was buzzing, news vans crowding the curb, reporters barking questions into cameras, protestors chanting from across the street, but Black and Walls didn't stop. They walked briskly to their unmarked sedan, slipped inside, and shut the noise out with the slam of the doors.

"Radio just came through," Walls said, starting the engine. "Unit's already canvassed the dock. Nothing solid, but they flagged something."

"Then let's see for ourselves."

The drive was long, almost two hours, highway stretching out under a pale dusk sky. Neither man said much; both were thinking of Levi Coaster's testimony, the way he had tied the docks directly to Grove and Waters. By the time they turned off the interstate, the air had changed…thicker, damp, heavy with the scent of brine.

The dockyard was nearly deserted when they arrived, with patrol cars parked in a loose perimeter, their flashers flashing red and blue against the rusted shipping containers. A uniformed officer waved them through.

Inside the perimeter, one of the evidence techs approached, holding up a sealed bag. "Detectives, this is all we've got so far. Found it near the loading ramp."

Black took the bag. Inside was a child's navy-blue jacket, faded at the edges, with a half-broken zipper. He turned it slowly in his hand, his jaw tightening.

"Was it abandoned, or dropped?" Walls asked.

"Hard to tell," the tech replied. "No blood. No prints yet. Just left there, like someone didn't care enough to hide it."

Black exhaled through his nose, staring out at the endless rows of containers. "If Coaster was right, this place was the hub. But they've cleaned it out."

They spent the next hour moving between containers, opening doors, sweeping beams of light through the cavernous emptiness. Dust. Trash. Rope fibers. But no children. No bodies.

Finally, Walls kicked at the dirt, frustration showing in the slump of his shoulders. "Nothing but ghosts."

"Yeah," Black muttered, tucking the evidence bag under his arm. "But sometimes one ghost is enough."

They turned back toward the entrance, the dock creaking beneath them as distant waves broke against the pilings. The afternoon air carried a chill, a reminder of the urgency ticking away with every hour.

As they walked toward the patrol car, Walls broke the silence first. "We should brief Lightening first thing. Even if it's thin, he needs to hear it."

"Agreed," Black said. "The Chief won't like it, but better he hears it from us than the press."

They slid into the sedan, the doors closing with a final thud. For a moment, they just sat there, the silence louder than the waves.

Walls spoke, voice low. "Nothing but ghosts, Black."

Black placed the bag carefully on the back seat. His jaw clenched, eyes fixed on the horizon. "Yeah. But this one ghost might be enough to haunt Grove."

The engine rumbled to life, headlights cutting through the sunlight as they pulled away. Behind them, the dock stretched into shadow, empty and endless, like a place that swallowed children whole and gave nothing back.

Chapter 30: The Jacket

The drive back from the dock was quiet, both detectives weighed down by the single piece of evidence in the backseat. A child's jacket, sealed in a bag, carried more weight than a hundred reports. But in a case this poisoned with corruption, they both knew it might not be enough.

By the time they reached the station, the evening streets were nearly empty. Black didn't wait; he carried the evidence bag straight downstairs to the tech room. "Get this processed for DNA," he ordered, his voice clipped. "Every fiber, every speck.... run it all."

Walls nodded and peeled off toward Chief Lightening's office. When he arrived, the door was cracked, and the Chief's voice carried out into the hall. Walls paused, just outside the frame, as Lightening spoke into the receiver.

"...I'll handle it. Not to worry, sir." The call clicked off.

Walls stepped in as if he hadn't heard. "Chief, we're back from the dock." Lightening leaned back in his chair, eyes sharp but unreadable. "And?"

"Evidence tech flagged a jacket," Walls said. "Child-sized. Looks like it could belong to one of the missing. Black's getting it processed now."

Before the Chief could answer, Black entered, holding a slip for the chain of custody. He handed it over, his tone brisk. "It'll be logged properly. If there's a DNA match, we'll know soon."

Lightening waved a hand, dismissive. "A jacket isn't a child. Until you've got bodies or live rescues, it's just noise. Don't waste resources chasing ghosts. Focus on keeping this trial steady. Witnesses alive, court moving forward. That's the priority."

Both detectives stiffened. Walls said nothing, but suspicion churned in his gut. He caught Black's eye as they left the office, and the unspoken message passed between them: something's off.

Back at their desks, the silence broke. Black leaned in, voice low. "I'm not dropping this. I'll call Hill. He deserves to know we're processing evidence. He'll be the first to hear if it matches."

Walls only nodded, his mind replaying the Chief's words on the phone. I'll handle it. Not to worry, sir.

Minutes later, Prosecutor Jackson Hill picked up on the second ring. Black briefed him quickly, promising updates. Hill's voice tightened on the line.

"Appreciate it, Detective. Keep me posted. In the meantime,…" A pause, then the decision. "I'll reach out to Francine Grove. We need to prep her for testimony. If she's ready, she could be the hammer that seals this case."

When he hung up, Hill stared at the phone a moment longer. Then he dialed again. Francine answered, her voice soft, cautious.

"Mrs. Grove," Hill said gently, "I'd like to stop by the community center to talk this evening. We need to be ready when the time comes." She agreed.

Hill and O'Hell left the office as the courthouse buzz died down for the evening, slipping into Hill's sedan. The city lights shimmered against the windshield as they pulled into traffic, exhaustion sitting between them like a third passenger.

Hill drummed his fingers against the steering wheel. "Tomorrow, the defense calls their last witness. After that, we'll be ready. I'll call Frannie once they're done and set her for the morning after. She needs to be the hammer, not just another nail in the board."

O'Hell leaned back, loosening his tie. "Do you know who they're putting up?" "Luna Turner," Hill said grimly.

O'Hell sat up straighter. "Again? They already crossed her a week ago."

Hill's mouth tightened. "Exactly. Which means they think they found a crack. Maybe a detail they can twist. We'll see tomorrow. But first, we need Frannie ready. She's the witness the jury will carry home with them."

By the time they pulled into the lot of the community center, the evening hum of the city had softened. There was minimal laughter from the game room that spilled faintly into the hall. The sight of children bouncing between pool tables and ping-pong paddles was almost surreal against the darkness of the case they were building.

Manny caught sight of them first, calling out, "Frannie, you've got visitors." He grinned at the kids and stepped in to take over her ping-pong paddle.

Frannie wiped her hands on her slacks, nodded to the children, and walked them toward the activity room. Once the door shut, the lightness she had carried in the game room drained away. They headed towards her office.

Hill didn't waste time. He closed the door, his expression firm but gentle. "Frannie, I want to thank you again for deciding to testify. It means more than you know."

She folded her arms, then let them drop, her shoulders sagging. "It's the right thing to do," she said quietly. Her voice carried conviction, but her eyes betrayed the storm beneath.

They sat, and Hill opened his file, reviewing the line of questions. "We'll keep it simple. I'll ask direct questions, and you'll have free range to tell the jury what you know. How did you discover Benjamin was using your center? Why you built it in the first place, the betrayal matters as much as the facts."

She nodded, fingers tracing the edge of her desk. "I've thought about this. Every angle, every word I might say. And it still feels overwhelming. Because…" Her voice broke, and she pressed her palm to her eyes. "…because I loved him. I love Benjamin. And part of me still doesn't want to see him in chains."

The silence in the room thickened. Hill exchanged a glance with O'Hell, then leaned forward. "Frannie, the jury doesn't need to hear you hate him. They need to hear the truth. That's what will matter. Not vengeance. Truth."

She nodded again, a tear sliding down her cheek. "Then I'll give them the truth." Hill and O'Hell shook Frannie's hand as they left her office. Relief flickered across her features, but it didn't last. They stopped at the reception desk, exchanging a few words with Manny, when a sudden crash split the air.

A cinder block smashed through the front window with a deafening crack. Shards of glass exploded across the lobby, glittering like knives in the fluorescent light. Children screamed.

The block landed inches from two boys frozen near the glass. Cuts streaked their arms and faces, blood trickling down tiny hands.

O'Hell threw his arm around Frannie, pulling her to the ground. Manny dove toward the nearest group of children, covering their small bodies with his own. Hill grabbed the closest girl and shielded her as glass rained down.

"Under the desk!" the receptionist shouted, her voice trembling as she ducked behind the counter.

Chaos filled the center…children crying, staff rushing them to the nurse's office. "Ouch, my fingers, there's glass in them!" one boy whimpered. Another clutched his head, blood soaking his hairline.

And then, from outside, a voice cut through the ringing silence:

"You'd better keep your mouth shut!"

The words hung like smoke, cruel and unmistakable.

Frannie's breath caught. "Benjamin? He wouldn't…" Her voice cracked. Hill and O'Hell locked eyes. Neither spoke.

They stayed until the last child was treated, every wound cleaned and bandaged. Frannie and Manny waited as Mr. Jenkin, the hardware store owner across the street, carried boards to cover the shattered glass.

Police arrived, notebooks out, asking questions no one wanted to answer. Hill texted Black: Center attacked. Children injured. Threat delivered.

Finally, the building was cleared. The staff helped escort children home under new safety protocols, walking groups down the sidewalks to try to rebuild their sense of safety. Still, the murmurs lingered.

"Why would someone throw a brick through our safe place?" "Who wants to hurt us?" a child said.

"Frannie…are you okay?" another child said.

She forced a smile. "Yes. Just…disappointed." But her eyes glistened.

When Hill and O'Hell stepped back into the night, silence filled the sedan. The city blurred past their windows, too quiet, too dark.

Finally, O'Hell broke it. "Grove. Would he?"

Hill shook his head slowly, disbelief weighing his voice. "I don't know. But one thing's certain…. her testimony can't wait."

Chapter 31: Recalled

Black sat slouched at his desk when his phone buzzed. It was Hill. The message was short, stripped of any legal polish: Center attacked. Children injured. Threat delivered.

Black's jaw tightened as he read. He exhaled slowly, then tapped a reply with stiff fingers: This case has gone too far.

Walls, perched on the corner of the desk with a cup of fresh coffee, watched him. "What now?" Black handed the phone over. Walls' brow furrowed as he read.

"Cinderblock through the window," Black muttered. "A couple of kids cut up. Hill said O'Hell pulled Francine out of the line of fire."

Walls cursed under his breath, setting his cup down with a sharp clink. "Waters."

Black nodded, his voice low. "I don't care if Grove goes down tomorrow, I want Waters exposed. We dig deeper, off the record. I'll handle the paper trail; you talk to your contacts at the docks. Something's bleeding between the two of them, and I'm not waiting for court to catch up."

He stood, gathering his coat. "Come on. Let's get out of here. Tomorrow's going to be another turning point."

Walls grabbed his jacket, and the two men left the station, their shadows stretching long in the flicker of the parking lot lights.

The next morning, the courthouse buzzed with anticipation. Reporters lined the steps, cameras flashing as the defense team swept in. Inside, the jurors filed into the box with heavy eyes, the weight of testimony from Levi Coaster still pressing on them.

When the clerk called the session to order, McMichaels rose smoothly, his suit crisp, his confidence palpable.

"Your Honor," he said, voice dripping with practiced ease. "The defense recalls Luna Turner to the stand."

A ripple ran through the gallery. Luna's name carried the memory of earlier testimony, the foster care worker who had confirmed Jonah Carter's placement. Francine, seated quietly in the second row, stiffened.

Lampson's gavel came down once. "Bring her in."

Luna entered, shoulders squared but eyes betraying nerves. She took her seat, adjusting the microphone as McMichaels approached with a measured smile that never touched his eyes.

"Good morning, Ms. Turner."

She nodded slightly. "Good morning."

McMichaels leaned on the podium. "Let's start simple. How many children are currently on your caseload?"

"About forty," she said, her voice steady at first.

"Forty," he repeated, drawing the word out. "And how often are you required to see each child?" "It depends on the severity of the case."

"Severity," McMichaels echoed. "And Jonah Carter? How severe was his case?"

Luna's throat tightened, but she answered clearly. "Stable. I was not aware of any issues. No reports of abuse, no truancy. He was attending school."

McMichaels flipped open a file, pages rustling loudly in the silence. "Stable, you say. No true issues." He looked up, his gaze sharp. "How often did you see him personally?"

"First of every month."

A pause. Then McMichaels tapped the file. "Funny. Because, according to your own notes, you only saw him once in the last three months."

Luna blinked, her composure cracking. "I… yes, I missed

two visits. But I staffed it with my supervisor, Ms. Keys. It was documented."

"And the reason you missed them?"

Her voice trembled, though she fought to steady it. "We were understaffed. My caseload doubled. It was an oversight, but I kept up the best I could. I love my job. I care about these kids."

McMichaels stepped closer, pouncing. "If you loved your job, Ms. Turner, then maybe Jonah Carter wouldn't have slipped through the cracks."

Gasps rippled through the gallery. Luna's face crumpled, tears streaking down her cheeks as she looked away.

"Objection!" Hill barked, rising from his chair. "Argumentative."

"Sustained," Lampson snapped. "Jury will disregard counsel's last remark."

"No further questions," McMichaels said.

"Ms. Turner, you may step down," Judge Lampson instructed.

Luna pushed back from the stand and walked stiffly toward the exit, covering her face as she passed the rows of spectators. The image of her breaking stayed with the jury, despite Lampson's instructions to forget.

Francine's stomach turned as she watched. Rage flared at McMichaels for twisting the truth, and at herself for ever doubting whether she should testify.

Hill stared at his desk, his fists clenched, jaw set. He knew McMichaels had just tried to weaponize the very system designed to protect children. And the jury had seen every moment of it. Lampson banged her gavel once, her voice sharper than usual.

"We'll recess for ten minutes. Jury, please refrain from

discussing the case among yourselves. We'll resume shortly."

The jurors shuffled out, murmuring as they exited. Hill leaned toward O'Hell, his jaw locked.

"I need to bring her back up. If the jury leaves with McMichaels' last word ringing in their ears, she's done."

"Then flip it," O'Hell muttered. "Remind them she did her job. Show them she's the one who cared."

When the court resumed, the jurors looked calmer, notebooks in hand. Judge Lampson adjusted her glasses and gestured toward Hill.

"Redirect, counselor. Have the witness return to the stand."

Luna reapproached, hands clasped tightly in front of her.

Hill rose slowly, giving her a reassuring nod before stepping forward. His voice was measured and calm, in contrast to McMichaels's attack.

"Ms. Turner," he began gently, "earlier, counsel questioned you about missed visits with Jonah Carter. Let me ask, when you realized Jonah was missing, what did you do?"

Luna straightened a little. "I immediately filed a missing child report. I called the police, then stayed after hours to update the case record. I followed every protocol we're trained to follow."

"And did you delay calling anyone?"

"No." Her voice grew stronger. "The moment I knew he wasn't where he was supposed to be, I called it in. There was no hesitation."

Hill nodded, pacing slowly. "And when Detective Black and Detective Walls responded, were you present?"

"Yes. I stayed until they arrived, and I remained with them through the search." She swallowed, but her voice steadied. "I was with them the day Jonah's body was discovered on Mr.

Grove's property."

A ripple ran through the gallery.

Hill let the silence hang, then leaned closer to the stand. "So, despite a doubled caseload, despite staffing shortages, when it mattered most, did you do your duty?"

Luna's chin lifted, her voice firm now. "Yes. I did my duty. I cared about Jonah, and I still do." Hill stepped back, letting her words settle into the jury's bones. He turned toward Lampson. "No further questions."

Lampson gave a curt nod. "Witness may step down."

Luna rose from the stand, this time walking with her head higher. She wasn't unscathed; the sting of McMichaels' words still clung to her, but Hill had stitched her credibility together just enough for the jury to see her as human, flawed but dedicated.

Lampson tapped her pen against the bench. "Very well. Counsel, please call your next witness."

Hill rose smoothly, adjusting his tie. The courtroom seemed to hold its breath. He didn't shuffle papers, didn't fumble. He already knew who he was calling.

"The State calls… Francine Grove."

Gasps rippled through the gallery like a wave. Even the jurors shifted in their seats. McMichaels and his defense team shot upright, shock flashing across their faces. Benjamin Grove's eyes widened, his jaw tightening as if the name itself had struck him.

Lampson banged the gavel sharply. "Order! This is still a court of law. Order!"

All eyes turned to the center aisle as Francine stood. Her frame was slight but steady, her bruises visible even under the courtroom's harsh lights. She smoothed her skirt with trembling hands and began her walk toward the stand.

Benjamin tried to catch her eye, but she never looked his way. The bailiff guided her forward, swore her in, and the courtroom stilled to a tense, humming silence. Francine Grove, the defendant's wife and leader of the community center, the woman with everything to lose, took her seat. And the trial shifted on its axis.

Chapter 32: The Breaking Point

The air felt heavier than usual, a thickness of anticipation and unease. Reporters leaned forward, jurors straightened in their seats, and Benjamin Grove sat stiff at the defense table, his jaw tight and his eyes fixed on the empty witness chair.

"The State calls Francine Grove."

The words dropped like a thunderclap. Gasps rippled through the gallery. Lampson's gavel cracked hard against the bench. "Order!" she barked, her eyes sweeping over the room.

At the defense table, Benjamin shot to his feet. "Frannie!" His voice broke, raw and desperate. "Frannie, I love you! Please…please don't do this to me!"

The jury gasped again, murmurs rising. Lampson slammed the gavel once more. "Mr. Grove! Control yourself. One more outburst, and I'll have you removed from this courtroom, again."

Benjamin's attorney, McMichaels, tugged him back into his chair, whispering furiously in his ear. But his eyes never left Francine as she stood and slowly approached the stand.

Her bruises caught the light, fading purple along her cheekbone, the swollen split at her lip, and the room fell into a hush. Every eye followed her as she raised her hand for the oath.

"Do you swear to tell the truth, the whole truth, and nothing but the truth?" Her voice trembled but didn't break. "I do."

She sat, straightened her shoulders, and folded her hands in her lap. She didn't look at Benjamin. Not once. Hill rose slowly from the prosecution's table, his tone calm, steady, coaxing. "Please state your name for the record."

"Francine Elizabeth Grove."

"And your relationship to the defendant?"

She hesitated, her throat tightening. "He…is my husband."

A murmur drifted through the gallery again, but Hill pressed forward, his voice a soft anchor. "Mrs. Grove, can you tell us how you first became aware that your community center might be involved in this case?"

Francine's eyes glistened. She took a breath and steadied her voice. "When the body of Jonah Carter was discovered on our property." The words scraped out, heavy and final. "I was out of town at the time. When I came home after a week, reporters were at my door, shouting things I didn't understand. My public relations team told me a child had been found on our property. I went to the police immediately."

Her hands were clenched in her lap. "That's when I learned my husband had been arrested. For conspiracy. For embezzlement. For human trafficking. For things I could not even wrap my mind around."

The jurors leaned forward. Benjamin shifted in his seat, his face flushing red.

Hill let her words sit before asking, "Do you own and operate Red Leaf Community Center?"

"Yes," she said firmly. "I built it from nothing. It was supposed to be a safe haven for every child who walked through those doors. Because when I was a child, I needed a place like that. I promised myself one day I'd create it. And I did." Her voice broke, just for a moment. "But Benjamin…he almost destroyed it. Destroyed me."

Hill's voice stayed even. "Why are you here today, Mrs. Grove?"

Francine swallowed hard, tears threatening to fall. Then she lifted her chin. "Because I cannot stay silent. Not after what I've seen. Not after what I found." She reached into her memory, voice trembling but growing sharper. "After our home was broken into, after those men beat me, I found a jump drive hidden in Benjamin's safe. Files of children. Dates. Locations. Money transfers. Hundreds of thousands of dollars."

The gallery gasped, and Lampson's gavel cracked again for order.

Francine's voice grew stronger, conviction surging through the cracks of her fear. "I love my husband. I do. But love doesn't erase truth. And the truth is, he used my community center to funnel children into trafficking. The very place that was supposed to protect them became their doorway into a nightmare. And I will not..." she stopped, her voice shaking with fury, ".... I will not be silent."

"Liar!" Benjamin erupted, slamming his fists on the table. "You don't know what you're saying! You're my wife!"

"Mr. Grove!" Lampson thundered, gavel slamming. "One more word and you will be removed!"

Marshals stepped forward. The jury stared, wide-eyed, some whispering, others shaking their heads.

Francine did not look at him. Not once. She turned her face back to Hill, tears sliding silently down her cheeks, but her chin unbroken, her voice unshaken now.

Hill nodded slowly. "No further questions, Your Honor."

The silence that followed was suffocating. Francine's testimony lingered in the room... undeniable, raw, unforgettable.

"McMichaels, you may proceed with cross," Judge Lampson said.

The air hadn't yet settled when McMichaels rose. He buttoned his jacket slowly, deliberately, giving the jury time to watch the calm, collected attorney reclaim his stage. His voice, when it came, was smooth, almost patronizing.

"Mrs. Grove," he began, pacing a step closer to the witness

stand. "You've just given this jury quite a performance. But I want to cut through the emotion and get to the facts. Is that alright?"

Francine met his gaze, steady and unflinching. "I'm not performing, sir. I'm telling the truth." A murmur rippled through the gallery, quickly silenced by Lampson's gavel.

McMichaels smiled thinly, feigning patience. "Of course. Let's start with this jump drive you claim to have found. You say it was in your husband's safe?"

"Yes."

"And you opened it yourself? Without notifying law enforcement first?"

"I did. Because men broke into my home, searching for it. They threatened me and bruised my face. I had to know what they were after."

McMichaels tilted his head. "So, no chain of custody. No guarantee that the files weren't planted, altered, or fabricated. Isn't that correct?"

Francine's jaw tightened. "What I saw was real. Transfers. Names. Children's names. I wish to God it wasn't real, but it was."

The jury's faces were a mix of shock and sorrow. McMichaels pressed harder.

"Mrs. Grove, you testified that you still love your husband." He paused dramatically. "So, isn't it possible that this...testimony of yours is less about truth and more about guilt? About trying to save face for allowing criminal activity to take place under your nose?"

Francine's hands trembled on the armrest of the witness chair, but her voice stayed calm, deliberate. "I am not here to save face. I am here because children were hurt. Children who trusted me. Children who walked into Red Leaf thinking it was safe. I cannot undo what happened, but I can speak the truth."

A few jurors nodded unconsciously. McMichaels noticed and pivoted. He tried to rattle her.

"Mrs. Grove, isn't it true you benefited financially from your husband's dealings? Your non-profit, your pride and joy, was funded in part by Benjamin Grove's political machine.

Contributions. Donors he courted. Are you denying that?"

Francine inhaled sharply, then leaned forward. "Yes, Benjamin raised money for the center. But I never asked him to turn it into a cover for trafficking children. I would rather Red Leaf burn to the ground than have one child taken from it."

Her words hit like a hammer. The jury shifted again.... toward her, not him.

McMichaels' smile faltered. He tried one last angle. "Mrs. Grove, your emotions are understandable. But emotions don't make facts. You admitted yourself.... You weren't even in town when Jonah Carter was found. You weren't present when these alleged transfers happened. So how can you claim certainty about any of it?"

Francine's eyes filled, but her voice didn't waver. "Because I saw it with my own eyes. Because I've been threatened in my own home. Because I know my husband, and I know the man he's become. And because if I stay silent now, more children will vanish. That is why I am here."

The courtroom held its breath.

McMichaels stared at her, lips pressed thin, his strategy collapsing. He turned slowly, walked back to the defense table, and muttered, "No further questions."

Judge Lampson's gavel struck once. "The witness may step down."

Francine rose, her legs shaky but her chin high. She didn't look at Benjamin at first. The jury, however, couldn't look away from her. Francine gathered her papers with trembling hands, then pushed herself up from the witness stand. The murmur of the courtroom was a low hum in her ears, but she blocked it all out. She stepped down carefully, each heel striking the polished floor like a verdict.

For a moment, she hesitated, then turned her head. Her eyes locked with Benjamin's.

His face, usually carved into a mask of confidence, faltered. Behind the anger and the bluster was something raw, almost desperate. Betrayal. Rage. A plea she refused to acknowledge.

Francine held his gaze, steady, unyielding. There were no words left between them, only the truth that now lived outside of their marriage and inside the courtroom.

Benjamin shifted in his seat, his lips parting as if to speak, but no sound came. His attorney placed a firm hand on his arm, pulling him back. Francine finally turned away, her chin lifted, her bruises stark under the lights. She walked back toward the gallery, past rows of jurors who couldn't look anywhere else. Every step was a declaration: she had chosen the children, the truth, over him.

And for the first time, Benjamin Grove looked like a man who realized he had lost everything. Benjamin shifted in his chair as if to rise, but McMichaels' hand shot out, forcing him back down. Lampson lifted her gavel. The sound cracked like thunder.

"Enough," she said sharply. "This court will not tolerate another outburst. We are adjourned for the day."

The jury startled at her sudden tone, then began gathering their belongings as Lampson continued, her gaze hard on them.

"You are reminded of your oath. Do not discuss this case with anyone, not even each other, until deliberations begin. Do not read about it in the papers, do not watch commentary on the news.

Tomorrow we will resume with closing arguments."

She paused, her voice steady but tired. "Until then, you are dismissed."

The bailiff moved to escort the jury out, their footsteps shuffling in uneasy rhythm. Reporters in the gallery scribbled furiously, their pens catching the last echoes of drama before Lampson swept from the bench.

Benjamin turned once more toward Francine, his mouth moving silently as deputies surrounded him. She did not return his stare. She adjusted her coat, lifted her chin, and walked towards the back of the courtroom.

Hill and O'Hell stood together, watching her go. The weight of her testimony lingered in the air, heavier than the gavel's crack.

The case was no longer just about Benjamin Grove. It was about silence being broken and truth laid bare. The courtroom emptied slowly, the echo of Lampson's gavel still vibrating through the walls. Frannie lingered by the door, clutching her purse as if it were armor. She waited until Hill and O'Hell finished gathering their files.

"I'd like to walk out with you," she whispered. "The press...they're waiting." Hill gave her a steady nod. "We'll get you through."

Together, the three of them moved toward the doors. The heavy oak swung open, and the hallway erupted like a hornet's nest. Cameras flashed, reporters surged forward, microphones thrust into her face.

"How do you feel now that you testified against your husband?" one shouted. "Mrs. Grove, what about the community center? Are the children in danger?" "Do you realize you betrayed him?"

Each question was a dagger, sharp and merciless. Frannie tightened her grip on her purse, her chest tightening. Black and Walls were already there, with two uniformed officers, forming a barrier as best they could. The crowd was relentless.

Then one voice cut through the others, direct and piercing:

"Why did you choose to speak today, Mrs. Grove?"

Frannie froze. For a moment, she considered pressing forward, head down, lips sealed. But something inside her snapped. Slowly, she turned toward the wall of cameras, her voice trembling but clear.

"I chose to speak," she said, "for the missing children to bring them home. I spoke to make it right. I spoke because the truth needed to be heard, even if it cost me everything. I spoke because if I didn't…" Her throat caught, and then she lifted her chin. "Then that would be my sin."

The hallway fell into stunned silence. For the first time all day, the reporters stopped shouting. Cameras still clicked, but the hallway seemed to hold its breath.

"Move her out," Black barked, breaking the spell. He and Walls flanked Frannie, guiding her through the sea of stunned faces.

As they pushed her toward the exit, Hill glanced back over his shoulder at the press pack, still frozen in place. "That'll be on every front page by morning," he muttered to O'Hell.

O'Hell shook his head, still shaken himself. "Good," he said. "It should be." Frannie kept her head low as Black and Walls shielded her through the crowd, past the barrage of cameras and microphones. Within minutes, she was in the back of the unmarked sedan, the door shutting out the noise. Her heart still hammered, the echo of her own words replaying in her mind: I spoke because if I didn't, that would be my sin.

The ride felt like a blur. When she finally reached Jessica's house, Mouse bounded out as soon as the door opened, nails clicking against the hardwood as he leapt into her lap. Frannie buried her face in the dog's fur, the sob she had held back all day finally breaking free.

Jessica ushered her inside, guiding her to the couch. "Tea," she said gently. "You need something warm to steady you."

Frannie nodded, though her mind was still tangled in the

courtroom, the flashes, Benjamin's eyes burning into her as she testified. She tried to smile as Jessica returned with two mugs, tried to make small talk about nothing at all, but her thoughts were elsewhere, still standing at that witness's stand, still hearing his voice shouting her name.

Then her phone rang.

The sound jolted her upright. She glanced at the screen; it was a collect call from the county jail. Jessica froze mid-sip, eyes widening.

Frannie's hand trembled as she set her mug down. Mouse whined softly, pressing closer to her leg.

She stared at the phone, the world shrinking to the single blinking notification.

Chapter 33: Between Love and Betrayal

Frannie hesitated, her thumb hovering over the green button, ready to let the call ring out. But something in her heart wouldn't let her. She pressed accept.

"Frannie," Benjamin's voice came through, low and trembling, stripped of all the bravado he had carried in the courtroom. "I'm sorry. For everything. For what I put you through, for what I did to the center. I let money cloud my judgment, and I destroyed the one thing you loved most. I'm not asking you to wait for me or even stay married; I'll probably be gone a long time. But I'm asking you to forgive me. Please. I love you."

The silence on the line stretched. She pressed her hand against her chest, fighting tears. She could hear him swallow hard, could almost picture him gripping the receiver, trying not to break down.

"Benjamin," she whispered, her voice heavy with grief. "I love you too. But I can't believe you used what I built, the center, my heart…to funnel children into darkness. You took my trust and shattered it. But…" She closed her eyes. "I forgive you."

On the other end, a sharp exhale, almost a sob, filled the silence.

"Thank you," he breathed. "Tomorrow…I'll see you tomorrow. And after that…it'll probably be the last time."

The line clicked dead before she could reply.

Frannie stared at the phone in her hand, her reflection caught faintly on the black screen. Her forgiveness was real, but so was the betrayal. She whispered into the silence, "Goodbye, Benjamin." Jessica set the empty mug on a coaster and touched the back of Frannie's hand. "You should sleep," she murmured.

"Your body needs the quiet."

Frannie nodded. Mouse thumped his tail against the couch and pressed his head to her thigh, as if he, too, were asking her to surrender the day. The house was still except for the soft hum of the refrigerator and the old clock over the mantle that ticked a slow, patient rhythm, mercy in seconds. She smoothed the dog's ears and stood.

"I'm going up," she said, voice papery. "If I don't close my eyes now, I'll hear the gavel all night."

Jessica rose with her and gathered the used tissues from the coffee table. "You were brave today." Frannie managed to make a tired smile. "Bravery feels like shaking hands."

"Then let your hands shake here," Jessica said, kissing her cheek. "Tomorrow, you can be brave again."

Upstairs, the guest room was familiar now: spare quilt, a photograph of a winter field by the window, the small lamp with a chipped base. Frannie sat on the edge of the bed and stared at her phone. The call log showed a collect call from the county jail. Under it, her mother's name. Under that, a number she didn't recognize, then Hill, then O'Hell. Life had become a list of voices demanding something of her. She turned the screen face down, crawled under the quilt, and whispered with knowing to: "Lord, make the truth louder than fear."

Sleep came in scraps. In one dream, she was back at the center as a child, standing in a room that hadn't existed then, walls lined with chalkboards covered in names. She was erasing, and the names kept coming back, fainter every time. In another instance, she was at the witness stand, but the microphone had no cord, so her voice went nowhere. She woke before dawn with her throat tight and the taste of dust at the back of her mouth.

Downstairs, Jessica had already left a note: Tea in the thermos. I'll drive you if you want.... J.

Frannie poured a cup, dressed, pressed her cheek to

Mouse's head, and told him to be good. When she stepped outside, the early light over Red Leaf was thin and gray, as if the day itself was tired of holding its breath.

The courthouse steps were already a throng of bodies.... reporters, protesters, and onlookers drawn to the gravity of judgment. Hand-painted signs bobbed in the morning chill: JUSTICE FOR THE CHILDREN; STAND WITH FRANCINE; GROVE LIED; one that read ENOUGH in block letters. Someone prayed softly near the bottom of the stairs, eyes closed, palms up. Another voice shouted that the city was rotten to its roots. The sound rose and fell like a tide.

Black and Walls were at the door with two uniformed officers, narrowing the entrance to a controlled channel. When they saw Frannie and Jessica approach, they stepped forward.

"Morning," Black said, not unkindly. "We'll get you through."

Frannie searched his face and found only the day's purpose there, not pity. She nodded. "Thank you."

Inside, the courtroom felt different, emptier and heavier at the same time. The jury box was seated, the judge's bench unoccupied. Lampson's clerk was arranging papers with brisk efficiency, and Henry Printerson, the court reporter, sat at his machine as if guarding a small box of gold coins. Hill and O'Hell were at their table with neat stacks of notes; McMichaels and his team, Winston to his right, Reddings a step behind...whispered in a tight cluster.

Benjamin was already in his seat, hands cuffed lightly in front, and a marshal was posted a pace behind him. He looked smaller today. The bruising hum of the room slid around him as if he were a post in a river. He glanced back only once. When he found Frannie across the aisle, his face opened with something raw, hope or pleading or the ghost of the man she'd married. She didn't look away. She nodded once, nothing more, and took her place in the second row beside Jessica.

"All rise," the bailiff called.

The room stood. Judge Lampson entered, robe falling like a dark wave. The case had thinned her a little, but her gaze was steady steel behind glass.

"Be seated," she said. "We will proceed with closing arguments. Counsel for the State, you may begin."

Hill rose. He didn't look at his notes. He looked at the jury.

"Members of the jury," he began, and his voice filled the room without strain, "you have carried a heavy weight these past weeks…names and faces, laws and facts, grief and anger, and the patience to sort them into something worthy to live by. I'm not going to rehearse every detail; you have them in your notes. I'm going to ask you to remember three voices."

He held up a finger. "First: Luna Turner. An overworked social worker who did her duty when it mattered most. She called the police the moment she learned a child was missing. She stayed late. She walked the dark with detectives. She stood here and told you the truth, even after the defense tried to reduce her to a mistake on a calendar."

He lifted a second finger. "Second: Dr. Savannah Houser. No emotion. No bias. Only the body of Jonah Carter, a thirteen-year-old boy, the ligature marks around his neck, and the soil that matched the property under Benjamin Grove's control. The science does not take sides; it tells you what happened."

A third finger. "And Francine Grove. She did something harder than most of us will ever have to do. She stood here, bruised, and told you her husband used the place she built for rescue as a gate for ruin. She found the money. She found the names. She found her resolve. And she chose truth over comfort."

He let his hand fall. "There are other voices, too…Levi Coaster, who named the dock and the orders, even after men tried to shut him up; Daniel Gray, who told you about a van and a container and the sound of seagulls by a body of water that is not near Red Leaf City. These voices harmonize. They don't contradict; they complete the picture."

Hill stepped closer to the rail. "The defense will tell you this is all a coincidence. That money flows strangely sometimes. That men with influence don't always know what their subordinates do. That a jump drive is just a jump drive. I'm asking you to remember that none of these pieces stood alone. They fit. They have fit from the moment Luna dialed the phone to the moment, Dr. Houser washed the muck from Jonah's hair. They fit from Levi's swollen eye to Francine's split lip. They fit in a pattern that points one direction: guilty."

He paused, then lowered his voice. "Please don't make silence holy just because it is quiet. Make truth your measure."

He nodded once to the jury. "The State rests."

When he returned to his chair, O'Hell exhaled, a breath he'd been holding since the first word. Hill put his palms flat on the table, closed his eyes a moment, and whispered something that was either a prayer or an inventory of thanks.

"Defense," Lampson said. "You may proceed."

McMichaels rose, straightened his jacket, and took his place within the invisible geometry between tables and jury. He smiled with the precise measure of a man paid to look unflappable.

"Ladies and gentlemen," he began, "you have heard passion. You have heard sorrow. You have heard the prosecution draw a shape and insist it's a man. I'm going to ask you to look again."

He paced slowly before the jury box.

"Where is the chain of custody for that jump drive? Who handled it? Who had access to it? Who could have altered it?" He paused, letting the questions hang. Then his tone sharpened. "But none of that matters, does it? Because that so-called evidence was *excluded* from this trial. And that, ladies and gentlemen, explains a lot about this mysterious flash drive."

Where is a single image of my client moving a child, directing a pickup, or standing at a dock? You don't have it. Where is proof that Benjamin Grove knew what some opportunists may have done under the banner of his wife's charity? You don't have it. What you have is a city in pain and a man easy to blame because he dared to promise he would fix it."

He leaned closer, voice softening in a way that solicited sympathy like an usher's hand. "The State wants you to make a moral conclusion and then backfill the facts. That is not justice; that is grief, dressed for church."

He spread his hands. "And the outbursts? The frustration? If a husband cries out to the woman he loves from the end of a table, is that guilt or is it the last human thing left to him? Don't convict a man because he cannot bear to see his marriage consumed by rumors orchestrated by men you never saw take an oath in this room."

McMichaels straightened. "The law requires proof beyond a reasonable doubt. There are doubts everywhere you look. Follow them home."

He sat. For a beat, there was nothing but the scratch of Henry's steno and the whisper of someone unfolding a cough drop wrapper.

Lampson gave the jury her instructions carefully and measuredly, with the language of the law laid out like tracks. She asked them to rise, to gather their notebooks, to remember the oath. She sent them away with the gravity of the city on their shoulders.

The door to the deliberation room shut with a sound too soft for what it carried.

Deliberations are always shorter on television. In life, they breathe. They stutter. They pause for sandwiches and take stock of a stranger's face when a voice shakes. They sent notes for transcripts, clarifications, and batteries for the broken wall clock. The courthouse grew a second nervous system…the hum of waiting.

Reporters lined the corridor outside like gulls on a rail. The protesters' chants echoed through the glass. Black and Walls worked their phones at the end of the hall, conferring with a federal contact who promised nothing and suggested less. O'Hell dug at the seam of a paper cup with his thumbnail. Hill stood at the window, staring down at the steps where the signs bobbed, and thought of a boy's jacket sealed in a plastic bag.

Frannie sat between Jessica and Manny, silent. She hadn't wanted Manny to come, but he appeared at the door of the courtroom anyway, smelling faintly of disinfectant and peppermint candy. He sat inside himself like a folded chair and said, "I'm here," as if that were the whole prayer.

The first note from the jury came after an hour: Request readback of Dr. Houser's testimony on the cause of death. Henry obliged, the tape of his own hands delivered through his voice. Another note: Clarify the financial exhibits, including routing slips from the Red Leaf Progress Fund. Hill and O'Hell arranged the folders like small children at roll call. The law clerk ferried them in. The clock hands slipped and clicked.

Around four in the afternoon, the bailiff appeared in the doorway with his chin lifted, the expression that means nothing else but the end.

"Counsel," he said. "We have a verdict."

The room drew a breath. People stood more carefully than they needed to, as if the floor had become a thin sheet over water. Hill put a hand on O'Hell's shoulder and squeezed once. Black and Walls slipped in at the rear, lining the wall, unreadable. Frannie felt the world narrow to the space between her heart and the rail in front of her.

"All rise," the bailiff said.

The jurors filed in, faces solemn, their eyes avoiding anything that might weigh as a promise. Lampson returned, sat, and nodded to the foreperson.

"Madam Foreperson," she said. "Has the jury reached a verdict?"

"We have, Your Honor."

The clerk stood, paper in hand. The sound of it unfolding was unbearable.

"On the charge of conspiracy to commit human trafficking, how does the jury find?"

"Guilty."

"On the charge of murder, how does the jury find?"

"Not guilty."

"On the charge of human trafficking, how does the jury find?"

"Guilty."

"On the charge of attempted kidnapping, how does the jury find?"

"Not Guilty."

"On the charge of embezzlement, how does the jury find?"

"Guilty."

The words fell into the room like stones into a well, each landing deeper than the last. Someone in the gallery sobbed. Another voice whispered, "Thank you, God." Outside, a muffled cheer rippled, reached the windows, and broke like a wave.

Benjamin sat very still, as if the metal of the handcuffs had conducted a current into his bones and frozen him there. Then he turned. For the first time all day, his eyes found Frannie cleanly, without flinch or panic. His lips formed the words slowly and deliberately: 'I love you.'

Frannie's mouth trembled. She lifted two fingers to her lips and then outward, a motion small as a moth's wing. He watched the gesture and closed his eyes, a nod that looked like surrender.

"Order," Lampson said, though the room was not disorderly, only complete. She thanked the jury, discharged them with a gratitude that sounded almost personal. She announced that sentencing would be scheduled and that custody would continue with the Marshals. Paperwork clicked.

Shoes scuffed. The spell loosened its knot.

Marshals stepped to either side of Benjamin. He stood when they asked him to. For a second, he was just a man following instructions, and then he was the center of attention again, the cameras across the aisle shifting like sunflowers in the light.

"Mrs. Grove," McMichaels said under his breath as he gathered his files, "for what it's worth…." but he didn't finish. Whatever he thought he could offer had no place in the air left between them.

Hill turned, found Frannie, and nodded. It was not victory, not in any clean sense; it was something more complicated that would only later be called justice because there wasn't another word for it.

Outside, the city spoke in many voices —rage and relief, lament and a long, slow exhale. A woman on the steps lifted a sign that said WE LISTENED and wept as if applause had weight.

Inside, Benjamin reached the door where the Marshals would take him down the short corridor that led to the belly of the building. He paused and looked back one last time. Not at the jury. Not at Hill. At Frannie.

She stood. She didn't wave. She didn't speak. She put her hand flat over her heart.

He nodded again. Then he disappeared into the hall, swallowed by the architecture that exists for endings.

The corridor outside felt colder when the doors opened. Reporters flooded the space with microphones, questions, and the eager smell of ink. Black lifted a hand, and the officers formed a living aisle. Jessica held Frannie's purse while Frannie walked between them, head up, eyes clear.

"Mrs. Grove...what do you have to say to the city?" a reporter called. Frannie stopped. The crowd swayed to a hush.

"Only this," she said. "Let the children hear more than our shouting. Let them hear us keep our promises."

She moved again, and the crowd opened. At the top of the steps, the protestors fell silent without anyone telling them to. The winter sun slid out from behind a high cloud and threw the courthouse into a sudden, honest light.

Hill and O'Hell stepped into that light and felt its weight. Walls checked his phone, and his jaw tightened. Black squinted toward the far street where an idling sedan sat too long, then filed the detail away where he kept the things he did not yet have words for.

In the mingled noise, a single whisper seemed to rise, no one could say from where...It's done, and then dissolve into the crowd like breath on glass.

Frannie descended the steps with Jessica beside her, Mouse's leash looped in her coat pocket for a home still waiting. Somewhere behind them, a door shut with the careful finality of a chapter turned.

Above the steps, on the carved stone lintel, the old words remained: EQUAL JUSTICE UNDER LAW. For the first time in a long time, they did not look like decoration. They looked like a vow someone had finally spoken aloud.

And down the block, where the idling sedan had been, an engine purred once and vanished into traffic, a shadow keeping its counsel for another day.

Chapter 34: The Price of Truth

Frannie switched off the lamp and let the quiet of the house press around her. The verdict still echoed in the hollows of her chest…guilty, and with it the strange, empty relief of a cut finally cauterized. She had told herself this night would end with sleep, or if not sleep, then at least stillness. The kettle on the stove ticked as it cooled. Somewhere, a radiator murmured.

She toed off her shoes and slid beneath the quilt on the couch, phone face down on the coffee table, its battery a thin red sliver she meant to address and didn't. Rest, she told herself…. rest.

In the county jail, a thin rectangle of paper whispered under a steel door.

Benjamin saw it first as a sliver of white, like a piece of ice under a dull light. He bent to pick it up, palms blackened with the dry grit of the concrete floor. No envelope. No signature. Just the words, block-printed in blue ink with a careful, joyless hand:

Your wife talked. It's over!

He read it twice. Then a third time, as if the edges might change, as if the words might improve with repetition. He folded the paper once and slid it under his mattress, and from the moment he lost eye contact with those letters, his mind began to pull them larger, to press them against his skull like someone was applying them from inside.

Who? he wanted to demand of the air. Which names? How would they know? Why send it like this?

He paced the cell…five steps, turn, five steps back, and the walls moved closer. Inmates murmured in the row. A cough somewhere. A steel toilet flushed and groaned. He pictured Frannie's face in the gallery that afternoon, the way she'd kept her chin up even as the word "guilty" landed like a hammer. He pictured her walking out to the parking lot alone. He pictured hands that didn't belong to him on her door, the broken-toothed grin of threats made good.

The thought lodged.

He stared at the phone that was nailed to the wall on the other side of the bars. Calls were done for the night. Morning would come; he'd try then. He lay on the bunk and felt the mattress coil press into his shoulder blade. The words on the page beneath him seemed to rise through the thin foam, spelling themselves against his skin. *It's over!*

He didn't sleep so much as drift…shallow, briny, little shocks of consciousness snapping him awake whenever a boot scuffed the corridor or a key rattled.

When dawn bruised the narrow window, Benjamin was already on his feet, waiting for the phones to come alive.

The moment the guard nodded, he punched in Frannie's number from memory.

It went straight to voicemail.

He hung up and tried again.

Voicemail again.

On a couch across town, Frannie slept facedown with the quilt tucked under her chin, the phone a blank weight under the thinning light. The red sliver of battery had darkened to nothing, the screen an untroubled, lifeless pane.

Benjamin left a message that was never recorded and clung to a dial tone that never took his voice. He called again, and again. After the third attempt, something old and cold settled in him. He pressed his palm to the glass of the window in the call booth, and only the callused heel of it warmed under the weak morning sun.

Lunch was at one. He'd have the phones after that, the guard had said. He told himself he could make it.

He made it through a turn in the yard with the sky cupped low and gray, through a set of push-ups that left his shoulders trembling, through the long rectangle of time that followed when he leaned his head against the cool cinderblock and breathed in, out, in.

At twelve-fifty, they cuffed them out for chow. Voices rose in a tired chorus down the hall…the ritual of trays and milk cartons and plastic forks. Benjamin filed in, eyes fixed on the clock above the CO's station. One o' one. One o' two. One o'….

"Hey!" A shout erupted by the far table, a clatter of trays, the wet smack of milk splashed across tile. Two men squared up, chests puffed, teeth bared with a dramatist's clarity. Chairs screeched back. A carton rolled, hit a boot, and spun.

"Break it up!" a CO barked, already moving, already calling for hands.

Benjamin glanced up, reflexively. Half the room surged toward the shouting. The other half leaned forward, hungry for spectacle.

He turned back to the line just in time to feel something brush his ribs, a breath against his ear, hot with the sour of cafeteria coffee.

"This is from the Boss," a voice said.

Pain bloomed. Not sharp at first, but huge, an impact that stole his air before he could make a sound. Then the second strike hit home, and the pain clarified, a clean, burning line that opened across his back like a zipper being pulled the wrong way. He folded, hands flattening on the stainless counter as if to steady an ocean. The third and fourth drives came low, frantic, and practiced. The man behind him eased him forward as if offering him to the floor.

Benjamin dropped to his knees. The world blurred at the edges, the fluorescent lights smearing into a pale, indifferent river overhead. He thought of Frannie's hands on a coffee mug, the chipped blue one she kept, though he'd told her to throw it out. He tried to say her name and coughed blood instead; the sound was wet and small.

Somewhere, the show at the far table found its crescendo, and the attending officers snapped back toward the line just as Benjamin toppled the rest of the way. One CO shouted for medical; another kneeled next to Benjamin, "Stay with me," he said, a voice above him as gauzy as the lights, a towel pressed to his side. Fingers counted something at his neck.

He thought of the letter underneath his mattress and the bed he would not return to. He thought, stupidly, stubbornly, that the phones would be open in fifty-five minutes, that he would try again, that she would answer, that she would say his name the way she used to, before, when his name meant something softer.

The towel turned dark. The world narrowed until it fit inside a single sound, the long, sliding hush of his breath leaving and the low thunder of boots around him. He could not find the next inhale. He tried again. He could not.

Across town, afternoon slid in through Frannie's blinds. She woke to the ache of a neck that had been sleeping on wrong and a tiny phantom of hope that the last twenty-four hours had been a dream someone had sold her while she napped. The kettle was cold. The house smelled like lemon cleaner and the quiet after a storm.

Her phone was a dead thing. She plugged it in, watched the blank screen transform into a logo, then a battery icon, and finally, life. Three missed calls, all from the jail. Each time stamp was marked in a column that felt like a trail she had failed to follow. Her stomach turned. She thumbed to call back, but she remembered that county jail calls are not returnable. Frannie slipped the phone into her back pocket, with 20% battery life, and stepped out onto the covered back porch. The air met her with its stillness, the kind that hummed faintly through the screen door. She sank into the old chair near the railing, wood creaking under her.

She hadn't called Manny. He was across town, probably watering his garden the way he always did when he wasn't working. She imagined the slow rhythm of the hose, the careful way he turned the handle as if time could be tamed by patience.

Frannie exhaled. The phone was heavy in her pocket. "Three times," she whispered to no one. The jail had called three times.

She tried to form the truth, but I was asleep. I let it die. But nothing came out. Only the ache of wanting to say it. Frannie drew her knees close and murmured, half to herself, "Plug in next time, huh?" The words sounded like Manny's voice in her head, soft as a sigh, not a rebuke, just something that kept her from falling all the way through.

Her phone rang in her back pocket, sudden and sharp. She flinched, fumbled it out, and stared at the screen as if it were a mirror.

Unknown…county jail, she answered. "Hello?"

A man's voice, official and mannered. "Mrs. Grove? This is Warden Fields from Red Leaf County." Her mouth went dry. "Yes. Is Benjamin…?"

"Mrs. Grove," he said, and stripped anything generous from his voice. "I'm sorry to inform you that Benjamin Grove passed away approximately three hours ago."

She stopped hearing the middle of the sentence; only the edges remained, the sorry and passed. The words lay heavy and senseless between them.

"What happened?" she managed. "It's under investigation."

"What happened?" She heard herself repeat it, flat, as if the question had been assigned to her and not chosen. "Was it…did someone….?"

"As I said, it's under investigation." He cleared his throat. Paper rustled, the script advanced. "There are procedures we have to follow."

"Procedures," she said, and a laugh escaped, jagged and wrong. "He was alive this morning." Her hand found the edge of the couch to keep herself steady. "He called me." She shut her eyes. "I didn't answer. He called me and I didn't…" She broke off, the sentence shattering before it fell.

"We'll be in touch regarding… arrangements," the Warden said, the pause around the word long enough to hold a shiver. "I'm sorry for your loss."

The call clicked off. He'd given her nothing that could hold weight, no detail, no time, no kindness. Only a lid. It was only a label that would not tell her what was inside.

She stared at the phone. Her hand trembled, tendons fluttering like wires about to snap. She dialed back. A switchboard answered…an indifferent voice in a world that had just ended. She hung up. Redialed. Hung up again. Then she set the phone on the coffee table as if it had burned her.

"Benjamin's dead."

The words fell out of her mouth like stones, heavy, senseless, final. She repeated them, louder, and the sound cracked through the room. "Benjamin's dead." Saying it made it less real and more unbearable, as if each syllable tore another inch from the picture of their life together. "Why won't they tell me how he died?" she whispered, her voice shaking. "Why won't anyone tell me?"

She stumbled into the kitchen, the air thick and wrong, the light too sharp. Her chest hitched as her throat tightened.

"I kept your secrets," she cried, her voice rising. "Until… I- I couldn't anymore. I needed to tell the truth, and now this, and you still left me with nothing but questions!"

The words came out raw, scraped from someplace too deep ever to heal.

She slammed her fist against the counter, the sound sharp as thunder.

"Truth wasn't supposed to kill us," she shouted, her voice breaking in two.

Then softer, almost pleading: "We forgave each other."

Her knees gave way. She slid to the floor, palms catching the cold tile. The house groaned, settling around her grief like a witness too afraid to speak.

She thought of the courtroom, the flash of cameras, the verdict, Benjamin's eyes finding hers one last time as the deputies dragged him away. His mouth had formed the words, "I love you." And I should have said it back.

"Why didn't I tell you too?"

Her breath came ragged, uneven. "I should have answered," she choked, pressing her palms against her face. The tears came in violent bursts…sobs that ripped through her chest until breathing felt impossible.

She stayed on the floor, eyes fixed on the ceiling as if it might offer an answer. Minutes passed…maybe hours. The house was silent except for the sound of her own broken breathing.

When she finally spoke, it came out as a whisper into her trembling hands…a prayer and a punishment all at once.

"What have I done?"

Acknowledgments

I want to thank God first and foremost for giving me the strength and purpose to bring this story to life. Writing Cracked Glass: The Sin of Silence reminded me that truth will always find its way to the surface, no matter how deep the lies run.

To my family and friends, thank you for your endless encouragement, prayers, and belief in my vision. To every reader who opens these pages, I hope this story reminds you to speak up for what is right, even when it's hard to do so.

Author's Note

This story was born from a single question: What happens when silence becomes a sin?

In a world where wrong is often overlooked, Cracked Glass: The Sin of Silence challenges us to confront injustice rather than ignore it. Inspired by James 4:17 KJV "Therefore to him that knoweth to do good, and doeth it not, to him it is sin," the story of Francine Grove reminds us that faith without action can shatter under pressure. If this book has touched your heart, let it serve as a reminder that one voice can still make a difference.

About the Author

Kimberly Cummings is a Christian fiction author and founder of The Cozy Scratchpad, a publishing imprint dedicated to stories of redemption, justice, and faith. Her books delve into profound moral questions through suspenseful, emotionally charged storytelling.

She is the author of the Red Cover Collection, which includes I'm Not Him, Love Only Me, Through the Storms, The Waiting Porch, A Different Echo, the Cracked Glass Trilogy, and others.

Learn more or connect with her at:

www.kimberlycummingsauthor.com

Instagram: @Scratchpadcreate

Sneak Peek from Book 2: Cracked Glass

No Turning Back

The bells tolled, low and mournful, each strike trembling through the stone walls of Red Leaf Church and sinking deep into Francine Grove's chest. The sound carried like judgment. She sat stiff in the front pew, her hands knotted around a crumpled tissue, the black veil over her face fluttering each time she exhaled.

The oak casket stood at the altar, polished until it gleamed under the church lights, but it might as well have been a locked vault. It held Benjamin now, her husband, her partner, her shame. She hated that the lid was closed. She hated even more that part of her was relieved. She could not bear to see his face again, to wonder if regret had found him before death did.

The sanctuary was filled with people, yet it felt empty to her. Mourners lined the pews, some family, some old colleagues, some strangers who had come for the spectacle. Cameras flashed even here, though discreetly, as if no one could resist stealing one last piece of the fallen politician. Their presence weighed on Francine like another burden she could not bear.

Pastor Wiley's voice rose from the pulpit, intoning Scripture, calling for mercy, reminding the living of the frailty of man. The words blurred, slipping past her ears. She caught fragments of forgiveness, rest…God's will, but they dissolved into the same gray fog that had swallowed her since the morning she watched the news declare Benjamin dead in custody.

Dead before sentencing. He died before he could speak for

himself. Dead before she could ask him why.

The question clawed at her, relentlessly: Why didn't you tell me?

A sound broke through the muffled roar of voices outside. Chanting, ugly, insistent. Protestors swarmed the streets beyond the church doors, their signs a forest of accusation: MONSTER...JUSTICE FOR THE CHILDREN. SHUT THE CENTER DOWN.

One voice pierced the walls: "He got what he deserved!"

Francine flinched, her fingers tearing the tissue in two. The congregation stiffened, but no one moved. Pastor Wiley cleared his throat and kept speaking, though his voice faltered.

Francine bowed her head, shutting her eyes tight. The noise outside was thunder, but inside her own body a louder storm raged. Her grief was not quiet; it screamed, hot and jagged, in the hollow of her chest.

She pressed the torn tissue to her mouth, muffling a sob. She had sworn she would not break here, not in front of them, not where every pair of eyes cut her open and labeled her complicit. But the tears came anyway, slipping hot down her cheeks, soaking into the fabric of her veil.

Memories ambushed her: the sound of Benjamin's laugh in their kitchen, the way he kissed her forehead before leaving for late meetings, the speeches he rehearsed in front of her as if she were his only audience. She wanted to hate him for what he had done, or what he had been accused of doing, but grief tangled with rage until neither would let go.

Someone behind her whispered, sharp enough to sting.

"She knew. Don't tell me she didn't know."

The words sliced deeper than the chants outside. She gripped the pew, her knuckles white, nails digging into the polished wood. Her lips trembled, but no answer came. She wanted to rise and scream No! I didn't know! I never knew! But her body stayed frozen, shackled by sorrow.

Pastor Wiley's voice carried on, a hollow comfort. "We commit this body to the Lord, who knows the heart of every man. May we find mercy in His truth and peace in His judgment."

Mercy. Truth. Peace. The words felt like smoke in her lungs.

The choir began to sing, their voices steady, but Francine's world tilted. The hymn blurred, her breath catching in shallow gulps. She folded forward, clutching her stomach as if holding herself together. She felt Manny's hand, a steady pressure on her shoulder from the pew beside her, but she couldn't look at him. If she met his eyes, the fragile wall she'd built would crumble entirely.

Another shout from outside rattled the windows: "Justice for the children!"

Her sob escaped then, raw and ragged. She bowed low, shoulders shaking. The church blurred around her, colors running together until she saw only the coffin.

Why didn't you fight harder? Why did you leave me with this ruin?

The final prayer ended, and the service dissolved into shuffling feet, murmured condolences, and the rustle of coats. Francine barely heard any of it. The police had been waiting. Two officers approached, their faces firm but sympathetic, and urged her toward the side aisle.

The flash of cameras ignited again. She turned her head away, clutching Manny's arm for balance. Her knees buckled as she passed the coffin, and for one breath, she nearly collapsed onto the polished lid. Her hand brushed against it, trembling. She whispered so low only the wood could hear:

"I never knew."

Manny steadied her, guiding her forward, but the words

echoed inside her skull.

The doors opened. The chants crashed in, deafening this time, as if the city itself refused to let her grieve.

"She knew!" someone screamed from the crowd.

"Don't trust her!" another shouted.

The barricades trembled. Signs waved. Faces twisted with anger and certainty. Police linked arms to shield her as they moved her down the church steps.

Francine kept her head bowed, the veil hiding her tears. Her grief pulsed louder than their fury, but she carried both now, her sorrow and their judgment, twin weights pressing her toward the ground.

She stepped into the waiting car, her chest burning, and the door slammed shut behind her.

Through the window, she saw the crowd one last time. The chants blurred into a wall of sound, but her heart knew the truth: Benjamin's death had not silenced the city. It had not silenced the questions. And it had not silenced the shadow that still clung to her.

She pressed her palm against the blank glass, as if to hold back the world. But inside, her grief screamed louder than all of them.

Reader Invitation

If this story moved you, please take a moment to leave a review on Amazon or Goodreads. Your words help other readers discover the message behind these pages and support independent authors who write with purpose.

www.ingramcontent.com/pod-product-compliance
Lightning Source LLC
Chambersburg PA
CBHW020754310726
48969CB00002B/542